BY CHRIS COLFER

LITTLE, BROWN AND COMPANY
New York Boston

Little, Brown and Company
Hachette Book Group
1290 Avenue of the Americas, New York, NY 10104
Visit us at lb-teens.com

First Edition: February 2017

Little, Brown and Company is a division of Hachette Book Group, Inc. The Little, Brown name and logo are trademarks of Hachette Book Group, Inc.

The publisher is not responsible for websites (or their content) that are not owned by the publisher.

ISBNs: 978-0-316-38344-8 (hardcover), 978-0-316-38341-7 (ebook)

Printed in the United States of America

LSC-H

10 9 8 7 6 5 4 3 2 1

To Ashley,
for being the best friend a guy could ask for.
Since your memory is much better than mine,
you'll have to remind me which parts of this
book actually happened.

Chapter One

CONVENTION INTERVENTION

It wasn't WizCon unless someone was trampled. At least that was how the employees of the Santa Clara Convention Center saw it. The success of the annual event was never measured by the number of attendees (sold-out crowds were always a given) but by the number of injuries the enthusiastic crowd inflicted on one another.

Thankfully, the WizCon incidents were never malicious; the patrons simply buzzed with so much excitement they became a danger to themselves and others around them. So, the more reported accidents, the more the event planners were confident they had done their job.

And as the early comers outside pressed their bodies against the glass doors, rabid with anticipation, the convention staff knew Wiz-Con 2017 was about to break new records.

"It's twelve-oh-one!" said a little boy dressed as a gray alien. "You were supposed to open at noon!"

"Come on, we've been waiting for hours!" said an old woman dressed as a headless Marie-Antoinette.

"Some of us have been here since yesterday!" said a very sleepy teenage girl from a group wearing dinosaur onesies.

The convention center was surrounded with a massive gathering of historical figures, extinct species, and extraterrestrial creatures. It was an alarming sight to every passing observer, but it was much more innocent than the psychedelic cult it appeared to be.

All these people were at WizCon because they were fans of the hit television series *Wiz Kids*. The show was an action/adventure series that followed a trio of young geniuses who travel through space and time in an invention they constructed out of a port-a-potty.

Naturally, when it first premiered the critics treated the show like a piñata. Each review of the "ridiculous premise" was more scathing than the last. Reviewers took great pleasure in ripping it to shreds and even became competitive with their convictions, each claiming to have "hated it the most." However, with each fatal blow *Wiz Kids* only received more and more attention. People tuned in to see the "absurdity" for themselves, but they were not repulsed as promised. Audiences found the show's campiness to be rather charming, its unique underdog spirit resonated with them, and a global phenomenon was born.

No, it wasn't Shakespeare, but on the bright side, *it wasn't Shakespeare.*

Seemingly overnight, the cast of young teens became household names. Their likenesses were plastered across T-shirts, lunch boxes, bedsheets, and various hygiene products, and their personal lives became the subjects of tabloid debates.

Nine seasons later, the *Wiz Kids* viewership was larger and more passionate than ever before. The self-proclaimed "Wizzers" dominated the Internet with more hashtags, trending topics, discussion forums, and fanfiction than any other show on air. And like a religious pilgrimage, every fourth weekend in June, Wizzers from around the world traveled to Santa Clara, California, for the sacred *Wiz Kids* convention to celebrate the show together.

"It's five past twelve!" said the mother of triplets dressed as Roman Soldiers. "Open the doors already!"

"Let us in! It's hot out here!" said a man dressed from head to toe as a Martian Slug.

"My mustache is melting off my face!" shouted a little girl dressed as Edgar Allan Poe (or so people hoped).

Finally, at ten past twelve, the doors opened and a stampede of alien creatures, deceased world influencers, and large reptiles stormed inside the convention center—*WizCon 2017 had begun*! Security guards cautiously ushered the excited crowd like they were herding a flock of explosive sheep. Medics stood by with their gurneys ready. The other convention center employees made bets on which guests were most likely to "snap."

The first Wizzers through the door made a mad dash to the convention center theater, where the "*Wiz Kids* Cast & Creative Panel" was happening later that afternoon. Only the first six hundred people would have seats; the other poor saps would have to watch from a telecast in the Exhibit Hall.

Desperate to see their favorite actors in the flesh, the teenagers in the crowd charged through the halls, knocking over booths of overpriced merchandise and unsuspecting senior citizens in their path. They squeezed through the narrow doors of the theater and threw themselves into the first available seats they could find. Within minutes, all the seats were filled with giddy young people. Pitying looks were cast upon the unfortunate souls without seats, as if they were third-class passengers on the *Titanic*.

Not a single Wizzer could sit still as they waited for the panel to start. The entire theater jerked and twitched like everyone had to pee so badly it hurt. The anticipation was suffocating and some had to breathe into paper bags to keep from passing out—but who could blame them? *This was it!* The panel they had been waiting for all year was just a few agonizing minutes away!

Their eyes darted back and forth across the stage, as they wondered which wing their heroes would enter from. A table was set on the stage with four chairs, four microphones, and four nameplates. The crowd squealed like hyenas as they read the names of the cast and creator of *Wiz Kids*, especially the nameplate of Cash Carter, the lead actor of the show.

Without a doubt, the Wizzers were more excited to see Cash Carter than anyone else on the panel. If they weren't in costume, almost everyone in the theater wore a T-shirt with a picture of his character, Dr. Webster Bumfuzzle. The doctor was famous for his thick glasses, green bow tie, and blue laboratory coat. The Wizzers whispered among themselves as they speculated what Cash Carter was doing at that exact moment and if he was as excited about the panel as they were....

From the greenroom backstage, the commotion in the theater sounded like the rumblings of a distant storm. Cash Carter found serenity in the bathroom, where the crowd was drowned out entirely by the hum of the fluorescent lights. He stood in front of the mirror with his eyes closed, enjoying the quiet while he still could.

Cash was not a jealous person, but he envied people with *quiet*. Only in absolute silence could he simply *exist* and not be reminded of who and what he was, or according to his critics, who and what he *wasn't*. But finding a space that wasn't dominated by the commotion of a television set, the rapid clicks of paparazzi cameras, or the murmuring of a hungry crowd was very rare. The bathroom may have had cracked tiled walls, peculiar stains on the ceiling, a terrible musky smell, and someone definitely had been murdered there in the past—but to Cash, it was a sanctuary.

His tranquillity was interrupted by a knock on the door.

"Mr. Carter?" asked an underpaid stagehand. "Are you still in there? We're hoping to start the panel in five minutes."

"Five minutes? I thought we weren't starting until two," Cash replied.

"It *is* two," the stagehand said.

Cash had been in the bathroom for over an hour without realizing it. He opened his baggy, bloodshot eyes and stared at his reflection. The twenty-two-year-old actor was thin, unshaven, and sported messy hair. He wore a black blazer over the T-shirt he'd fallen asleep in the night before and strong cologne to mask the fact that he hadn't showered in two days.

"Is everything okay?" the stagehand asked. "You've been in there for a while."

"I'm fine," Cash mumbled. "I just lost track of time. They can start the intro to the panel—I'll be out in five."

"Actually, the producers wanted to have a word with the cast before the panel begins," the stagehand said.

Cash grunted. "In that case, I'll be out in ten."

The stagehand let out a deep sigh. "Copy that," he said, and clicked a button on his headset. "He says he'll be out in ten—yes, I know we're already running behind. Let the crowd know we'll be starting closer to two thirty. Calm down, Gary—this is WizCon, not the Oscars."

The stagehand walked down the hall in a huff, granting Cash a few more moments of peace.

A rush of nerves swept through Cash's core like a flock of bats. Even after nine years of conventions, he always got anxious before appearing in front of an audience. Call him crazy, but there was something about walking into a room of screaming, applauding, and crying strangers that Cash just couldn't get used to. Although he never took the Wizzers' affection for granted, it was a lot of pressure being the source of so much happiness. With one slip of the tongue, he could emotionally scar a generation of young people for the rest of their lives and trigger a wave of resentment for the rest of his.

Being beloved was fucking tough.

Luckily for him, these days Cash had a little help to take the edge off. He reached into his pocket and pulled out three large pills and two marijuana gummy bears. He swallowed the pills, chewed up the gummies, and chased them with a sip from a flask tucked in his blazer. Sure, it wasn't exactly the *healthiest* combination, but the goodies always worked faster when they were taken together.

Cash closed his eyes again, took a deep breath, and waited for his secret weapons to do their magic. A moment later, there was another knock at the door.

"Mr. Carter?" the stagehand said. "It's been *fifteen* minutes. Are you ready?"

Poor time management was a side effect of Cash's special treats, but his anxiety was completely gone. In fact, Cash could barely feel anything at all. Everything felt light and easy around him, as if he were drifting through the clouds in a hot-air balloon. Only when he opened his dilated eyes and looked around was he reminded he was in a bathroom at all. His preconvention cocktail had done the trick!

"Mr. Carter? Did you hear me?" the stagehand asked, growing more impatient by the millisecond.

Cash giggled. There was something so funny about being called *Mr. Carter* by someone almost twice his age.

"Yeah, I heard you," he said. *"Showtime!"*

Cash begrudgingly left his porcelain sanctuary and followed the stagehand down the hall. The greenroom was more crowded than he thought it would be. Seven people were seated with their chairs facing him, and in Cash's delayed state, it took him a couple moments to recognize them.

Damien Zimmer, the creator of *Wiz Kids*, was seated in the middle with the show's executive producer, Jim Kaufman. To their right were Cash's cast mates, the beautiful Amy Evans and the hunky Tobey Ramous. To Damien and Jim's left were two middle-aged men and one woman, each wearing a designer suit. Cash knew they were executives from the network, but since executives were fired and hired so frequently, he didn't know their names.

"Well, this is a surprise," Cash said.

"Would you give us a minute?" Jim asked the stagehand.

The overworked man was desperate to get things started, but he gave them some space.

"Sit down, Cash," Damien said, and nodded to an empty chair.

"Um...okay," Cash said, and took a seat.

All of them stared at him with stern expressions—except his costars; they were looking down at social media on their phones. Cash could tell they were all pissed off at him for something—something much worse than taking his time in the bathroom. Perhaps he had said something uncouth in an interview or forgot to live-tweet during a rerun.

"So...," Cash said. "What's up?"

"Before we begin, it's important you know we're all here because we care about you," Jim said.

"Duh, it's WizCon," Cash said. "Everyone is here because they care about me."

The remark inspired several eye rolls and exhalations, but Cash wasn't trying to be a smart-ass. On the contrary, after three painkillers, two edibles, and a shot of whiskey, he was too numb to be anything but literal.

"This is serious, Cash," the woman executive said. "This isn't going to be a pleasant conversation, but it's a necessary one before things get out of hand."

"Out of hand?" Cash asked. "What the hell are you talking about?"

Everyone passed the responsibility of leading the conversation to the next person, until it landed in Damien's lap like a heavy stack of books—books he did *not* want to read.

"Things have always been rocky between us, so I'm probably not the best messenger for this," Damien said with a dramatic sigh. "Ever since we wrapped season nine and went on hiatus, you've gone totally out of control. At first we thought it was just a phase, but after two months of utter nonsense, we're afraid it's far worse. We've all cleared our schedules so we could be here today and address your recent behavior."

Damien was right—he wasn't the right messenger. In fact, he was the last person on earth Cash would listen to about behavior.

At just thirty-five years old, Damien Zimmer had the ego and the entitlement of all Hollywood's worst clichés put together. He began his career as a child actor on a cheesy sitcom called *Who's the Parent?*—which was more memorable for its obnoxious laugh track than its writing. When Damien was in his midtwenties, he developed *Wiz Kids* as a starring vehicle for himself. The network purchased the show but thought Damien was too old and forced him to cast younger actors. Even though *Wiz Kids* became a huge hit and made him filthy rich, Damien had always despised Cash for "stealing" his part and the spotlight that came with it.

"Hold up," Cash said. "Is this an *intervention*? Right before a convention?"

"Damn right it is," Damien said. "And I believe it's more than warranted. You've been seen getting wasted at clubs all over town, getting high in public places, speeding down Sunset Boulevard with hookers in the backseat of your Lamborghini, and the LAPD are at your house every other night to shut down a ridiculous party."

"First off, those were *strippers*, and I drive a *Maserati*," Cash clarified. "And it's not like throwing parties and getting drunk is against the law."

"No, but *child endangerment* is," Damien went on. "You're lucky you weren't charged after taking the Boys and Girls Club of America skydiving or those poor kids from Make-A-Wish to the shooting range."

"We're also aware you were caught trespassing," Jim added. "Someone filmed you climbing an elephant statue at the La Brea Tar Pits *naked* while screaming 'I'm the king of the mammoths.' You have no idea how much damage control the network publicists went into to keep it off the Internet."

Cash giggled. "You've got to admit, *that* was pretty legendary," he said. "By the way, could I get a copy of that? I lost my phone that night and it might show where I dropped it."

His request was denied with passive-aggressive silence.

"I believe you've entered a downward spiral of selfishness, stupidity, and self-destruction," Damien said. "You're ruining your reputation and jeopardizing the viewership of the show in the process. Even though we're not currently filming, you are still a representative of this network, this studio, and *my* production company—"

Damien recited the rant like a Shakespearean soliloquy, but Cash's eyes drifted away from him. His attention was completely captivated by Amy, who had started taking selfies with her phone. Cash couldn't think of anything more inappropriate to do in the middle of an intervention—it was like ordering a pizza in the middle of a funeral. Then again, he wasn't surprised. Amy's narcissism had always fascinated him.

Once when they were on set, Cash accidentally saw inside Amy's photo album when he confused her phone for his. Every picture was a different selfie with the same exact pose and her favorite expression— *sultry surprise*. He scrolled for miles but never found a single picture of friends or family—it was all just Amy. Sometimes he worried Amy wasn't actually Amy at all, but Amy's stalker wearing a suit made out of her skin.

"Cash, are you even listening to me?" Damien asked, and leaned forward to take a closer look at him. "Wait, are you *stoned*?"

"Not enough for this conversation," Cash muttered under his breath.

This got a serious rise out of his coworkers, especially Tobey Ramous, who was so annoyed he threw his phone aside.

"This is going nowhere!" Tobey said. "He doesn't give a shit about anything we're telling him. I'm supposed to be back in Los Angeles tonight for a night shoot. How much longer is this going to take?"

Tobey (or *Roids McRage*, as Cash called him behind his back) was referring to the set of *Moth-Man*, the multi-million-dollar comic book movie he was starring in. He had bulked up so much for the part, and so quickly, it was a miracle he could tie his own shoes. *Moth-Man* was an opportunity every actor dreams of and Tobey was using his entire hiatus from *Wiz Kids* to shoot it. Still, Cash found it very ironic that Tobey spent eighty hours a week dressed as a giant insect yet somehow thought his time was more valuable than anyone else's.

"Allow me to wrap things up," Cash said. "I understand my behavior has raised a few eyebrows, but after nine seasons of playing by the rules, always saying and doing the right thing and never rocking the boat, I think I've earned the right to *have a little fun*. Come on, guys, I've been doing this show since I was twelve years old. You're only young once—I just want to be *young* while I still can."

If the looks being exchanged were any indication, there wasn't an ounce of sympathy for him. No one gave a fuck about his desire to be young.

"Unfortunately, your definition of *youth* is a breach of contract," one of the male executives said. "You and your representation agreed to the studio's morality clause when you were hired, and then again during renegotiations in the sixth season. If your behavior doesn't change, we'll be forced to take legal action."

It was a very serious threat, but instead of trembling where he sat, Cash only laughed.

"You can only sue me if I'm still under contract," he said. "And at the rate I'm going, I doubt you'll be employing me much longer."

"So *that's* what this is really all about?" Amy said. "You're trying to get yourself *fired*? That's pathetic!"

"Dude, you're a fucking idiot," Tobey said. "If you get fired from the show you'll never work again and the fans will *hate* you!"

Cash was overwhelmed by the love and support coming from his costars. They were *nailing* this whole intervention thing. He was totally inspired to change his ways so *their* lives would be easier.

"Everyone, calm down," Jim said. "No one is getting fired. We're here to *help* Cash, not scold him or accuse him of anything."

They were obviously on different pages about the matter, because Damien was giving Cash the most scornful look to date. Not once in nine years had he ever turned down an opportunity to scold Cash.

"I feel so sorry for you, Cash," Damien said. "You're not mature enough to understand how lucky you are. There are millions of people in this world who would *kill* to be sitting where you are. Like it or not, you're the lead actor of a network's highest-rated show—they'd sue you for everything you've got before they'd fire you. So you're going to fulfill your contractual obligations and you're going to do it on your best behavior. I'd make peace with that if I were you."

Cash didn't know if he should be appalled or applaud him— Damien gave his best performances when he was ticked off. However, his allegations couldn't be further from the truth. Immaturity and ingratitude were languages Damien spoke, not Cash. The truth was, Cash *had* made peace with reality—he had made more peace than anyone else in the room could possibly understand.

"There's more than one way to get out of a contract," Cash said.

A wide grin spread across his face. No matter how much they tried scaring him, Cash knew he wasn't returning for the next season of the show. There was something he wasn't telling them—something he would have loved to confess just to prove them all wrong, but he had to be strategic about it. A better time would present itself.

The stagehand reentered the room very awkwardly, like he was walking in on his elderly parents having sex.

"Excuse me, I don't mean to interrupt," he said. "We told the crowd we were starting at two thirty and it's now two forty-five. Are we close, or should we tell them we've pushed it to three?"

"We'll put a pin in this conversation until we find time to finish it," Jim said. "We've brought our concerns to Cash, now it's his job to take them to heart. But let me reiterate, *no one* is getting fired and *no one* is leaving the show. We're here to talk about the upcoming season and *nothing* else. Now, let's go out and make the fans happy. None of us would have jobs without them."

No one objected. Everyone was relieved the conversation was finally over, especially Amy and Tobey. The meeting seemed to have taken a toll on them more than it had on Cash. He almost offered them some of the treats in his pocket, but thought it was probably tacky to offer drugs right after an intervention.

Jim and the executives left the greenroom to watch the panel from the audience. The stagehand escorted Damien, Tobey, Amy, and Cash to the stage and had them wait behind the curtain.

"When they call your name, step through the curtain and take your seat at the table," the stagehand instructed.

"Oh, is *that* how it works?" Tobey said, and did an impression of someone with special needs.

"Yeah, like we've never done this before," Amy said, and took another selfie.

Cash chuckled, but not at his costars. He thought it was funny how there was hydrocodone, weed, and alcohol flowing through his veins at a work event but *he* wasn't the biggest douchebag onstage.

"Sorry, they make me remind you every year," the stagehand said, and clicked the button on his headset. *"We're ready back here. Cue the introduction!"*

An energetic announcer was blasted over the audio system and filled the theater like the voice of God.

"Ladies and gentlemen, boys and girls, extraterrestrials, reptiles and insectoids, people from the past, present, and future, and Wizzers from around the world, welcome to the 2017 'Wiz Kids Cast and Creative Panel'!"

The audience went berserk. If the energy emitting from their bodies could be absorbed, it would power all the homes in Central America for a decade.

"Please welcome the former star of Who's the Parent? *and the creator of* Wiz Kids, *Damien Zimmer!"*

The words *former star* seemed to have sent a sharp pain down Damien's spine because he twitched uncomfortably. He stepped through the curtain and bowed before the audience. The Wizzers greeted him with warm applause but mostly tried to look past him to see the cast standing backstage.

"You know him as the goofy anthropologist Professor Fitz Luck-unckle! Please welcome to the stage the man who puts the 'buff' in 'history buff' and the star of the upcoming movie Moth-Man, *Tobey Ramous!"*

Tobey leaped through the curtain like a bull released from its pen. His silhouette darted across the curtain as he ran around the stage doing backflips and flexing his muscles for the crowd. Tobey was so amped up an elephant tranquilizer wouldn't have calmed him down.

"You know her as the mechanical engineer with the heart of gold, Dr. Jules 'the Tools' Peachtree! Please welcome actress turned supermodel and outspoken pescatarian the gorgeous and talented Amy Evans!"

Amy glided through the curtain like she was on a catwalk. She blew kisses, made heart shapes with her hands, and then took a selfie onstage—but oddly, didn't include the audience in it.

"Last but certainly not least, you know him as the lovable, nerdy, and quirky quantum physics expert Dr. Webster Bumfuzzle! Please give a warm WizCon welcome to the one and only Caaaash Caaaarter!"

Before the announcer was finished, the audience was screaming so loud Cash could barely hear his cue to come out. He stepped onstage and was hit with a tsunami of affection. The audience roared twice as hard as they had for the others. The stage lights made it very difficult to see anything and a tardy spotlight practically blinded him. All Cash could see was the manic flashing of cameras in the audience, as if he were facing an endless, pulsating galaxy.

When his eyes finally adjusted, he saw Wizzers shaking, crying, and jumping hysterically throughout the theater. He politely waved at the crowd, only causing the commotion to magnify. Cash found his seat at the table beside his coworkers, but the audience continued cheering until their voices went hoarse.

"Please welcome the panel moderators. From Entertainment Weekly, *Jennifer Smalls; from* The Hollywood Reporter, *Terrence Wallem; and YouTube personality Kylie Trig."*

Lights came up on the front row of the audience, where the moderators sat. Each had a handheld microphone and a *Wiz Kids* notepad with their questions.

"We'll start the panel questions with Jennifer Smalls," the announcer said.

"Thanks for having me, WizCon," Jennifer Smalls said into her microphone. "First off, it's so wonderful to be back at WizCon!"

If there was one thing the cast of *Wiz Kids* agreed on, it was that Jennifer Smalls was Satan in black leggings. Before she reported for *Entertainment Weekly*, Jennifer worked for a website called *Gotcha*, a gossip blog devoted to outing closeted gay actors, breaking up celebrity couples, starting pregnancy rumors, leaking nude photos, and making life as difficult as possible for anyone in the public eye.

When Cash bought his first home, Jennifer Smalls posted his address online, which was practically an invitation for paparazzi, Hollywood tour buses, and five very delusional people who refused to leave. It cost Cash hundreds of thousands of dollars to hire full-time security for his property and to expedite restraining orders. Needless to say, he wasn't Jennifer Smalls's biggest fan. The only reason she was invited to WizCon was because in 2004 she wrote an article claiming Damien Zimmer was robbed of a Best Supporting Actor Emmy nomination for *Who's the Parent?*

"You're always welcome here, Jennifer," Damien said into his microphone.

"My question is for Cash," she said. "We've noticed there is more and more stunt work each season. I was wondering what it was like to film episode 908—'Atlantis Falling.'"

"It was wet," Cash replied—and that was all she got.

His shortness was not just a tactic for Jennifer's questions, but for the convention in general. The less he spoke, the fewer pictures would surface of him in midword—those always made him look like he was having a stroke, and also seemed to be the *only* photos publications used with their articles anymore. Luckily, the audience found his shortness very amusing and no one was the wiser.

"Now we'll go to Terrence Wallem for the next question," the announcer said.

The Hollywood reporter from *The Hollywood Reporter* aggressively flipped through his notes as he formed a question. He was in his late sixties and one of the most feared television critics in Los Angeles. Terrence was infamous for finding something to dislike in everything he watched. He said *Game of Thrones* was "too soft," *Downton Abbey* was "juvenile," and *The Big Bang Theory* was "an insult to intelligent people."

Judging by the irritated look on Terrence's face, he would rather have been having a colonoscopy with no anesthesia than be sitting at WizCon among the Wizzers.

"My question is for Mr. Zimmer," Terrence said. "With all due respect, this show is all over the place. In the same episode your characters were swimming in the rivers of Ancient Mesopotamia during one scene, and then hiking through the craters of Mars in the next. What exactly inspired you to create this show?"

"I've always been a huge fan of science fiction and history, and no one had intertwined them yet—at least as well as I thought I could," Damien said, and ran his fingers through his hair. "Originally I wrote it for myself to star in, but once I began developing it with the studio, I decided the part wasn't right for me. I told them it would be better for the show if I stayed off camera and put all my creative energy into the writer's room."

"Right," Terrence said, and made a note of it. So far, the *creative* side of this panel wasn't impressing him.

"Our next question will be from Kylie Trig," the announcer said.

The audience cheered for YouTube personality Kylie Trig as if she were an actor in the show. Kylie stood and waved to her admirers like a pageant contestant. She was in her late teens, had bright blue hair, and wore cat's-eye glasses and a rainbow tutu. Even before she opened her mouth, she was a lot to take in.

"Helloooo, Wizzers!" Kylie said into her microphone with the energy of a coked-out toddler. "It's so good to be back at WizCon!"

It wasn't long ago that Kylie was just another *Wiz Kid* superfan following the cast from airport to airport, hotel to hotel as they traveled the country on press tours. Kylie started vlogging about her brief encounters with them (stretching the truth from time to time) and developed a following of her own. As the show gained an audience, so did Kylie's videos.

Today, she was one of YouTube's most watched personalities and had become a *New York Times* bestselling author when HarperCollins published her debut memoir, *Confessions of a Fangirl: A Wizzer Love Story*. According to *Forbes* magazine, Kylie Trig was now worth more money than the whole cast put together.

Interestingly enough, the success of *Wiz Kids* went to Kylie's head more than it went to the head of anyone officially attached to the show. The girl who used to wait outside in the rain for hours just to get a glimpse of Cash, Amy, or Tobey would now only go to *Wiz Kid* events if she was paid six figures and flown private. In Cash's opinion, Kylie Trig was the American Dream for a new generation.

"My first question is for Cash *and* Amy," Kylie said. "What is the fate of Peachfuzzle? And do you love Peachfuzzle as much as the Peachfuzzlers?"

Cash stared at Kylie like she was speaking another language, but he consciously kept his emoting to a minimum so his face wouldn't be turned into an obnoxious meme later.

"Huh?" Cash asked. "What's a *Peachfuzzler?*"

Kylie playfully rolled her eyes as if he had asked her if blue was her natural color. "The shippers who ship Dr. Peachtree and Dr. Bumfuzzle," she said. "I'm sure you've seen the hashtags."

"I thought they called themselves Bumtrees," Cash said.

Kylie shook her head. "We changed it."

Terrence Wallem looked from side to side in a daze. He had no clue what the hell anyone was talking about. Whatever Peachfuzzlers or Bumtrees were, they couldn't be appropriate for the children in the audience.

"Cash and I couldn't be more thrilled so many people care so deeply about the relationship between our characters," Amy said, desperate to say something before the panel was over.

"So will they be on or off next season?" Kylie asked. *"Cash?"*

This was a very tricky question, especially since Cash didn't have an answer. The "shippers" were the most passionate group of the *Wiz Kids* fandom. If Cash said something they liked, his social media would be flooded with pictures, videos, and GIFs of Dr. Bumfuzzle and Dr. Peachtree kissing or looking lovingly at each other. If he responded with something they *didn't* like, his social media would be bombarded with pictures, videos, and GIFs of decapitated animals, human feces, and militants destroying priceless artifacts. He had to be careful.

"Well, they've been on and off since season five," Cash said with a nervous quiver in his voice. "So, since they were mostly *off* last season, I would assume they'd be back *on* next season."

His answer was music to the Peachfuzzlers' ears. The shippers throughout the audience stood and applauded. It was an emotional moment of triumph for them, as if the football team from their hometown had just won the Super Bowl.

"For the next question, we'll go back to Jennifer Smalls," the announcer said.

Jennifer leaned back in her seat, retracting her head like a snake about to strike. Cash mentally braced himself for the venom coming his way.

"My next question is also for Cash," Jennifer said. "Over the last few weeks, I've gotten hundreds of tweets from people saying they've seen you stumbling out of bars or dancing erratically in clubs. Has the stress of Hollywood caught up to you? Is it true you're hanging up your role-model cape in exchange for a pair of bad-boy boots?"

The entire convention went dead silent. Apparently you could take the girl out of *Gotcha*, but you couldn't take the *Gotcha* out of the girl. To Cash's horror, Damien spoke on his behalf before he had a chance to respond.

"People forget Cash is just a normal twenty-two-year-old when he's off set," he said. "As long as things don't get out of hand, he has every right to have a little fun while he's still young."

Cash snapped his head toward Damien so hard it was a miracle his neck didn't break. He had never heard something so kind *and* backstabbing uttered in the same breath before. Cash was tempted to splash Damien with water just to see if he would melt.

"Couldn't have said it better myself," Cash said. "Work hard, play hard—that's my motto."

"The next question will be from Terrence Wallem," the announcer said, trying to change the subject.

"Really? Oh, all right...," Terrence said, and quickly thought of another question. "How many more seasons will *Wiz Kids* be on the air?"

The entire theater sat on the edge of their seats. If it were up to them, the show would never end. For most of the audience, the show had been on for the majority of their lives—for some, the show *was* their lives. They couldn't imagine a world without it. Losing it would be like losing a family member, maybe even worse.

"We'll be on the air as long as you keep watching," Tobey said, and made a fist in the air.

"We're as dedicated to the Wizzers as they are to us," Amy said, and tossed her hair.

For a split second, Cash considered telling the audience what he had almost shared in the greenroom. Finding out he wouldn't be returning for *Wiz Kid*'s tenth season would have crushed the fans, but letting the whole world know before confirming it with his bosses would have been sweet, sweet vindication. But as Cash looked around the room at all the eager faces staring up at him, he couldn't bring himself to say it.

"Yeah...*ditto*," he said, and looked down at his hands.

His answer was followed by a deafening roar of appreciation, but Cash was so far into his own head, he didn't hear it.

In all honesty, Cash's relationship with the fans of *Wiz Kids* meant more to him than anything else in the world. Getting to do what he loved and causing so much joy in return was the greatest thing that would ever happen to him. It made all the bullshit and challenges that came with fame worth every minute. Periodic cynicism was only a tool he used to shield the weight of meaning so much to so many people.

Disappointing the Wizzers was Cash's greatest fear and he knew his leaving *Wiz Kids* would devastate them. Watching all the happiness he had inspired over the years fade and turn into heartbreak and anger would devastate him in return. Sadly, it was inevitable.

However, leaving the show wasn't what concerned him the most. The *reason* he was quitting was far more disappointing than the exit itself. Even though he had very little control over the matter, once the story got out it would spread like wildfire and his life would change forever. The inconveniences he dealt with today for being famous were nothing compared to the hurricane that waited.

Cash Carter had a deep secret he was keeping from the world, and unfortunately for him, it was only a matter of time before the truth came out.

Chapter Two

A SUMMER TO REMEMBER

The excitement of WizCon stretched far beyond the crowded halls of the Santa Clara Convention Center. In all corners of the world, fans meticulously scanned the Internet for any glimpse of the panels, exhibits, and homemade costumes inside the convention. The Wizzers' collective efforts put the investigative teams of the FBI and CIA to shame.

In Downers Grove, an Illinois suburb twenty miles outside Chicago, recent high school graduate Topher Collins was glued to his laptop as if it were dialysis. He scavenged through the depths of social media and ogled complete strangers' candid photos like a cyberstalker. He kept browsers open to every nerdy blog covering the convention and refreshed the pages every twenty seconds for the latest and greatest. His in-box chimed continuously, like a toddler playing with a reception bell, as Google Alerts pointed him in more directions for another WizCon fix.

Topher was very tall and hunched over his desk like an adult at a kid's table. He could have easily been a basketball player if it wasn't for his absolute lack of athletic ability (newborn giraffes were more coordinated than he was). Instead, Topher had been gifted with a brilliant mind and proudly displayed his valedictorian medal over the corner of the most prized possession in his bedroom: a framed season-six poster of *Wiz Kids*—signed by the cast.

He refreshed a blog called *The Nerd Herder* and was mesmerized by a new photo from the convention. A voluptuous blond woman was dressed as the Nordic Alien Queen from season five; she had hand-glued individual sequins on her skin to create the character's infamously tight jumpsuit. She left very little to the imagination and Topher's hormones were drawn to her like a paper clip to a magnet. His face was so close to his laptop he could see the pixels of his screen.

Suddenly, a video message appeared on the screen and almost gave Topher a heart attack. It was his friend Joey Davis, calling from his own bedroom just a few blocks away.

"Hey, man," Joey said. "Did I *scare* you?"

Joey was black, super handsome, and unlike Topher, very coordinated. He had been the captain of the Hip-Hop Dance Team since freshman year, the lead in every school play and musical, and had recently been voted prom king. He was well liked by everyone who knew him and he always left the people he encountered with a smile. As far as Topher knew, being a devoted Wizzer was the closest thing Joey had to a flaw.

"Dude, have you seen the girl in the Nordic Queen costume at the convention?" Topher asked him. "Total MILF! I'm sending you the link."

Topher passed the link along. Joey had a look for himself and let out a loud snort.

"Bro, you might want to read the caption before you rub one out." He laughed.

Topher quickly read the credits under the photo. *"Timothy?"* he said in shock. "That's a *man*? Oh no, I was re-creating French independent film scenes with him in my mind!!"

"I'm sure Tim would be flattered—obviously he put a lot of effort into that look," Joey said, and scrolled through the rest of the blog. "Man, what do most of these people do for a living? How can they afford these costumes? I swear the fans have better production values than the actual show."

"I know, right?" Topher said. "I saw a man dressed as a cyborg with actual plasma screens attached to his body."

"It makes the android costumes we wore to WizCon 2015 look like crap," Joey said. "And we spent *hours* putting those together. I still have scars from the hot-glue gun."

Another video message appeared on both their computers. This time it was Sam Gibson, calling from her bedroom on the other side of town. Sam was petite, pretty without any makeup, and had very short dark hair. She was still wearing her yellow uniform and hat from her summer job at Yolo FroYo.

"I *literally* just ran all the way home from work!" Sam panted. "I tried looking at the blogs on my break but I couldn't get any reception. What have I missed? Have any spoilers for season ten come out?"

"Nothing too crazy yet, just some photos of the costumes and exhibits," Topher said. "Kylie Trig hasn't even posted her recap of the panel."

"She's been taking her sweet-ass time ever since she hit ten million subscribers," Sam said. "What time is she supposed to post it?"

"Her tweet said around five o'clock California time and it's already ten past seven here, so it should be up any minute now," Joey said.

"Have any videos leaked from the panel yet? There are usually a bunch by now," Sam asked as she rummaged through the Internet to catch up with the others.

"Just a couple, but everyone is screaming so loud and shaking so much you can't hear or see anything," Topher said. "You'd think it was footage from a Bieber concert or a natural disaster."

"Same difference," Joey quipped.

Sam shook her hands and shimmied in her seat, experiencing a personal earthquake of her own.

"*I can't wait!*" she said. "They better give us some clues about what to expect. I haven't been able to sleep since the season finale! Why'd they have to end it with Dr. Bumfuzzle trapped in that Reptoidian nest on Kepler-186 and Dr. Peachtree in the courtroom of the Salem Witch Trials? That was some Hollywood sadistic shit!"

A third video message popped up on their screens. Moriko Ishikawa (or "Mo" as they had called her since elementary school) was scowling into her camera with her arms folded. She was usually bursting with bubbly energy, but at the moment Mo was frozen with dissatisfaction.

"Excuse me, but it's been *three days* since I posted chapter four of my *Wiz Kids* fanfiction novel and none of you jerks have commented on it yet," she said.

Topher, Joey, and Sam looked into their cameras very guiltily.

Even though Mo had reminded them twice an hour since it was published, they had all managed to forget.

"Sorry, Mo, I've been serving cold, sugary fermented milk to upper-class families all week," Sam said. "I promise I'll read it tonight before bed."

"I've been busy with Billy," Topher said, referring to his younger brother. "I'll check it out later."

"And I'm not going anywhere *near* fanfiction," Joey said unapologetically. "It terrifies me, especially *yours*. The last story you wrote scarred me for life. I didn't know there were so many adjectives to describe Tobey Ramous's pubes."

"I never said you had to *read* it!" Mo said. "Just go on there and leave a comment. The more comments I get, the more Wizzers will be interested. I'm trying to start a following here—*throw the Asian girl a bone*!"

"Okay, okay, okay." Joey laughed. "Calm down—I'll go on right now and make something up. What's the novel about, anyway?"

Mo tucked her hair behind her ears and sat up in her seat, as if she was describing her work on a morning talk show.

"It's a story that explores Peachfuzzle's sexual awakening," she described. "Written in the style of Nicholas Sparks, the novel opens with Dr. Bumfuzzle and Dr. Peachtree traveling through the Andromeda Galaxy when they suddenly crash on a planet where physical contact is forbidden. At first, they submit to the laws of the alien world with little resistance. However, the longer they're marooned, the more an undeniable attraction grows between them. Tension rises with every passing hour. *An animalistic desire consumes them! Soon the temptation is too much to bear! They must confess their undying love for each other using a language only their bodies can speak!*"

"Jesus Christ, Mo!" Topher laughed. "Take a cold shower!"

"That sounds *exactly* like your last story," Sam pointed out. "Is Peachfuzzle all you ever think about? You know it sends subliminal degrading messages to women, right?"

The writer swiveled her head and rolled her eyes so her frustration was evident. It didn't matter how many times she explained herself, her friends never understood her work.

"I'm not actually writing about *Peachfuzzle*, I'm just using them to gain an audience," she said. "As soon as I get a book deal I'll change the names and locations so I don't get sued and *boom*—I'll have my own franchise! Laugh at me all you want. I'm sure people laughed at E. L. James, too, but look where writing fanfiction got her!"

"All right, I just left a comment on chapter four," Joey said.

"Awesome! You're the best, Joey!" Mo happily checked her comment box, but did a dramatic double take when she read his post. "All you put was 'Nice adjectives.' Is that *all* you could come up with?"

"Hey, *you're* the writer," Joey said. "Why don't you write your own reviews and have us post them?"

Mo was initially repulsed by the idea, but the more she thought about it, the more his proposal intrigued her.

"That's actually genius," she said. "Normally I'd be turned off by something so dishonest, but fanfiction is like the fricking Hunger Games—only the cunning survive. Check your e-mail tonight, I'll send you guys comments to post later."

The other three were curious and fearful about the words Mo

would put in their mouths, but they were always happy to support one another—even in the unsettling realm of fanfiction.

Topher, Joey, Sam, and Mo couldn't have been more different, but they had been best friends since the fifth grade. It started on the playground of Schiesher Elementary School in 2010 when they all dressed as Dr. Bumfuzzle for Halloween. It was a magical moment for the fifth graders—like when Tony spots Maria across the dance floor in *West Side Story*. Prior to that, making friends and fitting in at school had not been any of their strong suits, so finding other kids who were infatuated with the same television show was a remarkable discovery. It was the beginning of an unbreakable bond and the greatest joy of their lives.

For the past seven years, every Wednesday at eight o'clock, the unlikely quartet would meet up at a predetermined location and watch the newest episode of *Wiz Kids* together. They'd spend the following week stressing about the plot, overanalyzing it beat by beat, and making predictions of what the next episode had in store. The routine repeated week after week, month after month, until the season finale put them out of their misery. (Unless the season ended on a torturous cliff-hanger; then there'd be chaos until the show returned.)

Their enthusiasm for such an outlandish program was questioned and ridiculed by everyone they knew, but to them, *Wiz Kids* was so much more than just a trivial television show. It was their first memory of true excitement and gave their childhoods a purpose. It took them on otherworldly and educational adventures, showing them the world beyond the dull streets of Downers Grove. Most important, it was their first experience of camaraderie and gave them a sense of belonging they had never known before. The show was the corner-stone and driving force of their friendship, and they hoped it would continue for many years to come.

And *Wiz Kids* hadn't just introduced Topher, Joey, Sam, and Mo to one another, but also to passionate Wizzers from around the world.

A fourth video message appeared on their computers from their e-friend Davi, a thirteen-year-old boy from Macapá, Brazil. He was thin, had light brown skin, and had wide eyes like a doe. They could see the moonlit waves of the Brazilian coast in the distance behind him.

"Hey Davi!" everyone said together.

"Olá, fucktards," Davi said—his use of American slang was a work in progress. "Happy WizCon Day! Sorry it took me so long to join you. The cybercafe is busy as tits tonight."

"What episode is airing in Brazil?" Sam asked. "Has Dr. Bum-fuzzle gotten to Kepler-186 yet?"

"No, he and Professor Luckunckle are still fighting Nazis with General Patton," Davi said. "Are they going into space soon? I sure shitting hope so. All this American history is hard to follow."

"Oh just you wait!" Sam teased. "The season-nine cliff-hanger is going to blow your mind!"

Topher's e-mail chimed with a notification from YouTube.

"Guys, Kylie Trig just posted her recap!" Topher announced. "Let's go to YouTube and watch it together. We'll press Play on the count of three."

"No, we have to wait for Huda," Mo interjected. "She'll be devas-tated if we watch it without her."

"It's three o'clock in the morning over there," Joey said. "She's probably asleep."

As if Huda had been just waiting for an introduction, she appeared in a fifth video message on their screens. Huda was a fifteen-year-old Muslim girl from Saudi Arabia. She had a round face, big cheeks, and adorable dimples. Even though she lived on the other side of the world, Huda's knowledge of American pop culture and Hollywood gossip always impressed everyone. If it was a headline, Huda knew about it.

"Please tell me you haven't watched Kylie's recap without me!" she said, inches away from her webcam.

"Hi, Huda," Topher said. "Perfect timing. We were just about to go to YouTube and watch it together."

"Wait!" Huda objected. "They censor my shit over here—I don't get YouTube. Can't you play it on your iPad and hold it up to your camera for the rest of us? Pretty please?"

"Works for me," Topher said, and loaded the video on his iPad.

"Huda, if everything is so censored, how did you even know the video had been posted?" Joey asked.

Huda looked around her home to make sure no one was listening.

"The Wizzer anticensorship train," she whispered. "Whenever something notable happens in the *Wiz Kids* fandom, the Wizzers in Mexico message the Wizzers in Puerto Rico, who message the Wizzers in Cuba, who message the Wizzers in Japan, who message the Wizzers in China, who message the Wizzers in Russia, who message the Wizzers in Turkey, who message the Wizzers throughout the countries in the Middle East like me in Saudi Arabia. It's a very complex system and it took *years* to perfect, but we knocked through those firewalls like Jenga."

The others were impressed such a covert and proficient system had been set up in the Wizzer community, but they weren't surprised. It was a testimony to the official slogan of the *Wiz Kids*' viewership: "When there's a Wizzer, there's a way."

"That's incredible, Huda," Mo said. "If only diplomacy worked as efficiently as a fandom, there would never be war again."

"Kylie's video is loaded!" Topher said. "Should I play it?"

"*YES!*" everyone shouted, and leaned closer to their computers.

Topher pressed Play and held his iPad up to his computer's camera for the others to see. The video had only been up for three minutes and already had four million views. They impatiently sat through a fifteen-second ad for an energy drink called CherryInsulin, followed by the thirty-second-long introduction to all Kylie Trig's videos (in which she sang an obnoxious theme song and hit a tambourine off-beat to the music).

Finally, fresh footage appeared of Kylie lounging on a tufted chaise in the presidential suite of her Santa Clara hotel.

"*Whaaad up, Wizzer sluts!*" Kylie said. "Welcome to another episode of *Trig Talk with Kylie Trig*! How am I doing, you ask? Not too shabby.... Just got back from the 'Cast and Creative Panel' at Wiz-Con 2017.... No biggie.... We've got more to dish and dissect than a marine biologist, but first let me answer the question most of my subscribers want to know: Cash Carter confirmed that next season of Wiz Kids.... *Peachfuzzle is back ON, mothafuckaaaas!*"

Kylie shook a maraca and twirled her leg above her head like she was a human helicopter. Mo and Huda squealed so loud they almost blew out Topher's speakers.

"Here are the deets y'all Wizzer bitches need to know from the rest of the panel," Kylie continued. "First, let's talk about the cast: Tobey Ramous is looking buff as fuck—I would totally tap that ass if I wasn't afraid he'd crush me. *Memo to Amy Evans*: if you're going to take a selfie on a stage, make sure to include the audience so we can tag ourselves in it later—it's called *manners*. Cash Carter is rocking Robert Pattinson's *too-hungover-to-care* look these days, but honestly, he doesn't pull it off. By the way, he was *totes* flirting with me when I asked him about Peachfuzzle, not that I'm surprised—happens every year."

"Get to the season-ten details, you overrated stalker!" Sam yelled on behalf of everyone in the fandom.

"I don't mean to be *Frank and Beans*, but I was by far the best moderator at the panel," Kylie went on. "They paired me up with ol' Prostate McGee from *The Hollywood Reporter* and Jennifer Whogivesafuck from *Entertainment Weekly*. She had the *audacity* to call out Cash Carter on his recent benders in Hollywood. I know we've all been concerned about it—I personally hosted a candlelight vigil on the matter in my last video—but there are certain things you just *don't* bring up at WizCon! Anyway, shit got *reeeaaaal* uncomfortable. Luckily, *Has-Beener-Zimmer* put out the flames. Now let's get to what we learned about season ten...."

"Finally!" Joey said.

"The cast confirmed the show will stay on air as long as we watch it, so we can all just chill the fuck out about that—I'm talking to you,

WizzerJane97," Kylie said. "However, Professor Luckunckle will be absent for three episodes in the fall because Tobey Ramous is committed to *Moth-Man* reshoots—apparently Warner Brothers already knows the movie will need them. Also, if you don't like the storyline on Kepler-186, that's too damn bad. The Reptoids are sticking around until the middle of season ten."

"The Reptoids are *back*? No cocking way!" Davi said, and wrapped his arms around his head.

"That's the season-finale twist I was telling you about," Sam said.

"Don't talk about the season finale!" Huda begged. "The Wizzers in Turkey haven't sent it to me yet!"

"*Has-Beener-Zimmer* also said there will be three surprise guest stars in season ten," Kylie said. "He wouldn't say who, but gave these hints: one has an Oscar, one has a Grammy, and one has a sex tape. He also promised the fans he would not write another role for himself or force another *Who's the Parent?* reunion down our throats. Episode 907 was just as painful for him as it was for us—I'm paraphrasing of course. Well, that's all the info I've got for you today, Wizzer sluts. Tune in tomorrow for my recap of the *Wiz Kids* 'Post Production Panel.' And if you haven't subscribed to my channel yet—*kill yourself.* Peace!"

Kylie's video concluded with another thirty seconds of her obnoxious, self-performed theme song, but thankfully Topher clicked his iPad off before it finished. All the people on his computer were quiet and motionless as they processed the information Kylie had revealed. Once it was absorbed, they erupted in contagious spurts of exhilaration, like cheap fireworks setting each other off.

"That was awesome!" Joey said. "I wonder how they're going to write Professor Luckunckle off for three episodes."

"Or who the surprise guest stars are going to be," Sam said.

"I can't believe we have to wait eighty-one days until the next season!" Mo said. "That's practically a pregnancy!"

"Girl, please," Huda said. "That's a wink compared to how long I have to wait. I'll be lucky if I'm caught up with season nine by then."

"But *Reptoids*?" Davi asked, still stuck on the topic. "Are they dusting my balls? I *hate* the Reptoids!"

Topher was just as eager about the things his friends were pointing out, but they were overlooking the *best* news to come out of Wiz-Con 2017.

"I'm just happy they confirmed the show is sticking around," Topher said. "We were kind of counting on it."

With graduation in their rearview mirrors, Topher, Joey, Sam, and Mo would be splitting up soon to attend different colleges in the fall. Topher was staying in Downers Grove for community college, Joey was going to Oklahoma Baptist University for performing arts, Sam was headed to the Rhode Island School of Design to study interior design, and Mo would be attending Stanford to major in economics.

Regardless of their new locations, they were still very committed to their Wednesday night *Wiz Kids* ritual; they'd just be doing it over the Internet. Now with the certainty that *Wiz Kids* would continue throughout their college years, the pending good-bye was a lot easier to swallow. And since their time together was limited, Topher, Joey, Sam, and Mo had big plans to make the most of it.

"Are you guys excited for your road trip?" Huda asked. "You're leaving tomorrow, right?"

"You guys didn't tell me you were going on a road trip!" Davi said.

"We didn't want to brag, but it's going to be a lot of fun," Joey said. "Our parents helped us pay for it as graduation gifts."

"Speak for yourself," Sam corrected him. "I had to get a summer job to pay for my quarter of the costs."

"Topher's planned out the whole thing!" Mo added. "His mom is even letting us borrow her station wagon."

"Where are you guys going? How long will you be gone for? Tell me everything!" Davi said.

Topher rubbed his hands together as he informed their e-friends of their exciting itinerary. He looked like a criminal mastermind reciting his plan for world domination.

"We'll be gone for about two weeks," he said. "We're driving from Illinois to California. The first five days we'll be on the road checking out roadside attractions, historical landmarks, and national parks on the way. We're going to see the world's biggest rubber-band ball, the St. Louis Gateway Arch, the Lewis and Clark Museum, the Mark Twain National Forest, the Bundy and Claire Jailhouse, the UFO Observation Tower, Dinoworld, the Petrified Forest, the Arizona Meteor Crater, the Grand Canyon, and then, finally, the Santa Monica Pier. We'll be in Santa Monica for four days so we can explore Los Angeles, hang out in Hollywood, and take an exclusive tour of the *Wiz Kids* sets on the Sunshine Studios lot!"

"You've got to be fondling me!" Davi exclaimed.

"I am *so* jealous!" Huda said.

"Wish you guys could come with us," Sam said.

Mo suddenly let out a quick screech and everyone jumped. Topher's thorough description had reminded her of something very important she needed to do before the trip.

"Mo, are you okay?" Joey asked. "Did someone leave a nasty comment on your fanfiction?"

"No—I just realized I haven't even packed yet!" Mo said.

"Crap, me either," Joey said. "I've got to sign off and do some laundry. What time are we meeting in the morning?"

"Ten o'clock sharp," Topher said. "And we've got to be prompt so everything else in the schedule times out."

"Aye, aye, Captain," Joey said with a salute. "See you guys in the morning!"

"Bye, Huda, bye, Davi!" Mo said, and blew them a kiss.

Mo and Joey disappeared from their friends' computers screens. Davi and Huda's time zones were starting to get the best of them and they both yawned like newborn puppies.

"I have to say good night, too," Davi said. "It's late as douchebags down here and the cybercafe is about to close."

"I'm going to take a nap before breakfast," Huda said. "Have fun on your trip, guys! Post pictures as you go—I'll have my contact in Turkey keep an eye out for them!"

The Wizzers from abroad signed off and Topher and Sam were the only two left. They were usually the last two on their computers and sometimes continued the conversation until the wee hours of the morning. Topher had nothing against Joey and Mo, but he always looked forward to his alone time with Sam.

"What a night," she said. "I'm so overstimulated I doubt I'll sleep much."

"Don't worry, I'm taking the first driving shift tomorrow," Topher said. "You can sleep in the car if you need to."

Although he would never admit it, Topher had been crushing on Sam since the eighth grade. He had been in denial about it for five years and was constantly fighting off his feelings like they were symptoms of an oncoming cold—but nothing could cure him of *Sam*. There was something about her that was different from all the other girls Topher had ever known; it was something familiar that made her so easy to talk to and fun to be around. He was convinced there was no one else like her on earth.

There were many times Topher had suspected Sam might feel the same way about him, but she was a tough egg to crack. As close as they were, Sam had always been a very guarded person. But perhaps that was what Topher found most intriguing about her: Sam was a mystery waiting to be solved.

"I'm so excited about our trip," she said. "But it's kind of bittersweet, you know? In a couple months we'll be so far away from each other. Each time I try to wrap my head around it, I get so depressed."

"I know exactly how you feel," Topher said. "Look at it this way: our band isn't breaking up, we're just gonna take a sabbatical until our inevitable comeback."

Sam gave him a sweet smile and Topher melted inside.

"Yeah, I like that," she said. "Our road trip isn't our final tour, it's just to tide us over until the next adventure. Thanks again for taking the time to plan it, Topher. It means the world to us."

"Don't mention it," Topher said. "It'll be a summer to remember."

"You've got that right," Sam said. "Well, I'm gonna try to rest. Good night, see you tomorrow!"

"Good night, Sam."

She signed off and the only thing left on Topher's blank computer screen was his own reflection staring back at him. For the first time, a profound loneliness began to fill the pit of his stomach. Since he was the only one among his friends staying in Downers Grove for college, the upcoming farewell was much more harrowing for Topher. The others got to move on in a way he didn't—like he was a bird still stuck in the nest.

Staying in Downers Grove hadn't been Topher's first choice. He had applied and been accepted to MIT and had been looking forward to attending the prestigious school in the fall. Being in Massachusetts also meant he'd be close to Sam in Rhode Island, which really sweetened the deal. Unfortunately, life had other plans.

There was a soft knock on Topher's door.

"Come in," he said.

Topher's mother, Shelly Collins, stepped inside his bedroom. She was already dressed for her night shift at the hotel she worked at in Chicago.

"Hey," she said. "Hope I'm not interrupting WizFest."

"Mom, for the hundredth time, it's *WizCon*," Topher said. "And we just finished."

"Oh sorry, *WizCon*," Shelly said. "Well, I'm headed to work. Billy is already asleep downstairs so you don't need to worry about putting him to bed."

Topher's twelve-year-old brother had cerebral palsy and had been confined to a wheelchair for most his life. Even though he had limited speech and needed assistance eating, bathing, dressing, and using the restroom, *disabled* and *handicapped* were words Topher would never use to describe his brother. Billy was the happiest and most loving child Topher had ever met. He laughed and smiled at every opportunity he could, even if there was nothing to laugh or smile about. It was like Billy knew a secret the rest of the world hadn't figured out yet.

"Cool, I'll check on him before I go to bed," Topher said.

"Thank you, sweetheart," Shelly said, but lingered in the doorway.

"Anything else?" he asked.

There definitely was—Shelly had a look in her eye that told Topher she had something serious she needed to get off her chest. She had a seat on his bed so they could talk.

"I've felt so guilty I haven't had a chance to thank you," Shelly said. "What you're doing for your brother—what you're doing for our family—well, it's something that should've *never* been asked of you."

"Mom, you gotta stop feeling bad about it," Topher said. "If I went away to school, you couldn't juggle Billy and work all on your own. Dad's teaching gig in Seattle is only going to last two more years—that gives me plenty of time to get my GE degree here and transfer to someplace fancier when he gets back. It'll be a lot cheaper for me in the long run, too."

"Just because it makes sense doesn't make it right," Shelly said, and glanced up at his valedictorian medal. "You worked so hard in school so you could go to a good college. I never wanted your brother to set you back in any way, or give you a reason to resent him later."

Although a good portion of Billy's care fell on Topher's shoulders, he never resented his brother. Having a sibling with special needs was exhausting and stressful in ways people could never understand without experiencing it themselves, but the only resentment Topher ever felt was toward the people who *pretended* to know what it was like—or worse, the people who didn't even *try*.

In many ways, Topher had more reasons to be thankful for his brother. Living with someone who had actual struggles and genuine limitations gave Topher a unique perspective on his own life: Topher was an overachiever and a perfectionist because, in his mind, there was no reason he *couldn't* be. His daily inconveniences seemed so minor in comparison to his brother's. And knowing his brother would become his sole responsibility one day when their parents were gone, Topher never gave himself the option of failing.

Billy wasn't keeping Topher from success; he was the *key* to Topher's success.

"Mom, I would never blame Billy for this," Topher said. "This is my decision and no one else's. And it's not a setback, it's just a detour. MIT isn't going anywhere."

Shelly smiled, but the guilt never left her eyes.

"I don't know what I did to deserve a son like you," she said. "Now, speaking of detours, is everything set for your trip tomorrow?"

"I think so," Topher said. "Thanks again for letting us use your car and taking the time off work so I could go."

"It's the least I could do," Shelly said, and checked her watch. "I better get going so I'm not late—the drunks and stoners aren't going to check in themselves. I'll stop at the gas station on my way home so you can start your day tomorrow with a full tank."

She kissed her son on the forehead and left for work.

Topher would have been lying to himself if he said he was happy about the decision to stay home for college. Still, he knew the right decision wasn't always the easy one—that was a lesson Dr. Bumfuzzle had taught him in one of the early episodes of *Wiz Kids*.

He felt pathetic for thinking it, but even at eighteen, Topher held the fictional doctor in as much regard as he had when he was a child. Cash Carter's character had always been a source of strength and inspiration during rough times. To this day, whenever he faced a challenge, Topher asked himself, *What would Dr. Bumfuzzle do?* and an answer would present itself.

Even though the character didn't exist, Topher was often inclined to express his gratitude for his positive influence. So whenever the spirit moved him, he'd venture to CashCarter.com and write the actor a thank-you letter. It was either that or have a conversation with the poster in his bedroom.

> Dear Mr. Carter,
>
> It's Topher Collins again from Downers Grove, Illinois. I know I've said this to you a thousand times, but once again I feel the need to thank you for your work on the show. I understand as an actor you have very little control over the things your character does, but the way you've portrayed him through the years has had such a profound effect on my

friends and me. He's our hero and we have you to thank.

Watching *Wiz Kids* is what brought us together, and watching the show is going to keep us together. We recently graduated high school and are splitting up soon to attend different colleges. I don't know how we would stay connected if it weren't for our Wednesday-night viewing parties. I'm sure it isn't easy being famous or working on the same show for so long, but please know you have fans that couldn't be more grateful for everything you do.

I don't want to take any more of your time, but in case I get busy with school and don't have a chance to write you again, it's been a pleasure watching you and a privilege growing up with you.

Sincerely,
Topher Collins
Downers Grove, Illinois

PS—We leave tomorrow for a cross-country road trip. If you're free, we would love for you to join us! LOL.

Topher figured that was enough vulnerability for one letter and sent it in. Just like all the letters he had sent Cash Carter over the years, he was sure it would get lost among the thousands the actor received daily. Regardless, it felt nice to pay his respects.

Topher went downstairs to check on his brother and found Billy sound asleep in his favorite Captain America pajamas. He slept so peacefully it made Topher tired just looking at him. With a huge day ahead of him, Topher got a glass of water from the kitchen and climbed the stairs back to his room to put himself to bed.

When Topher returned to his bedroom, the first thing that caught his eye was a notification on his computer screen he had never seen before. It was an alert from CashCarter.com letting him know his letter had been received... and the actor had *replied*!

Topher's heart began palpitating and almost dropped into his stomach. *Was this real life?* He read the notification over and over again but it never changed. *Holy shit this was real life!* He dashed to his desk at lightning speed, tripped over his chair, and crawled on his knees to the edge of his desk. He clicked the link on the notification and the actor's response loaded. With two words, Topher Collins's life would never be the same:

What time?

Chapter Three

WHAT THE PSYCHIC SAID

Sam Gibson hated garlic with a fiery passion. At four o'clock, Monday through Saturday, the restaurant below her mother's apartment, Garliholic's, fired up its stoves and sent a strong aroma through the floorboards of Sam's bedroom. The odor clung to her clothes and was impossible to mask with perfume or cologne, so she carried it wherever she went like a smelly Scarlet Letter.

The only thing in Sam's arsenal to combat the zesty fumes was a collection of candles that rivaled the altar of a Catholic church. She had every seasonal and exotic fragrance imaginable laid out on her windowsill and lit them *all* to battle Garliholic's. Sometimes the combination of so many scents gave Sam a headache, but it was better than smelling the restaurant's sixty-clove chicken pasta specialty (which people ordered in droves every night despite all the one-star ratings Sam posted on Yelp).

The layered smell also acted as a repellent for Sam's nosy mother, keeping her away from Sam's room and out of her things—a happy byproduct.

Deep down, Sam was grateful for her intrusive mom and the garlic restaurant below them. Being smoked out of her own bedroom and preyed upon like a three-legged field mouse was perfect motivation to get the hell out of Downers Grove. As sad as Sam was about separating from her friends, she was counting down the days until she moved to Providence and attended the Rhode Island School of Design.

Sam was an extremely gifted artist for two reasons: she was *talented* and she was *poor*. She learned early in life that if she wanted nice things she would have to get creative and make them herself. And Sam was planning to make a career out of this skill.

Of all the credentials in her application, the Rhode Island School of Design admissions board had been most impressed with Sam's portfolio of the do-it-yourself furniture in her bedroom and the descriptions of how she created it.

Dumpster Diving Décor is how I would describe my unique style of design, Sam wrote.

> *The platform and headboard of my twin mattress are made from a stack of wooden crates I found on the side of the road. Above my bed, the suspended bookshelves were shopping baskets I found in an alley, painted red, and nailed to the wall. My lounge chairs used to be halves of a huge tire I rolled home from a junkyard. I lined the inside with red cushions and use the hubcap as a coffee table between them. My bedroom didn't have a closet, so I made a*

*wardrobe out of an old fridge from the restaurant
below my apartment. I painted the appliance
turquoise and stuck the handles of an old mop
and broom through it to hang my clothes.*

*The lighting in my apartment is terrible, so I took
a bicycle wheel, wrapped it in Christmas lights,
replaced the bulbs with empty liquor bottles to
magnify the light, spray painted everything gold,
and created a chandelier any rock star would be
envious of. I made a stand for my record player
and vinyl collection out of a stack of 1950s suitcases
from my late grandfather's attic. I covered a wall
with the record covers and now the Rolling Stones,
the Smiths, the Knack, Gang of Four, and the Killers
watch over my bedroom like rock guardian angels.*

*My mother made the mistake of giving me her old
vanity set. She expected me to keep it in pristine
condition, but I painted it black, beat it with a chain
(that part was just for fun), covered it with hundreds
of witty bumper stickers, and now I use it as a
computer desk. I'm not a big fan of mirrors, so I
covered the oval plate of glass with pictures of
my friends and magazine cutouts of my favorite
television show, Wiz Kids.*

All it took was one glimpse of Sam's portfolio and anyone could
tell she had a gift. (The portfolio also made it obvious Sam was in
desperate need of financial aid to attend RISD, so she passed it along
to every scholarship program she applied to as well.) However, recy-
cling objects of convenient shapes and sizes was much more than just
a hobby for her. Restoring what others had cast aside, giving it a new

purpose, and granting it a new identity was Sam's greatest therapy. She only wished transforming herself could be as easy as upgrading the trash she found—but Sam would need much more than a fresh coat of paint for what she had in mind.

"Well, I'm gonna try to rest," Sam said into her computer. "Good night, see you tomorrow!"

"Good night, Sam," Topher said back at her.

Just as Sam logged off her computer, her mother, Candy Rae Gibson, walked into her bedroom without knocking. She had a bulging shopping bag in one hand and a vodka gimlet in the other. If there were a statue erected in Candy's honor, it would need these items to look authentic.

"Good Lord, Samantha," Candy said, and winced at the smell of the candles. "Do you really need *all* those going at once? It's like a séance in here—but I can't tell if you're summoning the dead or scaring off the living."

"Mom, you're violating my privacy when you don't knock," Sam said.

"Oh, please," Candy said, and rolled her eyes. "I wish there was something going on in this room that *warranted* privacy. The day I catch you watching pornography or smoking a joint I'll die of shock."

"Noted," Sam said under her breath.

The fact that Sam was Candy Rae Gibson's daughter was proof God had a sick sense of humor. In Sam's opinion, her mother was feminine to a fault. Candy always had big hair, long nails, wore too much makeup, and hadn't owned a pair of pants since the eighties. She was very friendly but not very bright, and often reminded people of a large cocker spaniel.

Candy worked as a hairdresser at a local salon and told all her clients at great length and in great detail how she was crowned Miss Georgia Peach 1999 at just eighteen years old—not that any of them asked. Coincidently, she had also been pregnant with Sam at the time, which made her cry on demand better than all her competitors. The open floodgates following the "world peace" question were what secured her the crown. Occasionally, after Candy had one too many vodka gimlets, Sam would find her waltzing around the apartment in her old tiara and sash.

"What do you want, Mother?" Sam asked as if her presence was causing her physical pain.

"I just got back from the store and picked you up some clothes I thought you'd like for your trip."

Candy emptied the shopping bag on Sam's bed. To her daughter's horror, it was a pile of tank tops, miniskirts, lacy bras, and neon panties. They were clothes for a barbecue at Barbie and Ken's, not a cross-country road trip with her friends.

"You know I wouldn't be caught dead in any of those," Sam said.

"Would it kill you to add a little color to your wardrobe?" Candy asked. "Everything you own looks like it was bought at a nineties grunge concert. You've got the same figure I had when I was your age; I wish you'd let it show once in a while."

"That's how I dress," Sam said. "It's what I like to wear, it's what I'm most comfortable in, and that's always how it's going to be."

"You might change your mind one day," Candy said with a shrug.

The hopeful hairdresser looked from side to side as if she knew something Sam didn't.

"Mom, you're doing that thing with your eyes again," Sam said. "If you have something to say, please just spit it out."

"You want to know the truth? Fine, here it is," Candy said. "I stopped by the psychic on Fourth Street after work today. She told me a bunch of really interesting things. Apparently I was royalty in a past life, I'm going to make a good investment soon, Grandpa says hello, *yada yada yada*.... But the most interesting stuff she had to say was about you."

"The psychic told you I needed new clothes?"

"No, she told me there's a *boy* in your life that you aren't telling me about!"

Sam's eyes bulged so large they almost rolled out of her head.

"What?" she said.

"I told her that couldn't possibly be true because I would have known if you were dating someone," Candy went on. "But Madame Beauffont was adamant about it. She couldn't give me his name or age but described him in great detail. He sounds perfect for you—I'm talking soul mate material! He listens to the same music as you, likes making things out of trash, and he even watches that ridiculous show you're so obsessed with. Now, I know I'm the last person you like to talk to about these things, but if there was a boy, or a boy you had your eye on, I thought you might want a cute outfit to wear around him."

Sam tried to stop her mom from talking with every gesture she knew, but her mouth was like a runaway train with no conductor.

"Seriously, Mom?" she said. "I've told you a million times there are no boys in my life. Are you going to take Madame Beauffont's word over mine?"

"She's a world-renowned clairvoyant, Samantha," Candy said. "Why is it so hard for you to talk to me about these things? Having a boyfriend is perfectly natural for a girl your age. I'm trying to be supportive but you freak out every time I bring up the subject. Are you a lesbian or something?"

"No, I'm not a lesbian!"

"Then what are you so ashamed of, Samantha?" Candy asked.

Sam went quiet. She knew *why* it was such a touchy subject; she just wasn't ready to have the conversation with her mother yet. It was beyond Candy's level of comprehension.

"I'm not ashamed of anything," Sam said. "Boys just aren't a priority for me right now. I wish you'd respect that."

Candy threw her hands in the air in surrender and put all the clothes back into the shopping bag.

"I'm not trying to be disrespectful, I'm just impatient," Candy said. "I'll take these back to the store tomorrow. Now I've got to get out of this room before those candles give me a migraine."

Candy left Sam's room in a dramatic and defeated sulk. The psychic had been so accurate about everything else—how could she have been so wrong about this?

However, if Candy could read her daughter as well as Sam read her mother, she would know her daughter wasn't being completely truthful. The psychic was *right*: There was a boy Sam had been hiding from her mother, but it wasn't a boyfriend like Candy so desperately hoped. The boy in her daughter's life *was* her daughter.

There were very few things Sam Gibson knew for a fact, but she knew with all her heart, body, and soul that *he* was transgender.

When he was young, Sam never thought twice about his hatred of wearing dresses, his reluctance to let his mother put his hair up in a bow, or his preference for playing with the boys in his neighborhood as opposed to the girls. He despised the phrases *little girl* and *young lady,* but that was because they were always followed with instructions to sit up straight or behave a certain way. Sam didn't realize until he was much older that these were subtle hints his true self was sending him.

Sam had always been different from other girls, but it was around the third grade when his feelings surpassed *being different* and something felt blatantly *wrong.* For the first time, he and his classmates were no longer *students,* but divided into groups of young *men* and *women.* The segregation seemed to come with an invisible set of new rules, expectations, and restrictions that he had never put on himself. It made him uncomfortable but he didn't understand why. He knew he was a girl—that was obvious—so why didn't he feel like one? Why did he feel like a boy on the inside? Why did he want to be treated like one?

It was confusing, frustrating, and unfair all at once and the feeling got stronger the more time passed.

Sam's childhood was haunted with questions he couldn't answer. Was he a freak of nature? Was something broken inside of him? Had God made a mistake with him? Was God punishing him for something? He attended Sunday school with his friend Joey so he could learn how to pray and ask God to *fix* him. Every night Sam prayed to wake up the following morning in the correct body, but his prayers were never answered.

In the sixth grade, the beginning stages of puberty felt more like a hijacking than a natural progression. His body wasn't growing as much as it was *betraying* him. Every day he was altered a little more into something he wasn't meant to be. It didn't matter how many health videos he watched in preparation, the thought of emerging from his teens as a *woman* seemed foreign and improbable, like a caterpillar emerging from its cocoon as a spider.

Sam thought if he ignored the changes, his body might reject or reverse them. Instead of asking for a bra, Sam wrapped an ace bandage around his developing breasts until his chest appeared flat. The more they grew, the tighter he'd suppress them—sometimes the bandage left bloody cuts around his torso. Eventually he purchased a sports bra that gave the same effect, but it strangely felt like a moment of defeat; he was losing the war with his own body.

It was all so difficult for Sam to grasp; he didn't expect anyone else could possibly understand. He was afraid his friends and mom would treat him like Frankenstein's monster if they knew the truth, so Sam put up a strong guard, preventing anyone from getting too close and preventing himself from letting anything telling slip out. Sam thought this prevention was the only way he could protect himself, but sadly it sent him into an asphyxiating isolation. Even when surrounded by his closest friends, Sam felt completely alone.

It wasn't until middle school that Sam even heard the word *transgender*. Of course he had *read* the word once or twice before, but something about *hearing* it opened his eyes to its meaning. He was flipping through television channels late one night and came across a rerun of an old talk show. The headline read *Transgender in America* and the host interviewed two trans women and one trans man. Sam was on the edge of his seat as he watched the program. The trans guests talked about the struggles of growing up as the opposite gender, the frustration of living in a world that didn't understand them, and the freedom that came with their transitions.

As if the dust had been cleared off the windshield of his mind, Sam realized for the first time that he was trans, too. He couldn't be a freak of nature, or God's mistake, and he certainly wasn't a monster when there were millions of people just like him around the world. Sam was embarrassed it hadn't clicked before, but *transgender* wasn't a term used regularly on the streets of Downers Grove.

By the time Sam reached high school, he wasn't tormented by questions about *who* he was, but was besieged with questions like: *What should I do next? What are the steps of transitioning? How many do I want to take? Do I tell my friends and family? Will they accept me for who I really am? Am I strong enough to get by if they don't?*

The information Sam found and the people he spoke with online were helpful, but many recommended he find a counselor he could talk with in person. Besides covering his share of the road trip (and wanting to leave for college with a little cash in his pocket), one of the reasons Sam got a summer job at Yolo FroYo was to pay for sessions with a therapist. He made his first appointment with Dr. Eugene Sherman, a clinical psychologist whose office was walking distance from his work.

The psychologist was older than Sam was expecting, he had more hair growing out of his ears than his head, he didn't make eye contact with his receptionist, and he displayed a framed picture of himself with George W. Bush in his waiting room. There were plenty of warning signs, but Sam was so thankful to finally have someone to talk to, he ignored them.

"So you believe you're a man trapped inside a woman's body?" Dr. Sherman asked.

"Oh gosh, I hate it when people put it that way," Sam said. "That sounds like dialogue from an eighties' sitcom. I'd just say I'm a female-to-male transgender person—it sounds much more factual and less like a punch line."

"Have you shared any of this with your friends?" Dr. Sherman asked.

"No," Sam said. "My friend Joey comes from a really religious family, so I'm not sure what he would think. Mo can be really dramatic, so she's not the first person I want to tell. And Topher—well, the news might be hardest on him."

"You don't think he'll accept you?"

"It has nothing to do with acceptance," Sam said. "Don't get me wrong—Topher's like a saint. He could have gone to any college he wanted, but he's staying in town to help his mom take care of his disabled little brother. Telling Topher the truth will only be difficult because...well, because he has a crush on me."

"Is the feeling reciprocated?"

"You mean, do *I* have a crush on *Topher*?" he asked. "I'm not sure I've ever thought about it. I'm definitely attracted to men, if that's what you're asking. But I've been so focused on *being myself* that *being with someone else* hasn't really been a priority. Does that make sense?"

The psychologist made a note of it.

"And what do your parents think?"

"My mom couldn't handle it," Sam said, and shivered at just the thought of telling her. "She cries at every episode of *Grey's Anatomy*—I can't imagine what this would do to her. She'd probably take me to a witch doctor or hide estrogen pills in my food."

"And what about your father?"

"Oh, I've never met my dad," Sam said. "He was long gone before my mom found out she was pregnant."

"Have you ever had a stable father figure in your life?"

"Lots of figures, but never *stable*." Sam laughed. "My mom bounced from boyfriend to boyfriend, job to job, and city to city, dragging me all the way up the Mississippi River until we settled in Downers Grove. She made me call her 'Big Sis' until I was eight. If that doesn't paint the family dynamic I'm working with, I don't know what will—*hence why I'm here*."

Dr. Sherman found this remarkably interesting and made several notes.

"Well, Ms. Gibson, I have wonderful news," the psychologist said. "You're not transgender."

After spending almost an hour sharing his deepest secret, this was the last thing Sam expected to hear.

"Excuse me?" he asked.

"Growing up without a father and with an undependable mother, I assume there were many times in your childhood when you had to act as your own parent," Dr. Sherman said very confidently. "You had no choice but to assume the role of caretaker, not only for yourself, but at times for your mother as well. In the absence of a male presence, *you* had to be 'the man of the house,' so to speak. Therefore, it is perfectly understandable why you desire a male identity."

Sam felt like he had driven his car to a body shop for repairs and the mechanic was calling it a horse.

"I'm sorry, but I don't think that's accurate," he said. "I'm transgender because I identify with a sex that differs from my body. It has nothing to do with not having a father figure in my life."

"Yes, I understand you *believe* you're transgender, but it is my professional opinion that you're suffering from identity confusion—"

"I'm not confused about anything," Sam said. "This has been something I've struggled with and kept hidden since I was a child. I don't think you understand how hard it was to come here and tell someone about it. I came here for advice on what to do next and how to tell my loved ones, not to be treated like I'm crazy."

Dr. Sherman took off his glasses and set his notes aside. The next two words that came out of his mouth made Sam realize the psychologist would never understand and he had made a grave mistake in coming to see him.

"*Young lady,*" the psychologist said. "I have studied the human mind for more than four decades. I understand the appeal of joining the transgender community, but I promise you, the transgender movement is nothing short of a trend for nonconformists. In fact, it is still considered a mental illness by the World Health Organization. I would very much like to help you, but mutilating your body is not something I will recommend when your issues can be worked out through counseling."

Sam was at a loss for words but with an abundance of emotion.

He felt his whole life had been spent in a straitjacket, and the first person he had asked to loosen it only made it tighter.

"I'll make you a deal," Dr. Sherman said. "Go home and look up the unemployment rate, the poverty rate, the harassment rate, and the victims-of-violence rate of transgender Americans. If you are still confident that it is the lifestyle you'd like to lead, I'll be happy to recommend another psychologist. But until then, I'm afraid there's nothing more I can do for you."

Sam had expected to leave Dr. Sherman's office feeling liberated, confident, and enthusiastic to pursue the life he was meant to lead. Instead, as Sam walked home he felt more depleted, scared, and isolated than ever before. If he couldn't get support from a clinical psychologist, could he find it in his friends and family? Could he make the transition without them? Could he find the strength to transition all by himself?

The only thing that could help him answer his latest batch of questions was *time* and time alone.

Every night since his awful visit with Dr. Sherman, Sam watched his favorite episode of *Wiz Kids* to cheer himself up before falling asleep. Episode 313, "Prisoners of the Asteroid Belt," followed Dr. Bumfuzzle as he chiseled through hundreds of asteroids and freed an alien species imprisoned inside them. The Celestial Angels, as they were called, were a beautiful race with pale transparent bodies and wide holographic wings. Once freed, the angels happily fluttered off into space, eager to rejoin their families in their home galaxy across the universe.

"Prisoners of the Asteroid Belt" resonated with Sam more than any other episode of *Wiz Kids*. At times he felt just like a Celestial Angel trapped inside an asteroid, but Dr. Bumfuzzle wasn't going to appear and save him. If Sam wanted to be freed, he would have to free himself—he just needed to find the courage to start. Even if he had to make the transition on his own, finally feeling at home in his own body and finally being acknowledged as the person he truly was would make the journey worth every minute.

What Sam didn't know was that a helpful hand was on the way, and it was a lot closer to Dr. Bumfuzzle than he could ever have predicted.

Chapter Four

OVERACTIVE IMAGINATION DISORDER

Mo Ishikawa set a *Wiz Kids* folder on her pink bedspread and faced the large mirror in the corner of her bedroom. Unlike her friend Sam, Mo *loved* mirrors—possibly a bit too much. She had three of them in her room and never passed an opportunity to check herself out, strike a pose like Amy Evans, or say "hey girl" when she passed by.

At the moment, Mo was staring into the eyes of her reflection for a very serious, nonquirky matter. She took a deep breath and recited a speech she had been working on for three months. She had practiced it so much it was ingrained in her memory like the Pledge of Allegiance.

"Dad, we need to talk," Mo said. "I don't mean to ambush you, but we need to discuss my education. I know it's always been your dream to see me attend Stanford, but after a lot of thought and reflection I've decided it's not for me. I never told you this, but after I applied to Stanford, I also applied to the creative writing program at Columbia University. I was accepted there, too, and that's the school I'm planning to attend in the fall."

She opened the *Wiz Kids* folder and spread her Columbia acceptance letter and the information about the university's creative writing program across her bed, pretending to show her father.

"I understand why you think writing isn't a secure profession, so to make you more comfortable, I'm planning to minor in economics. I apologize for not bringing this up earlier, but I knew you would be upset. I sent enrollment deposits to both Stanford and Columbia to buy some time so I could work up the courage to tell you, but I need to start choosing classes before they all fill up. Here's a list of all the courses I'd like to take during my first semester."

Mo set the list on top of the business school information.

"I don't want to live with regrets, and going to Stanford for business will make me miserable. I'm a writer, Dad—it's in my blood and it's what I want to spend my life doing. As you've taught me, being an adult is about making tough decisions, so I hope you see this as an example of maturity and not disrespect. Now please look over the materials I've provided and let's have a conversation about it in the morning. Thank you. *How was that, Peaches?*"

Mo anxiously glanced at her gray cat, Peachfuzzle "Peaches" Carter, who was lying on a pile of stuffed animals in the opposite corner of the room. The cat was twenty-one pounds of pure judgment and wore a jeweled collar that perfectly matched his demeanor. He looked at Mo the way he always looked at people—as if the voice inside his head was saying, *Go fuck yourself.*

Mo was used to her cat's unsympathetic expression. Peaches's green eyes had been filled with resentment since the day he was brought home from the animal shelter—like he knew his existence was a tribute to a fictitious television couple.

Naturally, Mo knew it was unlikely an animal that pooped in a box of sand, lived off canned salmon, and slept twenty hours a day was holding a passionate grudge against her. However, Mo had to remind herself the truth about most things from time to time. Her imagination had a mind of its own.

"I wonder how mad Dad will be when he finds out," Mo pondered as she paced the room. "I mean, *technically* he can't force me to go to Stanford. Then again, my college fund is *technically* his money. What if he keeps it from me? What if I have to pay for a Columbia education with student loans? What if I never get paid to write after I graduate? How will I get out of debt? I'm going to have to sell my organs on the black market!"

Mo had suffered from OID (overactive imagination disorder) since childhood. The condition wasn't officially recognized by the United States Department of Health (because Mo had made it up) but the disorder was just as taxing and consuming as any.

"Snap out of it, Mo!" she said, and slapped herself. "Your father is not going to let you sell your organs to pay for college. You're his only child—he'll need you to take care of him when he's old. God, if I just had an older sibling I wouldn't be dealing with this crap."

Then again, if Mo had a brother or sister, she probably wouldn't be an aspiring writer. Growing up an only child was what sparked her creativity and cursed her with a lifetime of OID. With no one to play with, Mo had to invent alternative ways of entertaining herself.

For example, when Mo was two years old she took the caps off absolutely everything in the house and kept them in a Tupperware container under her bed. Her only reason for doing this was to frustrate her father and giggle as she watched him search for them.

At three years old Mo developed an obsession with the mirror. The lonely toddler spent hours every day looking, talking, and making funny faces at herself. The mirror was much more than a sheet of glass that housed her reflection—it was a window into a world where her doppelgänger lived. To this day, if Mo passed a mirror without making eye contact or saying "hey girl," she felt she was neglecting an old friend.

When Mo was four years old she named every object in the house so she'd always have someone to talk to. Not only did she bestow identities upon the furniture and appliances, but she also gave the objects pastimes, preferences, and political views. She didn't know what the terms *Republican* and *Democrat* meant, but she told her parents in great detail how the washer wasn't speaking to the dryer because he voted for John Kerry in the 2004 presidential election.

Mo's mother thought her daughter was funny and inventive, so she encouraged the personification. Unfortunately, Mrs. Ishikawa's supportive parenting backfired on her and her husband. Having names also meant every object in the house had a *soul*, so whenever the time came to replace or recycle something, Mo acted as if her parents were committing murder.

When the Ishikawas threw out Bruce, the wobbly bar stool, Mo cried for a week. She was never the same after she saw Anthony, the broken television, get kidnapped by two garbage men. Mo ran after the truck for six blocks, memorized the license plate number, and called 911 when she got home. The call resulted in a very awkward conversation between her father and the two police officers who showed up at their door.

Her mother had no choice but to tell her that Meredith, the dented lampshade, ran away to join the circus. Mo received postcards from Meredith until she was five years old, telling her all about her adventures on the road. Thankfully, Mo never noticed how similar Meredith's handwriting was to her mother's.

Mo's personality assignments continued into the backyard as well. Every tree, plant, and rock had a complex backstory she was eager to create and share with her mother.

"I had no idea the maple tree lived in Switzerland before moving to our backyard," Mrs. Ishikawa said. "What made him decide to move to the United States?"

"Because he was in love with the cedar tree and they wanted to get married and start a tree family," Mo said.

"That's the same reason Daddy moved here from Japan," Mrs. Ishikawa said. "What about that boulder? Why does he or she live with us?"

"That only looks like a boulder, Mommy," Mo explained. "It used to be a shooting star and flew through the galaxy for a million years before it crashed there!"

"That's incredible, sweetheart," Mrs. Ishikawa said. "I love your stories so much. Could you do Mommy a favor? I have to go to some meetings soon—just grown-up stuff, nothing exciting—and I would love it if you wrote your stories down so I could take them with me. They'd give me something to smile about."

"I would love to, Mommy!"

Mo was beyond excited to have a project and took the task very seriously. Using the few words she knew, Mo wrote elaborate stories about the bugs in the garden, the birds that lived in the trees, and the stars in the night sky. Sometimes the plots became very complicated as she unraveled them, so Mo would make visuals with crayons and markers so her mother wouldn't get confused.

"These stories are wonderful, Mo-Bear!" Mrs. Ishikawa said. "They're exactly what I need. Listen, I've got even more meetings coming up soon. Do you think you could keep writing stories for me? They're the highlight of my day."

"You bet I can!"

Every day that Mrs. Ishikawa had a meeting, Mo handed her a new story as she walked out the door. Her father always drove her mother to her meetings, leaving Mo in the care of her aunt Koko, and by the time they returned, Mo would already have a new story for her mother to take to the next meeting. Soon the meetings became very frequent and Mo found it challenging to keep up with the quota she had set for herself.

"I'm so sorry, Mommy," Mo said. "I didn't finish my story about the neighbors' dog for you."

"That's all right, sweetheart," her mother said. "Mommy's feeling a little tired—I probably won't do much reading today anyway. Why don't you finish it and I'll read it at my next meeting?"

Mo was so devoted to supplying her mother with stories, she hadn't noticed that Mrs. Ishikawa's energy level had lowered significantly since she started having all those meetings.

"Mommy, why are you so tired all the time?" Mo asked one day. "Do your meetings make you sleepy?"

"Why yes, they do," Mrs. Ishikawa said. "Adult stuff is important, but it can be very boring. It makes me sleepy just thinking about it. But don't worry, Mo-Bear. Mommy will be her usual self once her meetings end."

Her mother's energy level wasn't the only thing changing. Mo also noticed Mrs. Ishikawa was much frailer and paler than she used to be. The more meetings she went to, the smaller and weaker she became.

"Mommy, why are you so skinny?"

"Um...well, sometimes I forget to eat lunch at my meetings," Mrs. Ishikawa said.

"What happened to your eyebrows and eyelashes? Did they fall out?"

"Oh...maybe I'm shedding like the neighbors' dog? You know, summer's just around the corner."

"Mommy, people don't shed. What's *really* going on?"

"Sweetheart, come have a seat with me and I'll explain," her mother said. "I've been meaning to talk to you about something, but I've been waiting for the right time. You see, the meetings I've been going to every day are at the hospital with doctors."

"Why are you going to the hospital, Mommy?"

"Because...because...," Mrs. Ishikawa said with difficulty. "Well, because the doctors think Mommy might have *superpowers*! They've been running tests to find out."

"Superpowers?" Mo laughed. "You're teasing me!"

"How else would you explain all my changes?" her mother asked playfully. "Your mommy is the Incredible Sleepy, Shrinking, and Shedding Woman, but we have to keep it a secret so none of your friends get jealous."

"Is that why Daddy has become so quiet? Because he's keeping your superpowers a secret?"

"That's *exactly* why he's been so quiet," Mrs. Ishikawa said. "But not to worry, Daddy will be back to normal once I'm done with all my superhero tests."

"What can you do with your superpowers?" Mo asked, still unsure of the story her mother was telling her.

"That's what the doctors are trying to figure out. It's taking them a long time because they don't have very much imagination. Boy, I wish I knew someone who could help them out with *that*."

Mo lit up with bright eyes, and a big smile grew.

"But, Mommy, *I've* got a great imagination!" she said. "If I wrote stories about the Incredible Sleepy, Shrinking, and Shedding Woman, maybe it would help the doctors out!"

"Mo-Bear, that is the best idea I've ever heard!" Mrs. Ishikawa said. "I start another round of meetings soon—this time I'm staying in the hospital for a couple nights for more superpower tests. How about you write some stories for me and we can read them together when I get home?"

"You've got it!" Mo said.

While her mother was away at the hospital, Mo religiously worked on her stories about the Incredible Sleepy, Shrinking, and Shedding Woman. She wrote how her mother used her superpowers to sleep through the loudest noises on the planet, how she shrunk to the size of a mouse to retrieve things that fell under couches and behind dressers, and how she shed her hair into food to get free meals at restaurants.

Mo couldn't wait to share her new stories with her mother, knowing they would make her laugh harder than all the other ones had. Her aunt Koko didn't appreciate her creativity like Mrs. Ishikawa did, so Mo was very eager for her parents to come back. After almost a week, her dad finally returned home, but Mrs. Ishikawa wasn't with him.

"Daddy, is Mommy done with her superhero tests?"

"No," Mr. Ishikawa said. "No more tests."

Mr. Ishikawa had trouble looking his daughter in the eye and Mo worried he was mad at her for something.

"When is Mommy coming home?" Mo asked.

"Mommy isn't coming home," he said.

"Why not? Where is she?"

Mr. Ishikawa paused like he always did when he mentally translated his words into English. However, this time he knew exactly *what* to say, he just didn't want to say it.

"Mommy is *gone*."

"Gone? But where did she go? I have to give her my new stories."

Mo tried to hand her father her stack of stories but he wouldn't take them from her.

"No more stories, Moriko," he said. "Mommy died."

In time, Mo learned her mother had been battling cancer for over two years before she died. Then, during a simple procedure at the hospital, Mrs. Ishikawa went into kidney failure and was too ill to recover.

She had never thought her and Mo's conversation about the Incredible Sleepy, Shrinking, and Shedding Woman would be their last.

However, none of this was explained to Mo by her father. After his wife passed away, Mr. Ishikawa never spoke of her again and barely spoke at all. He worked late six days a week to avoid their house and spent his days off alone in his den watching Japanese television. He didn't have friends—most of his family still lived across the world— and the only communication he had with his daughter was to give her commands such as *Clean your room*, *Study for your test*, and *Go to Stanford*. Mo felt closer to her deceased mother than to her father—*he* was the real ghost in their house.

Even after thirteen years, Mo and Mr. Ishikawa had never adjusted to being a family of two, but became more and more like strangers living under the same roof.

"Dad's staying extra late at the office tonight," Mo said, and glanced at her clock. "What's taking him so long? How many Japanese people need legal advice this late on a Saturday?"

Her bedroom rattled as the garage door opened below it. She heard her father park his car and enter the house.

"Oh gosh, he's home," Mo said. "Here I go! Wish me luck, Peaches."

The cat gave her a look that said, *Go jump off a bridge* instead. Mo neatly organized the information about Columbia University in the order she planned to disclose it. She walked down the stairs and found her father in the dining room. He was eating a bowl of soup and reading a Japanese newspaper.

"Hi, Dad. How was work?" she asked.

Mr. Ishikawa never looked up from his newspaper.

"Fine, fine, fine," he mumbled. "Are you all packed for your trip tomorrow?"

"Almost," Mo said, and cleared her throat to begin her prepared speech. "Dad, we need to talk. I don't mean to ambush you, but we need to discuss my education—"

"Ambush?" Mr. Ishikawa asked. "What's an *ambush*?"

She hadn't planned for any interruptions but wasn't surprised. Most of Mr. Ishikawa's English died with his wife, consequently turning his daughter into a tutor/interpreter extraordinaire.

"Oh, an ambush is like a surprise," Mo explained.

"Surprise?" he asked. "You're going to surprise me?"

"There's no surprise, Dad. I just need to have a conversation with you and I didn't want you to be caught off guard by the subject matter."

"Is something wrong?"

"Well, that depends on *you*," she said, and went back to her speech. "I know it's always been your dream to see me go to Stanford—"

"Oh yes," Mr. Ishikawa said with a big nod. "Stanford is a great school. A great school will lead to a great job, and a great job will lead to a very successful life."

"Um...*right*," Mo said. "But after a lot of thought and reflection, I've decided Stanford may not be—"

"*Reflection?*" Mr. Ishikawa asked.

"Yes, to *reflect* on something also means to *think* about a certain situation."

"Oh yes, yes, yes," Mr. Ishikawa said. "You're a smart girl and *smart girls* think quite a bit. That's why you were accepted to Stanford."

This was more difficult than Mo thought it would be and she had thought of almost every scenario possible—including a war breaking out in the middle of her speech. She tried to stick to the words she had prepared, but it was harder and harder to focus the more her father interrupted her.

"Stanford is what I'm trying to talk to you about," she said. "You know, adulthood is about difficult decisions, and I don't want to live with regrets. I've been thinking that Stanford may not be the right choice for me."

"You're being too hard on yourself, Moriko," Mr. Ishikawa said. "You've studied very hard and earned very good grades. You deserve to go to Stanford as much as any other student. Don't be afraid."

The only thing Mo was afraid of was not getting her point across and she started to panic that she wouldn't. Her father had trouble with English, but he was no dummy. Mr. Ishikawa probably knew what his daughter was up to and wasn't as lost in translation as he appeared.

"Dad, you're not listening to what I'm saying—"

"So many people applied to Stanford, but only the smartest were accepted."

"Yes, I heard you loud and clear, now if you could just hear me out—"

"Stanford is a great opportunity and guarantees a great career—"

"DAD, I DON'T WANT TO GO TO STANFORD!"

Mo was more surprised by her outburst than her father was. Mr. Ishikawa dropped his spoon in his soup and stared across the table at the empty chairs. There was dead silence between them until Mo mustered up the courage to place the *Wiz Kids* folder in front of her father.

"I've been accepted into the creative writing program at Columbia

University in New York," she said. "*That's* the school I want to go to and *that's* the school I'm planning to attend. This is the information about the program and the courses I'm going to take. I know it's not what you want, but this is *my* life and I'm a *writer*, not a business-woman. Please support me in this."

Mr. Ishikawa opened the folder and flipped through the papers inside but never looked at anything long enough to read it. He slid the folder back to Mo and crossed his arms.

"Columbia is a *mistake*, Moriko," Mr. Ishikawa said. "Stanford is a smart choice."

"Dad, Columbia is a great school and has a wonderful economics program I can minor in."

"Writing isn't a real profession. You need a respectable job to be a successful person."

"You've never even read my writing! Maybe if you looked at it you'd change your mind—"

Mr. Ishikawa forcefully hit the table with an open hand, causing Mo to jump and his soup to splash on her Columbia acceptance letter.

"*No more discussion!*" he ordered. "*You will go to Stanford and that is final!*"

"*Dad, please!*"

Mr. Ishikawa silenced his daughter, not with another aggressive gesture, but by looking into her eyes for the first time that night.

"*Make your mother proud,*" he said softly.

The aspiring writer had never in her life been at a loss for words, and suddenly she was speechless. Her father hadn't mentioned her mother in thirteen years, and now it wasn't to *comfort* her, but to *control* her.

"Go to your room," Mr. Ishikawa said. "Get some rest before your trip tomorrow."

Mo took the *Wiz Kids* folder from the table and returned to her room in tears. She shut her bedroom door, picked Peachfuzzle off the pile of stuffed animals, and cuddled him on her bed against his will.

"Looks like we're moving to California, Peaches." Mo sniffled into her cat's ear. "I don't know what I was thinking. There's no reasoning or sympathy in Dad—just regulations and standards."

Peachfuzzle eventually clawed his way out from under her tight embrace. With zero compassion from her father or her feline, Mo went to her computer and found the empathy she so desperately needed in the only place she could find it: *her writing*.

Teardrops fell on her keyboard as she typed the opening paragraph to the next chapter of her *Wiz Kids* fanfiction novel. Its tone wasn't as erotic as the previous chapters.

CHAPTER FIVE

The solar winds of the Andromeda Galaxy echoed through the crater's canyons like a pack of coyotes howling at the full moons above. The winds frightened Dr. Bumfuzzle and Dr. Peachtree and they reached for each other throughout the night, but with the consequences of physical contact looming over their psyches, their open hands retracted before their fingertips met. They didn't know how or when, but the Earthlings knew they had to find a way out of this affectionless world, even if it was the last thing they did.

Mo continued writing into the early hours of the morning before going to bed. The names, the faces, and the places weren't her own, but the love between Dr. Bumfuzzle and Dr. Peachtree was the greatest love in her life. It may have been a fictitious relationship, but Mo figured vicarious compassion was better than no compassion at all. So she held on to Peachfuzzle like a life vest, hoping it would carry her through another dark and unforgiving storm.

Chapter Five

PASSWORD-PROTECTED

Joey Davis's family was so picture-perfect that the people of Downers Grove often accused them of having made a deal with the devil. The claim was supposed to be ironic, since everyone knew Joey's father was the pastor of the Naperville First Baptist Church—the second-largest Baptist congregation in Illinois.

Pastor Jeb Davis was a bit of a local celebrity in the tristate area. He shared the word of God with such confidence and passion the members of his church were convinced he was channeling Jesus himself. People drove in from miles away to hear his sermons every Sunday morning, and their daughters came along to gawk at the pastor's handsome sons.

This was among the many reasons why Joey hated church. There was something very uncomfortable about getting winked at by teenage girls while listening to your father preach about the last temptation of Christ.

"When are you going to get a girlfriend, Joey?" was the question he got asked the most at church.

"As soon as I find the right girl," Joey would reply, when he really wanted to say, *Did you* not *hear my dad's sermon about abstinence last week? Would* you *want to date with a father like that?*

"What's next for you after high school?" was the second question he got asked the most at church. "Are you going to become a missionary like your brothers?"

"Actually, I'm going to Oklahoma Baptist University for college," Joey would reply, resisting the urge to say, "Absolutely not. Rewarding poor villagers with clean water and AIDS medication in exchange for memorized Bible verses isn't my cup of tea."

Joey was the middle child of five strapping Davis boys. His older brothers, Matthew and Jeb Jr., were doing the Lord's work in Uganda. His younger brothers, Noah and Peter, were spawn of Satan that Joey had the misfortune of sharing a bedroom with.

"You goddamn heathens!" Joey yelled at them. "Where did you guys hide my phone charger? It was on my bed twenty seconds ago!"

He only had an hour before he and his friends left on their road trip and he was still packing. His little brothers weren't making it any easier and kept hiding his belongings every time he left the room. The boys acted perfectly innocent as they lay in their bunk beds playing *Moses: Escape from Egypt* on their Game Boys.

"Matthew 7:8," Peter said. " 'For everyone who asks receives; the one who seeks finds; and to the one who knocks, the door will be opened.' "

"I'm gonna knock open your skull if you don't cough it up!" Joey threatened.

"He hid it in his whale," Noah said. "I saw him do it when you were packing your toiletries in the bathroom."

"Tattletale!"

Joey yanked a plush whale out from under Peter's head and found his charger inside its zipped-up mouth. He hit his brother with the whale so hard a plush Jonah popped out of it.

"Now where the hell is my wallet?" Joey demanded.

"Matthew 13:50," Noah recited. " 'And throw them into the blazing furnace, where there will be weeping and gnashing of teeth.' "

"You won't have any teeth to gnash if you don't tell me where my wallet is!" Joey said, and raised his fist.

"He put it in the air-conditioning vent!" Peter said.

"Snitches get stitches!"

Joey used Noah's Popsicle-stick model of the Tower of Babel as a footstool to retrieve his wallet, crushing a dozen clay figurines under his feet.

"All right, I'm done packing," Joey said. "If either of you messes with my stuff before I leave, 'Cain and Abel' will look like *Milo and Otis* by the time I'm done with you."

"Boys, come downstairs!" their mother called from the bottom of the stairwell. "Your father wants to say a prayer for Joey before we go to church!"

Joey and his brothers climbed down the stairs and joined their parents in the living room. There was a framed painting over their fireplace of Pastor Jeb and Jesus Christ embracing in matching robes, as if the two were on the same boxing team. The pastor was standing just below the painting, with one hand on the mantel and the other holding the notes for his upcoming sermon. His wife walked around him, brushing his suit off with a lint brush and snipping any loose threads she found.

As Joey watched his parents get ready for church, he found it hard to believe Jeb and Mary Davis were capable of causing a scandal, but they were the talk of the town when they first moved to Downers Grove in the late 1980s. Since Joey's mother was white, the interracial couple faced some troubling times as they formed a church in the conservative part of town. Pastor Davis's early days at the pulpit were challenging, but the more he spoke out against the discrimination he and Mary received, the bigger his following became. Today, many people gave Pastor Davis credit for bringing the community together.

The stories made Joey so proud, but also confused him. His parents had faced obstacle after obstacle on their way to acceptance, only to use their platform to discriminate against others in the same way. Pastor Jeb's sermons were very compassionate, but he was never shy about condemning those he found "unfit" for God's love.

Joey wondered if his parents simply ran out of compassion, or if all social trailblazers become hypocrites in the end.

The pastor finished going over his notes and tucked them away in his lapel. *"God is good, God is good, God is good,"* he sang to himself. "Okay, boys, gather 'round. We're going to pray for Joey's trip before he leaves."

The Davis family formed a circle around their coffee table, joined hands, and closed their eyes. Noah and Peter always played a game of who could kick the other the hardest without getting caught whenever their father led them in prayer—a game Matthew and Jeb Jr. invented when they were kids.

"Dear Heavenly Father," the pastor began. "We'd like to take a moment on this beautiful Sunday morning to thank you for all you have blessed us with. We thank you for our home, we thank you for our family, and we thank you for allowing us to share your glorious word."

Whenever Joey prayed, he always imagined God as Ian McKellen lounging on a cloud and listening to the receiver of a golden rotary phone. He wondered if God appreciated all the gratitude in his father's prayers or if he ever thought, *Just get to the point, you little kiss-ass!*

"Heavenly Father, you've provided us with so much to be thankful for and we come to you now with a humble request," the pastor went on. "Please watch over Joseph as he embarks on a cross-country road trip with his friends Christopher Collins, Samantha Gibson, and Moriko Ishikawa—"

"Yeah, Daddy!" said a loud, breathy voice.

The Davis family unanimously opened one eye and glanced at one another, but none of them knew where the voice had come from.

"What was that?" Mary asked.

All three of her sons shrugged and Pastor Jeb continued his prayer.

"Heavenly Father, we ask you to keep Joseph and his friends from harm's way and shield them from any hidden dangers on the road.

Please give them the wisdom to make smart, responsible, and safe choices. May the fear of disobeying your word prevail over the temptations of sin. Allow him to return a better, a wiser, and a more holy man than today—"

"Yeah, Daddy!" the mysterious voice sounded again.

"Boys, electronics off when your father is speaking to the Lord," Mary reprimanded. "You know the rules."

"My Game Boy is upstairs!" Peter said.

"So is mine," Noah said. "It must be coming from Joey's phone."

"My phone doesn't make sounds like that," he said.

Joey pulled his phone out of his pocket just to be certain. As soon as he saw the screen his eyes doubled in size. He was wrong—it *was* coming from his phone.

"Yeah, Daddy! Yeah, Daddy!" the breathy voice moaned as two new notifications appeared.

Faster than lightning, Joey switched his phone to airplane mode and shoved it back into his pocket before anyone in his family could see it.

"Joseph, what was that?" Mary asked. "Why was your phone making such a provocative sound?"

"Sorry, it was just *Candy Crush*," he lied. "I have four new levels to beat. Back to you and the Lord, Dad."

His mother gave him a stern look and the pastor finished his prayer.

"Heavenly Father, please allow Joseph to enjoy these final weeks with his friends before they go off to college. Also, we ask you to continue watching over Matthew and Jeb Jr. as they spread your good word throughout Uganda. In Jesus's name we pray. *Amen.*"

"Amen," the others repeated.

"Noah and Peter, give your brother a hug good-bye and get in the van," Mary said.

Joey's brothers stepped on his feet as hard as they could, then ran out of the house before he could grab them by the collars.

"Boys, you're making Satan smile!" Mary called after them, then gave Joey a hug and kissed his cheek. "Stay safe out there, and make sure you call us and give us updates as you go."

"I will," Joey said.

His mother left the house and followed his younger brothers to the van. Instead of embracing his son, Pastor Jeb placed both hands on Joey's shoulders and looked him right in the eye.

"We're up against some troubling times, Joseph," the pastor said very seriously. "It's a scary world you're about to travel through. Don't let anyone turn you into a cautionary tale, you understand?"

"I won't," Joey said. "You don't have to give me the talk again, Dad. If anyone tries to give me trouble, I'll just walk away like you told me to."

"Good," he said. "And remember, son, *the Lord is watching you.*"

The pastor froze for a few seconds to let his words sink in.

Joey gulped. "I'll miss you, too."

The pastor gave Joey a strong pat on the back and headed for the door. Once his family was out of the house, Joey ran upstairs to his room and watched them in the driveway below his window. They climbed into their van and drove down the street, but Joey waited until they were completely out of sight before looking away. He shut the blinds, leaned a chair against the door in case they returned, and then pulled out his phone to read his recent notifications:

You have four unread messages on ManNip.

Joey clicked on the notification bubble and a gay hookup app loaded on his phone. The mascot of ManNip was a winking cat with sharp teeth, bulging biceps, and washboard abs. The app showed a map with the locations of gay men sprinkled across the nearby cities. It also had an itinerary option, so the gays of other towns could know when you were traveling.

Most important, the app was *free*, so it would never show up on his parents' phone bill—a real plus for a church boy in the closet.

Joey had only downloaded ManNip the night before and couldn't believe he had already been messaged. He had created a fake profile using the name Jay Davison, who he said was a twenty-two-year-old Anthropology student at Northwestern University in Chicago. He had uploaded photos of his torso, cropping his head out except in pictures taken at a great distance so no one could recognize him.

His stomach filled with butterflies as he pulled up the messages a guy named Brian K had sent him.

Hey sexy! ☺

Saw you were going to be in Oklahoma City tomorrow night.

I've been here since Thursday for a job.

Wanna meet up? ☺

Joey scanned through Brian K's profile before responding. He seemed tall, had really big arms, and a very bright smile. Brian claimed to be a twenty-eight-year-old architect from San Diego and had several pictures of himself in a hard hat with blueprints at construction sites to prove it. Joey knew people weren't always truthful on hookup apps (he being one of them), but Brian was pretty convincing.

After fifteen different drafts, Joey responded to Brian's message.

> Hi, Brian.
>
> Would love to meet up.
>
> Just name the time and the place. 😊

A strong surge of nerves went through Joey's core like a train speeding past a metro platform. He had never even talked to another gay guy before and here he was, mapping out his first sexual experience. It gave him a thrill, like he had successfully robbed a bank.

Of course, he knew having sex or being gay wasn't against the law (well, at least not anymore) but Joey had been programmed since birth to believe both were major sins. According to Pastor Jeb's sermons at church, Joey was most definitely going to burn in hell for giving in to his homosexual urges. But if his father was accurate about all his condemnations, hell sounded like an awfully crowded place.

Perhaps God had changed his mind about gay people to save space?

Joey could picture the scene as if it was from a movie: God (played by Ian McKellen) walked into a long boardroom in heaven and was joined by Moses (played by Denzel Washington) and Jesus (played by Idris Elba).

"Boys, I've changed my mind about the homosexuals," God said. "Perhaps acting out the physical urges they're born with is *not* as bad as committing murder, rape, and theft. I don't think they deserve to go to hell and I regret ever implying it."

"I think that's a great decision," Moses said. "We've been getting some complaints that hell is maxed to capacity. We weren't sure how to respond because, you know, *it's supposed to be hell.*"

"I couldn't agree more, Dad," Jesus said. "I've said from the beginning that *I love everyone.* The message has gotten mixed up over the years, but it's not too late to remind people."

"Then it's settled," God said. "We'll start by making the gay men remarkably attractive and the lesbian women capable of absolutely everything so everyone knows they have my blessing. The gay people will teach the rest of the world how to have fun, slowly winning them over, until there's acceptance and marriage equality in every country on earth."

"What about the people who still believe it's against your will?" Moses asked. "Trust me, I know how stubborn people can be when it comes to change."

God thought about it for a moment, and then came up with a great answer.

"We'll make the gay community so accepting of every race, culture, and nationality, it'll be obvious they're representing me," he said.

"But what if people choose to look past that?" Jesus asked. "I had some trouble convincing them I was representing you, too, remember?"

God scratched his beard and pondered that for a moment.

"I've got it," he said. "We'll make it very common for the people who discriminate against gay people to ignore the signs of global warming, inherently making homophobes responsible for ruining the planet. No one will want to side with them and gay people will finally be accepted by all."

"Terrific!" Jesus said. "That should do the trick!"

"Fantastic plan," Moses said. "That's why *you're* God."

The scene was projected frequently at the theater inside Joey's mind, but it was a show his family would never buy tickets to. No matter how much the world changed, the Davises and their church refused to evolve with it. Even as other churches and denominations moved forward, the congregation of Naperville First Baptist *proudly* held their gearshift on reverse.

The people in Joey's life were so offensive and vocal with their disdain for homosexuality, he worried he'd drown in the shame and guilt their words caused him. Other times, he was almost thankful for their honesty. Knowing he would never be accepted meant he never had to torture himself with the *question* of acceptance.

Luckily, Joey never had to worry about the truth slipping out like most gay teens did. Being the son of a pastor may have given him a mountain of issues, but it also gave him the perfect front when he needed one. Over the years he had become a master at dodging questions and changing subjects, and on the rare occasion he couldn't deflect, he just blamed all his sexual reluctance, reservations, and ignorance on his family's faith.

Joey had also become a master at suppressing his physical desires. He'd known he was gay since middle school but put off the idea of fooling around with another guy like it was a trip he'd take someday in the future; sex was something for the bucket list, not his immediate agenda. It was increasingly difficult to postpone the older he got and the stronger his hormones became. His sexual urges were no different from other guys his age—it was like a big horny Hulk was caged inside of him, desperate to be unleashed. But unlike his straight peers who made jokes and talked about it constantly to relieve the pressure, any outlet Joey used would only lead to suspicion.

The feeling came to a peak in his senior year of high school. He felt like he might explode if he didn't have a physical experience—it wasn't just sex that he craved, but something—*anything*—that made him feel alive and not compressed in his own skin. It was unlikely he'd get his rocks off with anyone at Oklahoma Baptist University, so he needed to do it before he left for school. If he just had that one experience—that one memory he could take to college—he might be able to suppress his feelings for another few years.

The summer road trip was the best opportunity he was going to get. He and his friends would be so far from home, if he hooked up with a guy along the way they would never know who he was, and it would never get back to his family in Downers Grove. It was perfect, and he set a plan into motion.

"Yeah, Daddy! Yeah, Daddy!" Joey's phone chimed with new notifications from ManNip.

I'll message you tomorrow with a plan to meet up.

See you then, sexy. XO Brian

Knowing he was *hours* away from (hopefully) losing his virginity made Joey's heart race. The front of his pants became tighter and tighter as his eagerness grew inside and out. It was almost time to meet up with his friends, but Joey needed some *release* before hitting the road.

Joey opened his laptop and clicked on a folder marked SCHOOL. Like he was navigating a digital labyrinth, he traveled through a series of strategically labeled folders—COLLEGE APPLICATIONS, ACCEPTANCE LETTERS, etc.—and finally came to a password-protected folder marked OBU. The folder was filled with pictures of actresses in bikinis and topless photos of models, but this was just a smokescreen in case one of his brothers managed to get this far into his hard drive. What Joey was after was in a second password-protected folder marked SINFUL.

SINFUL was an erotic treasure trove with photos of shirtless actors, athletes, and male models—including pictures of Cash Carter and Tobey Ramous from *Wiz Kids*. There were videos and stills from professional and amateur gay porn Joey had saved from the Internet. Whatever he could possibly want to fantasize about was at the fingertips of his free hand.

Joey was glad he had managed to conceal his collection so

efficiently, but going to such lengths to hide it was painfully disheart-
ening. The dishonesty he lived with every day weighed on him like a
ball and chain. Each time he opened SINFUL, the weight got heavier
and heavier. Joey had carried it for so long, he couldn't imagine life
without it.

Just like the pornography on his computer, Joey was also hidden
under a series of misleading layers, and it would take a very skilled
hacker to bring him to the surface.

Chapter Six

THE FIFTH PASSENGER

"The engine likes to play possum, but it always starts after the third or fourth try," Shelly Collins explained as the keys of her 1994 Chevrolet station wagon dangled from her fingers. "The headlights take a few seconds to click on, so don't panic if you don't see them right away. The windshield wipers are broken, so just pull over and wait for the rain to stop if you get caught in a storm. Also, the gas gauge only works when it wants to. Make sure you fill up the tank every three hundred miles regardless of what it says—*Topher, are you listening to me?*"

Topher was so lost in thought he hadn't heard a word his mother said. The only thing he could think about was the message he had received the night before from CashCarter.com.

"I totally comprehend," he lied. "Relax, Mom. You've had that car longer than you've had me. I know what works and what doesn't."

Topher reached for the keys but Shelly yanked them away as if she was taunting a kitten.

"Are you sure you're okay to drive? You look tired."

Topher wasn't tired, he was *exhausted*. How could anyone sleep after receiving a message from his childhood hero? The words *What time?* flashed in his mind all night like a dying lightbulb.

"I'm perfectly rested," he lied again. "I'm just anxious to get on the road. What time is it, anyway?"

Topher glanced at all the clocks in the house, but they said different things. Shelly checked her watch.

"It's nine fifty-five," she said. "What time are Joey, Sam, and Mo meeting you?"

"They should be here any minute now," Topher said. "In fact, I'm going to wait outside so we can leave as soon as they show up. Can I have the keys now?"

Shelly held the keys above her head, forcing her son to hug her before she handed them over.

"Please drive safe and come back to us in one piece."

"I promise," he said. "Thanks again for letting us use your car."

Topher grabbed his suitcase and headed for the door, passing Billy on the way.

"Later, dude," Topher said. "Stay out of trouble while I'm gone, okay? No wild parties without me."

"Finally, I'll get to watch something on TV besides *Wiz Kids*," Billy said as clearly as he could.

"It's all yours, little bro," Topher said. "Just don't overdose on *Ancient Aliens*. And take care of Mom while I'm gone."

Topher gave Billy's good hand a fist bump, then hurried out the door. He loaded his suitcase into the back of the station wagon, then paced the driveway, scanning his neighborhood street with the intensity of an FBI agent looking for a wanted fugitive.

"Get ahold of yourself, Topher," he thought aloud. "It wasn't really *him*. Some web programmer is just busting your balls—they're probably laughing at you right now."

Suddenly, a black SUV turned onto his street. Topher had never seen the car in his neighborhood before and his heart started to race.

"Then again, what if he's never been on a road trip before? What if he's always wanted to go on one and was just waiting for someone to ask him? *Oh my God what if he's in that car right now?*"

The SUV got closer and closer, making Topher's heart beat faster and faster. To both his relief and disappointment, it turned down another street before it could pass his house.

"God, I'm so gullible." Topher laughed. "I can't believe I was up all night wondering if—"

"Who are you talking to?" said a voice directly behind him, causing Topher to jump a foot into the air. He quickly turned around and saw Joey and Sam with their luggage in hand.

"Jesus, you guys are stealthy!" Topher said.

"Good morning to you, too." Sam giggled. "Were you talking to yourself just now?"

"*What?* Of course not," Topher said. "I was just going over our itinerary in my head. I wasn't expecting you guys would get here so early."

"You're the one who *insisted* we get here at ten o'clock sharp," Sam reminded him. "That may mean fifteen past ten in Mo time, but Joey and I are usually prompt."

"I know, I just wasn't expecting you guys to appear out of the mist like that."

"Dude, you've been so skittish lately," Joey noted. "I hope you aren't taking Adderall again."

"Please, I learned my lesson during finals week," Topher said, and changed the subject. "Well, happy first day of the road trip! Can I help you with your bags?"

He took their luggage and put it in the back of the station wagon with his own. Joey and Sam shared a look as he loaded the car—something was off about him.

"Topher, are you feeling okay? You seem a little stressed," Sam asked.

"Nah, I just didn't sleep much last night," Topher said.

"Were you up late watching *Naughty Nurses* again?" Joey asked.

"No—it wasn't like that," Topher said. "And I told you about that in confidence."

"Then what was it? Did Billy have another rough night?" Sam asked.

For a second Topher considered keeping it from them out of fear of embarrassment, but he figured they'd all get a good laugh out of it.

"Last night before I went to bed, I went to Cash Carter's website and wrote him a letter," Topher explained.

"A *letter*?" Sam said—already getting amusement out of it. "What kind of letter? Did you profess your undying love?"

"No, I just thanked him for entertaining us over the years," Topher said. "I also mentioned we were going on a road trip and invited him to come along."

"You did *what*?" Joey said with a laugh. "Oh man, I hope you didn't include our names on it. That's next-level lame."

"It was just a joke—anyway, getting to the point, I got a *response*."

"From the website?" Sam asked. "What did it say?"

"Let me guess," Joey said. " 'Dear Friend, thank you so much for this message blah blah blah I'm too busy to respond to everyone blah blah blah *Wiz Kids* Wednesday nights at eight.' Something like that?"

"No, it said 'What time?' " Topher said. "So I responded with my address and the time we were leaving but didn't hear back after that. I was up all night stressing over whether or not Cash Carter was planning to show up this morning."

He pulled the exchange up on his phone so they could see it for themselves. Joey and Sam looked at each other, looked back at Topher, and then burst into laughter. They laughed so hard tears came to their eyes. Their amusement was contagious and Topher snickered at his own stupidity.

"Pretty dumb, right?" Topher said.

"Oh gosh, that's hysterical!" Joey laughed. "Someone at his website was totally messing with you! And you *believed* it!"

"This is just like that thing during freshman year," Sam said. "Remember when Mo thought she was Facebooking with the real Tobey Ramous? But it turned out to be a creepy old man with an Asian fetish!"

"Oh come on, it wasn't *that* bad," Topher said. "At least mine came from a reliable source."

"I still can't believe you thought there was even a chance *Cash Carter* would show up in Downers Grove." Joey laughed. "Can you imagine any celebrity driving cross country in an old station wagon? You should never have told us, because we aren't *ever* letting you forget about it."

Suddenly, the sound of screeching brakes caught them by surprise. They turned just in time to see a shiny black town car pull up to the curb. The driver hopped out and hurried to open the passenger door. A cigarette butt was flicked out of the backseat first and was followed by a very good-looking man in his early twenties. He wore thick sunglasses, a black leather jacket, dark jeans, and designer boots. The passenger yawned and stretched before turning toward Topher and his friends.

"Howdy," the passenger said. "Are one of you guys Topher Collins?"

Topher, Joey, and Sam went numb from head to toe. They couldn't feel, they couldn't think, they couldn't even breathe—all they could do was stare at the newcomer as if he were Bigfoot.

"Holy fuckballs." Joey gasped. *"You're Cash Carter."*

Cash eyed the paralyzed trio over his sunglasses.

"Yup, this is definitely it," he announced.

It took them a few moments to realize who he was because Cash looked nothing like the nerdy quantum physics expert he played on television, but more like a modern James Dean. His hair was messy, he had stubble and poor posture. Without the benefits of a well-lit set, for the first time they noticed his pores, the lines on his forehead, and a hint of crow's-feet.

"Thanks for the lift, Larry," Cash said. "Sorry it was scheduled on such short notice."

The driver popped the trunk and handed Cash a black backpack with golden zippers. The actor slipped his driver some money and shook his hand.

"No problem at all, Mr. Carter," Larry said. "Enjoy your trip and let us know next time you're in the Chicago area."

Larry returned to the driver's seat and drove off, leaving Cash alone in the presence of three very still, quiet, and bewildered teenagers.

"No, you're not dreaming—I'm really here," Cash said playfully, but still didn't get a response out of them. "Oh come on, you can't be *that* surprised to see me. You did invite me, after all."

"Yes—*we did*! I mean—*I d-d-did*!" Topher stuttered. "I'm Topher Collins. It is such a pleasure to meet you, Mr. Carter."

Topher stepped forward and shook Cash's hand so aggressively he almost broke it.

"That's quite a handshake you've got," Cash said.

"Oh shit, I'm sorry!" Topher said. "Forgive us, but we're kind of freaking out right now. I hoped you might come, but I didn't expect you'd actually show up. *Wait*—you're not here because you think I'm *dying*, right? I hope no one told you I was sick or something, because I'm perfectly healthy."

Cash shrugged. "Nope, I'm here totally of my own volition," he said. "Joining a bunch of strangers on a road trip isn't something I make a hobby out of, but I figured, *why the fuck not*? You only live once. Unless you're a Buddhist, then you come back a couple times, apparently—just something I read on the plane. Reincarnation, they call it. Are these the friends you wrote about?"

Joey and Sam sheepishly stepped forward to greet him.

"*Hello, sir,*" Sam said, and bowed like he was approaching royalty. "My name is Sam. Can I just say, it is an *honor* and a *privilege* to be in your presence—an *honor and a privilege.*"

"I'm Joey—*Joey Davis,*" he said, unsure of what to do with his hands. "Big fan, man. *Big fan!*"

"That'll change once you get to know me," Cash said with a wink. "Is this all of us? *Aventura de cuatro amigos?*"

"We're still waiting for our friend Mo," Topher said. "She's running a few minutes late, but she always does. *Not that she's a bad person or anything—that's not what I meant to imply!* She's going to lose her goddamn mind when she sees you."

"Sorry I was running a little late myself," Cash apologized. "I was in Santa Clara for the *Wiz Kids* convention and booked the first flight I could get to Chicago."

"I'm glad you got a ticket," Topher said. "What airline?"

"Oh, I don't do airlines anymore," Cash said. "I fly private. It's pricey but beats having to take my shoes off in public, you know what I mean?"

The thought made Sam squeal excitedly, as if he'd said he had flown a dragon.

"Is this our chariot?" Cash asked, and nodded to the car.

He went to the station wagon and walked around it in a circle, like he was inspecting a car for sale.

"Yeah, *sorry,*" Topher said with a nervous laugh. "I'm sure it's not what you're used to—"

"Is that *real wood* on the sides?" Cash said. "Huh, I've seen these kinds of cars in John Hughes movies, but I didn't think they still existed. This is gonna be an adventure."

"You can say that again," Joey peeped.

They heard wheels rolling down the sidewalk nearby. Mo appeared a moment later, pulling her large pink suitcase behind her and carrying a large pink cardboard box.

"Hey!" Topher said. "Boy, do we have something cool to tell—"

"I'm sorry I'm late, but you guys aren't going to believe what happened to me this morning," Mo said. "I was halfway here when I realized I hadn't packed a swimsuit, so I had to turn around and go home. I walked into my bedroom and saw Peaches had taken a huge dump in the middle of my bed, so I had to clean it up and put my comforter in the washer. Then, on my way back, I realized I was *starving* and figured since I was late anyway I would stop and get doughnuts at the corner store for us to snack on... *Why are you all looking at me like I have mouth herpes?*"

Her friends were shocked she hadn't noticed Cash yet. They nodded toward him and when Mo's eyes finally landed on the actor it only took a second for it to sink in. She dropped the box of doughnuts and let out a scream so loud dogs could hear it in Indiana.

"You must be Mo," Cash said.

Chapter Seven

TRUTH-SHAMING

As Topher drove through town toward Interstate 55, he spent more time looking at Cash in the rearview mirror than at the road ahead. Sam sat beside him in the front while Joey and Mo shared the back-seat, and none of them could take their eyes off their surprise guest, either. They expected the sound of their alarm clocks to wake them from a dream at any moment. However, the strange alternative reality was never interrupted. *This was real life!*

"So . . . Downers Grove, huh?" Cash said as the community passed by his window. "What exactly goes on in Downers Grove?"

The actor was stretched out across the very back of the station wagon, using the others' luggage as oversized pillows. Everyone knew it was against the law for him to be without a seat belt, but none of them were about to reprimand their favorite television star.

"Absolutely nothing," Joey said.

"Gotcha. It's kind of a bummer name for a town. Is it named after someone in particular or is there an Uppers Cove nearby?"

"It was named after Pierce Downer," Sam said. "He was an evangelist who founded the town in 1832. At least that's what a plaque at the post office says."

"Solid fact, Sam," Cash said. "I can't tell if it looks more like the location of a Hallmark movie or a slasher film."

"Why are you with us?" Mo blurted out. She had been holding it in since they got in the car and couldn't contain it anymore. "Sorry, that came out wrong. I'm glad you're here, but what possessed you to join four strangers on a road trip?"

"Well, I've never been on a real road trip before and thought it'd be fun," Cash said. "Besides, it's a nice way to get to know some of my biggest fans a little better, say thank you, give back—*all that shit.* By the way, don't post anything on the Internet about me being with you or we'll get trailed by all the Wizzers in the Midwest."

"Copy that," Topher said. "Thanks again for joining us. We're going to remember this forever. It's the coolest thing that's ever happened to—"

"Do you guys mind if I smoke in here?" Cash asked.

The request took Topher off guard. "Um...actually, this is my mom's car, so—"

Sam elbowed Topher in the ribs and shot him a look that said, *Shut your mouth or I'll slit your throat with my pinkie nail.*

"Yeah, it's totally fine," Sam said.

Cash searched his pockets and found a pack of cigarettes in his jacket and a lighter in his jeans. He also found condoms, a joint, and matches from a strip club, but tucked those away before the others saw them.

"Mind opening your window for me, Mo?" he asked. "I don't want to fumigate you guys with secondhand smoke."

Mo rolled it down but looked slightly disturbed about it.

"Something wrong?" Cash asked her.

"No, I just didn't know you were a *smoker*," she said as if it were a derogatory term. "It's really bad for you, you know."

"*WHAT?*" Cash laughed as he lit his first cigarette. "*Since when? Who told you that?*"

"*You did,*" Mo said. "In a *D.A.R.E.* video we watched in the fifth grade, you said smoking kills and then taught us the anti-addiction dance with a man dressed in a lion costume."

Cash took a long drag of his cigarette and nodded as the memory returned to him.

"Oh yeah," he said. "Ironically, that lion was *wasted* the whole shoot. He kept a flask in his snout."

Mo's mouth dropped open like a child learning the truth about Santa Claus.

"So what's it like being famous?" Joey asked. "I'm sure you get asked that question all the time, but I'd love to know."

"It fucking sucks," Cash moaned.

"*Really?*" Joey asked. It was not the answer he was expecting. "But isn't it wonderful to have such a big following and to mean so much to so many people?"

"That's not fame, that's *respect*," Cash said. "Fame is the complete opposite of respect. *Fame* is getting interrupted every time you have a meal—it's getting asked favors by complete strangers whenever you step outside—it's getting asked advice on how to break into the industry from the guy taking a dump in the stall next to you—*it's getting criticized by the whole world and never getting to defend yourself!*"

Cash closed his eyes, slowly exhaled a long gust of smoke, and counted to ten to calm himself down. The others looked at the actor like he had momentarily transformed into a werewolf.

"Sorry about that," he said. "I didn't mean to go all *Black Swan* so soon after meeting you. I just hate that our society values it so much. It's like, *plant a fucking tree*, you know?"

Joey made a mental note not to bring up the subject again.

"So . . . what's it like being *respected*?"

"Oh, it makes fame worth it," Cash said cheerfully. "It's not like either comes with a handbook or anything. I think not being able to separate the two is why so many celebrities struggle with it. But I'm not a fucking psychologist."

The others nodded politely, but their faces were noticeably longer than before. Just like the actor's appearance, they were slowly learning Cash's personality was nothing like Dr. Bumfuzzle's.

"Tell us what it's like to work on *Wiz Kids*," Topher said. "Is it as much fun as it looks?"

Cash hesitated. "Um . . . *sure*," he said, and quietly faced the window.

"Anything else?" Topher asked teasingly. "Come on, we've never met an actor from TV before. We're dying to know."

The actor paused, forming the most politically correct and positive answer possible so he wouldn't upset them.

"Well, a lot of actors love working on television, but every show is different. Our show is more difficult to shoot because of all the special effects and stunts. We're in production fourteen hours a day, six days a week, nine months a year—so it's a lot more work than people realize. Sometimes I go days without seeing the sun."

Mo laughed like he was telling a joke, but there was no punch line.

"Wait, you mean *you don't like it*?" she asked.

"That's not what I said. I'm just suggesting it's difficult to keep up your energy and enthusiasm when you've been on a schedule like that for so many years—no matter how fun it can be. That's understandable, right?"

Clearly it wasn't, because Mo looked like someone had taken her childhood, ripped it in half, and thrown it out the window.

"But…but…but you make so much money and make so many people happy in the process. Doesn't inspiring people make it all worth it—don't *we* make it all worth it?"

Cash let out a long sigh. Mo was making him uncomfortable, but not nearly as uncomfortable as she was making her friends.

"*Hey, Mo?*" Topher interjected. "*Why don't we change the subject and stop berating the man who just flew two thousand miles to be with us.*"

"No, it's all right," Cash said. "Look, the five of us are going to be together for a while. I'd like this experience to be as authentic as possible, but part of that is getting to *be* as authentic as possible. I'm glad you like the show and I'm happy to answer as many questions as you want, as long as you stop *truth-shaming* me."

"Truth-shaming?" Joey asked. "What's that?"

"It's like fat-shaming but for honest people," Cash explained. "It's the reason famous people can never be totally truthful when they speak publicly. Think about it—everyone usually has the answer they want to hear before they ask the question, *especially* from celebrities. However, if we answer *honestly* and it differs from what people want to hear, unintentionally bursting a bubble or two, we get shamed for it. We're called ungrateful, selfish, disgraceful—everything but truthful. Alternatively, if we give the answer everyone wants to hear, but it doesn't seem *genuine* enough, we'll get shamed for that, too. It's a real mind fuck."

"So you have to constantly *lie* to make people happy?" Joey asked.

"Not constantly—that would be exhausting," Cash said. "I'll give you an example. One of you guys pull up my *Rolling Stone* interview from last February. Read the answers I gave the writer and I'll tell you if they're honest or not."

They weren't sure they wanted to play this game, but Sam got on his phone and found the article online anyway.

"Okay, first question: *How does it feel to be the face of a global phenomenon?*" he read. "Your answer: *Oh gosh, I'm not sure how to answer that. You say that like I'm single-handedly responsible for the show's success, when it really takes a village to make the show work. Our crew deserves as much credit as I do.*"

"See, that was completely honest," Cash said. "There wasn't a single white lie in it. Next?"

"*What's it like to be beloved by so many Wizzers around the world?*" Sam read. "Your answer: *I don't know how to describe it. Entertaining people and giving them a break from reality is why we become actors, isn't it? I'd say it's validating, but it's much more than that—it gives me purpose and I don't take it for granted.*"

"Also 100 percent true," Cash said. "Next?"

"*What's next for your career?*" Sam read. "Your answer: *I'm busy finishing the ninth season of* Wiz Kids *but have a few film projects lined up for our hiatus and maybe even a play in the West End.*"

"Bold-faced lies," Cash said. "I didn't have a single project lined up for this hiatus. You gotta say that shit so no one labels you as a future has-been—that'll kill a career. Even if it's obvious you'll never do anything but the show you're on, you can't admit it."

"But you've done more than *Wiz Kids*," Joey said. "You did that independent movie *Lucky*, about the blind and deaf soldier who lost his leg in World War II."

Cash was shocked. "You guys saw that?"

"Opening night," Topher said. "We had to drive to a bad neighborhood in Michigan to see it, but we were there."

The actor was touched and the corner of his mouth curved into a grin, but it only lasted a second.

"No one else saw it," he said somberly. "The critics were vicious, but I think they were still mad *Wiz Kids* had become a hit and were taking their aggression out on me. Funny how movie reviews can be scathing yet never mention a thing about the plot or characters. Long story longer, no one's going to cast me in another movie again. Back to you, Sam—*this is fun!*"

Cash flicked his cigarette out the window and then lay across the luggage in the back with his hands behind his head.

"*Damien Zimmer has said the* Wiz Kids *cast and creative team is like a family. Would you agree?*" Sam read. "Your answer: *Definitely.* That's all you said."

Cash groaned. "Damien Zimmer has despised me from day one. Every time I get any recognition he writes me into a coma or puts me through something horrendous as punishment. After I was on the cover of *TV Guide*, he put a dangerous stunt into a script and it broke my ankle. After I won a People's Choice Award, he put my character in a coma for twelve episodes. The list goes on. Next?"

"*Your costar Tobey Ramous just booked the lead role of a huge studio franchise. Are you jealous of his success?*" Sam read. "Your answer: *Not at all. Having a friend in a huge movie just means I get to attend a huge premiere to support him.*"

"Of course I was jealous," Cash confessed. "But Tobey really needed that gig for his self-esteem. We were really close friends until *Us Weekly* did a poll asking which of us was hotter. For whatever reason, I won and Tobey didn't take it well. He started lifting weights and doing steroids to cope and our friendship shriveled up with his balls. Next?"

"*Are the rumors that you and Amy Evans are more than friends true?*" Sam read. "Your answer: *No. That's a rumor the Wizzers who like our characters' relationship started. I'm glad they're so invested in the show, though.*"

Mo was anxious to hear his real answer and sat up in her seat like a puppy waiting for a treat.

"The only relationship Amy Evans is in is with herself," Cash said. "Meanwhile, every girlfriend I've ever had has been harassed and chased away by the Wizzers who refuse to accept the show isn't a documentary. Right before she dumped me, my last girlfriend got a box of hair in the mail. It came with a note that said, *We know Amy and Cash are in love. Get out of their way or this will be all that's left of you! Sincerely, the Bumtrees.* The police traced it back to a group of fourteen-year-olds in Moose Jaw, Canada."

Mo cleared her throat. "For the record, that's *exactly* why the shippers changed their name to the Peachfuzzlers," she informed the car. "The Bumtrees were giving the fandom a bad name . . . or so I heard."

Cash gave her a suspicious look over his sunglasses.

"*Right . . . ,*" he said. "Let me guess, you're one of them?"

Mo shook her head but her blushing cheeks told a different story.

"Oh come on, Mo," Joey said. "Your cat's name is Peaches and Dr. Bumfuzzle and Dr. Peachtree's relationship is all you ever write about?"

"You *write* about it?" Cash asked. "As in *fanfiction*?"

"Fine, I'm a Peachfuzzler—there, I said it," Mo confessed. "But in my defense, the events of *today* are much stranger than any fanfiction I've ever written or read."

"*Nothing* is stranger than fanfiction," Cash said, like a sailor recalling his encounter with a horrible sea creature. "Well, that's enough of that. Hope I didn't ruin *Wiz Kids* for you, but that's what growing up is all about—learning nothing is sacred in this world."

Topher, Sam, Joey, and Mo each looked a little more devastated than the next. Perhaps driving across the country with their favorite actor wouldn't be as thrilling as they thought? They were only twenty minutes into their trip and Topher already regretted inviting him.

"I can't tell you how therapeutic it is to speak so openly for a change," Cash said with a big grin. "Being deceitful is so draining, and I'm only dishonest when I have to be. I can't imagine what it's like to be one of those people whose *whole life* is a lie and who have to keep the truth from their friends and family."

Although they didn't notice each other, Sam and Joey both went quiet and looked out their windows. They knew exactly what it was like and didn't want anyone to catch the truth in their eyes.

"Lord, I'm as exhausted as a religious picketer in Vegas." Cash yawned. "I'm going to take a nap back here. Would you guys wake me when we stop for lunch? I'd set my alarm, but I lost my phone last week."

"Sure," Topher said.

Cash got comfortable but then quickly sat back up, as if remembering an important piece of information to share.

"By the way, I made up half the shit I just told you, but I think you get the point I was trying to make. *See you at lunch!*"

Chapter Eight

MADNESS AT MCCARTHY'S

As the 1994 Chevrolet station wagon cruised down the interstate, the picturesque suburbs of Chicago faded from view and were replaced with the vast cornfields of southern Illinois. The fields were beautiful as they swayed in the light summer breeze, but the conscious passengers were afraid mentioning it would wake the actor in the back and subject them to another upsetting lecture about truth-shaming.

Although Cash was the only one asleep, the whole car suffered through his sleep apnea. He snored like a polar bear and twitched like a cocaine addict with PTSD. It was the most *restless rest* any of them had ever witnessed. Joey kept a hand wrapped around the Ichthys key chain on his backpack in case an exorcism was needed.

After the first one hundred and thirty miles of their two-thousand-mile journey, the travelers were ready for lunch. And judging by the strange gurgling noises coming from Cash's stomach, he was ready to eat, too. Topher evaluated each roadside establishment they drove past and figured a diner called McCarthy's was their best choice, so he pulled into their parking lot.

"Hey, *Cash*," Topher called from the driver's seat. "Does this diner look okay for lunch? *Cash?*"

The actor slowly regained consciousness. "Where are we?" He yawned.

"Somewhere near Lincoln," Topher said. "There probably won't be anything else until we get closer to Springfield. This is the first place I've seen with a health grade on display."

"Fine by me," Cash said, and read the ads painted on the diner's windows. "Oh look, they've got a three-pound burger for three ninety-five. Doesn't get more American than that."

They got out of the station wagon, letting Cash out through the rear, and went inside. The tables were set around a giant jukebox and the staff were dressed as celebrities from the 1950s.

"Oh cool, it's got a fifties theme," Topher said. "I've always thought that'd be a fun era to live in."

"Speak for yourself," Joey, Mo, and Sam said in unison.

After a couple of moments waiting in the front, a hostess dressed as a sad Shirley Temple greeted them.

"Welcome to McCarthy's," she said. "Table or booth?"

"Either works for us," Topher said.

Cash did a quick scan of the diner. It was pretty busy for a restaurant off the highway. He pushed up his glasses and lowered his head.

"Actually, we'll take whatever's most inconspicuous," he said.

The hostess stared at him blankly. "Does that mean, like, away from the bathrooms?"

"It means that booth in the very back would be perfect," Cash specified.

"Okay, suit yourself," the hostess said. "Right this way."

The five roadies squeezed into a booth meant for four, sequestered from the other patrons, and the hostess passed out menus.

"Your server will be right with you," she said, and returned to the front.

"Do you always have to sit in the back of a restaurant?" Mo asked.

"Not always, it's just better to be safe than sorry," Cash said. "Going out in public is always a gamble. You never know where Wizzers might be lurking, *no offense*. One time I went to a movie theater by myself and caused such a scene the LAPD had to escort me back to my car."

"Seriously?" Joey asked.

Cash scrunched his forehead and thought about it. "Or was it mall security?" he pondered. "Hmm...I can't remember if that actually happened or if it was a story I embellished for a talk show. It's a thin line between being a storyteller and bullshitter. Which reminds me, I gotta hit the can. Will one of you order me a McCarthy's Milk Shake?"

He headed toward the bathrooms on the other side of the diner. Mo watched him, waiting until he was out of earshot before unloading her thoughts.

"He's terrible," she said.

"Mo, you're just saying that because he ruined your Peachfuzzle fantasy," Topher argued.

"No, I'm saying that because it's what we're *all thinking*," she said, and glared at Joey and Sam until they nodded along with her.

"He's more negative than I would have expected," Sam said. "It's kind of jarring since he's always full of positive affirmations on *Wiz Kids.*"

"He's *nothing* like Dr. Bumfuzzle," Joey said. "I've always known he was acting on the show, but damn, I never knew he was *that good* of an actor."

Topher laughed defensively and tried playing devil's advocate since it was his fault the actor had joined them.

"Okay, but that doesn't mean he's *terrible*," he said. "Just because he's not like the character he plays on TV doesn't mean we can't have a good time with him. Mark my words, I bet by the end of this trip we'll like *him* more than Dr. Bumfuzzle."

Mo gave him an epic eye roll. "Topher, you're going to go blind from looking on the bright side," she said. "This is our last adventure before college, and I don't want him to ruin our trip. We should ask him to leave before he spoils *Wiz Kids* forever."

"Ruin our trip? Spoil *Wiz Kids*?" Topher asked. "Now you sound crazy. Every Wizzer in the world would *kill* to be in our shoes right now. We're getting to know the *real person* behind the character we've idolized since we were kids. He's a little jaded, I'll give you that—but after all the joy he's given us over the years, the least we can do is let him be a *human being*. From what he's told us so far, I don't think he gets many chances."

Mo, Joey, and Sam folded their arms and sank into their seats. They knew Topher was right, but they weren't wrong, either.

"*Shhh*...he's back," Joey whispered.

"Okay, this place officially gives me the creeps," Cash said as he squeezed into the booth. "I think *McCarthy's* stands for McCarthyism. I just peed in a bathroom marked *No Commies Allowed.*"

The others were quiet and their body language had changed significantly from when he'd left the group.

"Why the long faces, Downer party?" he asked. "Are you worried I'm going to totally ruin your road trip and you won't be able to watch *Wiz Kids* ever again?"

"Of course not!" Topher said.

"No way!" Joey said.

"Never!" Sam said.

"Why would you say that?" Mo asked.

"I don't know, these days people always act like I've crushed all their hopes and dreams whenever I speak my mind. Thanks for letting me be honest in the car and being so cool about it. Well, except Jane Austen over here."

Cash nodded to Mo and she hid her face behind a menu.

"Good afternoon, ladies and gentlemen," said a waitress dressed as Marilyn Monroe. "Apologies for the wait, we're a little understaffed today. May I start you off with something to drink, or do you know what you want?"

"Hmmm," Topher said as he looked over the menu. "I'll take a McCarthy Milk Shake and the Red Scare special."

"Now, that burger is cooked *very rare*, hence the name. Is that all right with you?"

"I'll take it medium rare," Topher said.

"That sounds good—I'll have the same," Sam said.

"Me too," Mo said.

"Me three," Joey said.

"Me four," Cash said.

"Great, thanks for making my job easy," the waitress said. She wrote down their orders but froze when she saw Cash. "Do I know you from somewhere? Did we go to high school together?"

Topher, Joey, Sam, and Mo tensed up—afraid they were about to be featured in a future talk show story. Cash played it cool; in fact, he almost seemed to enjoy not being immediately recognized.

"I don't think so," Cash said. "Where'd you go to high school?"

"Richwoods High, and yourself?"

"I was homeschooled in California," he said.

The waitress was positive she knew him from somewhere and couldn't let it go. "No, I *know* we've met before. Or maybe you just have one of those faces?"

"I get that all the time," Cash said. "By the way, could we also get the 'Hollywood Ten'-Piece Appetizer? With onion rings and mozzarella sticks, please."

"You've got it," the waitress said. "That's five medium-rare Red Scares, five McCarthy Milk Shakes, and one 'Hollywood—'"

It suddenly clicked where the waitress had seen Cash before. She turned bright red, placed a hand over her heart, and lost her breath.

"Oh my God you're that guy from TV!" She gasped. *"I've never seen your show—I don't even know your real name—but you were in my* People *magazine crossword! What in the world are you doing here?"*

"Just eating lunch," Cash said.

"*Oh right...duh!*" the waitress said. "*Well, I'll be...I'll be right back with your milk shakes.*"

Topher, Joey, Sam, and Mo had embarrassed themselves so much when they met Cash that it was nice seeing someone else make a fool of themselves, too. They wanted to bust up laughing, but Cash was completely unaffected by the exchange.

"So what'd I miss while I was in the bathroom?" he asked.

"Nothing," Mo said. "We were just going over the schedule for the trip."

"Cool!" Cash said. "I'm anxious to know where we're going. Probably should have asked before I chartered a jet to be here, but I was too excited. Would you bring me up to speed?"

"I've got the whole trip down to a science," Topher said. "This afternoon we're going to stop by the world's biggest rubber-band ball on our way to St. Louis. In the city, we're going to spend the evening at the Lewis and Clark Museum and the St. Louis Gateway Arch. Then we're staying at the Paul Bunyan Hotel a few miles outside the city near the Mark Twain National Forest."

"The hotel is made up of little cabins," Sam added. "And they have huge statues of Paul Bunyan and Babe the Blue Ox out front. It's a great Instagram opportunity!"

"Tomorrow we're going to spend the day hiking through the Mark Twain National Forest, then drive to Oklahoma City and spend the night at the Vacation Suites," Topher explained.

"It's nothing fancy, but it's cheap," Joey said apologetically.

"Tuesday we're driving to Amarillo, Texas. We're going to take a tour of the Bundy and Claire Jailhouse, where the outlaws had their famous shootout with the police, and then we'll stay at the Teepee Inn."

"All the rooms are shaped like teepees!" Mo said. "It isn't politically correct, but it's still adorable!"

"Wednesday we're driving to Albuquerque, New Mexico. Along the way we're going to stop at the famous UFO Observation Tower, built on the spot where extraterrestrials allegedly crashed in 1948, then we'll visit Dinoworld, the largest collection of life-size dinosaur statues on earth, and then we'll spend the night at the Albuquerque Vacation Suites."

"We get a discount from also staying at the one in Oklahoma City," Joey said.

"Thursday we're going to visit the Petrified Forest, the Arizona Meteor Crater, hustle to see the sunset over the Grand Canyon, and then stay at the Grand Canyon Hotel. It's ambitious, but as long as we stick to the schedule, we should be fine. Friday we'll get up early and drive to Santa Monica and spend four days in Southern California— but you probably won't be interested in any of the touristy things we have planned there."

The Downers Grove natives were giddy as they listed the stops on their agenda, but Cash wasn't as enthused—*it was the dullest trip he had ever heard of.* The actor forced himself to smile to hide the underwhelming gaze in his eyes.

"*Cabins and teepees and canyons, oh my!*" he said. "So all of this sounds *fun* to you guys?"

"Oh, absolutely!" Topher said.

"We've been planning this for months," Sam said.

"We each picked out two locations we wanted to see on the way," Mo said.

"Except the Grand Canyon and California," Joey clarified. "We've all wanted to see those since we were kids."

Cash nodded but still wasn't convinced it would be as thrilling as they thought.

"Very nice," he said. "Hey, here's an idea! Since you guys already picked your stops, would you mind if I threw a few into the mix when the schedule allows? For example, while you guys are with Lois and Clark, maybe I could find something fun for us to do tonight?"

Everyone looked to Topher and waited for him to answer. After weeks of carefully organizing the schedule, it was his call.

"I suppose that'd be fine," Topher said, liking the idea the more he thought about it. "Although we're working with a tight budget. We won't be able to do anything expensive."

"Don't worry about money," Cash said. "You guys were kind enough to let me crash your trip. Whatever I add to it is on me. I insist."

A waitress dressed as Grace Kelly delivered their milk shakes. She never looked away from Cash as she set them on the table, then hurried back to the kitchen.

"That was weird," Joey said. "What happened to Marilyn?"

"Oh, this happens every time I eat outside Los Angeles," Cash said. "The first waitress went into the kitchen and told the whole staff I'm here. They didn't believe her, so now they'll take turns bringing our food to see me for themselves."

Like a prophecy fulfilled before their eyes, the staff of McCarthy's did exactly what Cash predicted. A different waiter or waitress brought the appetizer and each burger separately and stared in disbelief at Cash like he was a zebra wearing human clothes. Then, like a relay, a waiter or waitress returned every thirty seconds to get their second look at him.

"Care for another milk shake, sir?" asked a waiter dressed as Elvis Presley.

"Sure, thanks," Cash said.

"I'd love another, too!" Sam said, but the waiter was gone before anyone else had a chance to tell him.

In the blink of an eye, a waitress dressed as Lucille Ball returned with his refill, but was too scared to stay longer than a split second. Cash slid his new milk shake across the table to Sam.

"I knew they'd do that," he said with a wink. "Figured you wanted one—I ordered this for you."

As they ate their food, they could see word of Cash's presence had spread beyond the staff. A few of the patrons started whispering among themselves and pointing to the sequestered group in the back.

"People are looking this way," Mo said.

"Let me guess," Cash said. "The table with the little boy in the red shirt, the booth with the elderly couple, the table with the men wearing trucker hats, and the booth with the teenage girls and their moms."

"How do you know that with your back turned to them?" Joey asked.

"They clocked me on my way back from the bathroom," Cash said. "At first they didn't believe it was me, but after watching the staff freak out, it's been confirmed. Seriously though, I've gotten so good at judging people's mannerisms over the years."

"I'd say so," Topher said. "You could work for the CIA!"

Cash raised an eyebrow. *"Who says I don't?"*

Marilyn Monroe returned to the table with their check. Cash put a wad of money on the table and stood up.

"Lunch is on me," he said. "Now let's bounce—we've got a schedule to stick to!"

The party of five walked to the front door and all the other heads in the restaurant watched them like dolls in a haunted house. The little boy in the red shirt suddenly leaped into their path, blocking them from the exit.

"Are you on TV?" he asked Cash.

"Um... *guilty*." Cash shrugged.

"Can I get a picture with you?" the boy asked.

"You know, I'd love to, but my friends and I are on a really tight schedule...."

Cash looked to Topher for help, but it was a big mistake. Topher wasn't properly trained for a rescue mission.

"No, it's okay," he said. "One picture isn't going to set us back."

As soon as the first picture was granted, everyone in the restaurant jumped up from their tables and surrounded Cash like wolves around a wounded animal. All the waitstaff emerged from the kitchen and joined in as well. It was a sight straight out of a Black Friday shopping spree, and Cash was the hottest electronic of the season.

Forty-five minutes later, Topher, Joey, Sam, and Mo were sitting in the car outside while they waited for Cash to finish taking pictures with every patron and employee at McCarthy's diner.

"This is my fault," Topher said. "How was I supposed to know everyone else would want one, too? He's a TV star—not the Loch Ness Monster."

"Half the people in there don't even know who he is," Mo said. "I know that because they've already posted their photos online. Listen to this caption, *No idea who this is, but apparently he's famous.* There's something so wrong with that."

"Sure is," Joey agreed. "Looks like he's almost done, though—oops, spoke too soon. Here come the fry cooks."

"I thought he was exaggerating about that whole LAPD thing, but now I don't think he was," Sam said.

Finally, the photo requests inside the diner ceased and Cash was free to go. He climbed into the station wagon through the back and collapsed on the pile of luggage as if he had just returned from war.

"Cash, I'm so sorry, dude," Topher said.

Cash looked up and glared at him through the rearview mirror.

"What did we *learn*?"

Chapter Nine

THE WORLD'S BIGGEST RUBBER-BAND BALL

Topher sped down the highway, eager to leave the chaos of McCarthy's in the past. He felt terrible for not helping Cash avoid the situation, but didn't know how he could have foreseen it. The anguished driver repeatedly apologized to the actor to squash any hard feelings that might have been forming.

"Once again, I am *so sorry* for turning you into a human photo op," Topher said. "I won't let that happen again."

"Will you stop apologizing?" Cash said. "How were you supposed to know they'd come at me like piranhas? I've gotten stuck for a lot longer in worse places. This one time, I was at a checkout in an Ikea for eight hours."

"You were taking pictures for *eight hours?*" Mo asked.

"Nope—I was just buying a lamp. *Ba-da-bum!*"

Cash laughed wildly at his own joke and Topher was relieved to see he was in good spirits. The actor had been in a much better mood after taking two white pills from his backpack. Whether they were for pain or anxiety, nobody asked, but they figured it was warranted after the ordeal at the diner.

At roughly a quarter to four o'clock, and two hundred and twenty miles into their trip, the car passed Exit 178B and Topher knew they were getting close to their first roadside attraction.

"We're almost at the world's biggest rubber-band ball!" he announced.

Cash looked out the window but all he saw were fields and trees. "How do you know that? I didn't see a sign."

"I've got the entire route memorized," Topher said. "We just passed Exit 178B and the world's biggest rubber-band ball is off Exit 180A. It should be coming up in a couple minutes."

"You *memorized* the exit numbers?" Cash asked in disbelief.

"Topher's got one of those brains," Sam said. "He took more AP classes than anyone else at school and was valedictorian of our class."

"Thank God, too, because none of us would have passed Algebra 2 if he didn't tutor us," Mo added.

"Color me impressed," Cash said. "Where are you planning to go to college, Toph? Are you gonna be one of those Ivy League hotshots?"

"Not exactly. I'm staying in Downers Grove to get my GE and I'll transfer later. I'll get to save money that way and I can help my mom with my little brother—he's got cerebral palsy."

"Topher's the best brother in the world," Joey bragged. "And I would know—I have two older and two younger ones. But we don't treat each other with an ounce of the compassion Topher has for Billy."

"In that case, I call dibs to the film rights of your life story," Cash said. "What does the future hold for the rest of you? College? Peace Corps? *Sea Org?*"

"I'm going to the Rhode Island School of Design," Sam said.

"Stanford," Mo said.

"*Fancy.* What about you, Joey?"

"I'll be majoring in performing arts at Oklahoma Baptist University," he said.

"You're going to *Oklahoma* to study performing arts? Isn't that like going to Florida State to be a ski instructor?"

"*Well...*" Joey paused as he came up with a defense. "It's a really great program, it won't be too far from home, and a lot of talent has come out of Oklahoma—Brad Pitt, Blake Edwards, Kristin Chenoweth, James Marsden."

"I *suppose* you're right," Cash said. "Sorry, I didn't mean to shit on your parade, you clearly know what you're doing. I imagine it'll be hard meeting other gay people at a Baptist school, though."

Joey suddenly sat straight up in his seat like he had been electrocuted. "*I'm not gay,*" he said.

Cash was stunned, as if Joey had just denied being African-American. He looked to Joey's friends, but they didn't second-guess the objection.

"My bad," Cash said. "I meant it as a compliment. You look like you take care of yourself and seem really put together—like most gay people I know. I probably misread the whole *performing arts* thing."

"Compliment accepted," Joey said with a nervous laugh. "By the way, speaking of school, that reminds me, I have to attend this stupid registration meeting tomorrow night in Oklahoma City."

"A *meeting*? This early before the semester?" Topher questioned.

"Ridiculous, right?" Joey huffed. "It's something all students from out of state need to do before the school year starts. I figured I'd just get it out of the way since we're going to be there. It'll save me another trip."

His friends were bummed they'd miss a night with him, but understood the convenience and didn't fault him for it. Cash, on the other hand, thought it was a little *too* convenient. Something else was definitely going on, and Joey was terrible at hiding it—Cash knew a bad performance when he saw one.

"I see Exit 180A!" Topher declared. "First stop, here we come!"

The station wagon took the exit and pulled off the highway. They traveled a couple of miles away from the interstate, then turned onto a dirt road lined with a metal fence. The world's biggest rubber-band ball was at the very end of the road and perched on the top of a tall grassy hill. It was the size of a house, and a wooden observation deck wrapped around it.

Topher parked at the base of the hill but there weren't any other visitors. He and his friends got out of the car, let Cash out of the back, and stared up at the attraction for a couple of moments before approaching it.

"What a *dump*," Mo said.

Their first roadside attraction was a complete letdown. It was severely sun damaged and all its colorful bands had turned gray over time. Several pieces of wood were missing from the deck and termites had feasted on what remained.

"Even *I* couldn't fix up that pile of garbage," Sam said.

"Maybe it looks better close up," Topher suggested—once again blaming himself for the disappointment.

They climbed the hill to get a better look but it was even more decrepit up close. The whole deck had been tagged with graffiti, and several bird nests had been built within the looser bands.

"The pictures online looked way better," Sam said. "Granted, they were taken in the forties."

"Of which century?" Mo quipped.

"It's still a landmark," Topher said. "We still get to tell our grand-children we saw the world's biggest rubber-band ball. That's pretty cool, right?"

Cash was the only one brave enough to climb up the steps and walk around the observation deck. He seemed to see a much different attraction than the others did.

"I sympathize with it," he said. "This thing has spent its whole life on display, amusing and delighting families decade after decade, only to spend its final days covered in bird shit and with the stench of roadkill. It reminds me of an old actress I know."

"You think it bounces?" Joey asked.

Cash shrugged. "Let's find out."

He leaned back on the railing and kicked the giant ball with both of his feet as hard as he could, trying to set it free. The whole deck shook and pieces of wood started breaking off.

"Can we *not* damage public property?" Sam asked. "Some of us have applied for scholarships and will be denied if we get arrested."

"It's stuck anyway," Cash said, and ended his assault on the landmark. "This place is a dud. Let's get out of here. If we leave now, maybe we can make up the time we lost at the diner."

The travelers headed down the hill to the station wagon, but stopped when they heard a series of loud *snaps* and *crunches* behind them. They turned back to the attraction at the top of the hill and saw the observation deck start to crumble and collapse beneath it.

"That can't be good," Mo said.

The world's biggest rubber-band ball began to wobble and break free from the barriers containing it. The giant ball slowly rolled out from the deck's debris and descended down the hill, headed straight toward its visitors.

"*RUN!*" Topher yelled.

They bolted for the station wagon and threw themselves into the car. Topher cranked the ignition, but the engine didn't start.

"*Why isn't the car starting?*" Sam shouted.

"*Because it never starts on the first try!*" Topher reminded her, and tried again.

At first the enormous ball of rubber bands moved at a leisurely pace, but it gained speed and momentum the farther it traveled. Soon it was racing down the hill like a rubber avalanche.

"*Hurry! It's getting closer!*" Mo shouted.

"*I just need a second!*" Topher said.

"*We don't have a second!*" Joey screamed.

Finally the station wagon roared to life. Topher yanked the

gearshift into reverse and slammed his foot on the accelerator. The car rocketed backward right before the moving landmark could flatten it. The passengers cheered, but their worries weren't over.

"It's still coming toward us!" Sam hollered.

"This is just like Indiana Jones*!"* Cash laughed.

The giant ball ricocheted off the metal fence like a pinball and chased the station wagon down the dirt road like Godzilla. Everyone inside the car screamed except Cash, who sang the *Indiana Jones* theme song at the top of his lungs. Right when Topher worried they'd all be goners, the car reached the end of the dirt road and he swerved out of the rogue attraction's path.

The world's biggest rubber-band ball bounced into the horizon like a deer recently freed from captivity.

Topher, Joey, Sam, and Mo sat quietly as their hearts recovered from the traumatic experience. They were out of breath, sweating profusely: their whole lives had just flashed before their eyes. Cash erupted into a wildly inappropriate fit of hysterical laughter.

"What's so funny?" Joey shouted. *"You almost got us killed!"*

"Sorry." The actor snickered. "But at least I answered your question."

Chapter Ten

ROSEMARY'S ABORTION

At six thirty-five on Sunday evening, Topher, Joey, Sam, and Mo were enjoying the exhibits of the Lewis and Clark Museum in the heart of downtown St. Louis. The museum was rather dull and its displays were in serious need of a renovation, but the gang wasn't complaining. After narrowly missing being killed by the world's biggest rubber-band ball, they found the lackluster halls of the Lewis and Clark Museum very comforting.

They had dropped Cash off at a coffee shop earlier so he could find something "fun" for them to do later that night (and they feared whatever suggestion was coming their way). Being with the actor was turning into more of a babysitting job than a dream come true, so they enjoyed the peaceful museum while they could.

"*Sacagawea was a Native American woman from the Lemhi Shoshone tribe,*" Mo read from the pamphlet they received at the museum's entrance. "*She played an essential role in Lewis and Clark's exploration of the Louisiana Purchase, guiding the explorers from North*

Dakota to the Pacific Ocean, and established communication with the Native American populations they encountered."

Mo and her friends observed a tacky depiction of the explorers' first interaction with their celebrated tour guide. Lewis and Clark were handsome mannequins with blond hair and blue eyes, and had chiseled torsos peeking out from their colonial garb. Sacagawea was a slightly terrifying wax figure with a wandering eye, a smashed nose, and a crooked head. She looked more like a Halloween decoration than a national treasure.

"Typical," Sam said. "She did most of the work, yet they named the museum after the boys. Why can't there be a *Sacagawea* university, or public library, or high school?"

"Because white people are too immature to handle a name like *Sacagawea*," Topher said.

They heard a commotion at the front of the museum and saw Cash at the entrance. He was trying to purchase admission but the cashier had recognized him and was so surprised she forgot how to work the register. Once she recovered from the shock, she sold him a ticket and he happily jogged across the museum to rejoin his fellow roadies.

"Guys, I found the perfect thing to do tonight," he boasted. "I got us tickets to see Rosemary's Abortion live in concert! They're in St. Louis for one night only! They were completely sold out, but luckily I found a guy on Craigslist that had some tickets for sale!"

"*Rosemary's Abortion?*" Mo asked. Her imagination did her no favors and filled her head with gruesome assumptions. "I'm afraid to ask."

"It's only the coolest, hippest, and trendiest punk rock band in the Midwest," Cash explained.

"Is that an oxymoron?" Joey asked.

"They've got ten thousand likes on their Facebook page, three independently released albums on iTunes, and were avid Bernie Sanders supporters," Cash pitched. "I've never heard of them personally," he added, "but after checking every social events calendar on the Internet, it's our best bet for a fun Sunday night."

The actor excitedly passed out tickets to Topher, Joey, Sam, and the Sacagawea statue—mistaking it for Mo.

"I'm over here!" she said.

Cash took a second look at the wax figure and jumped a foot backward. "What the hell is that thing? An Ewok?"

"That's supposed to be Sacagawea," Sam said.

The name didn't ring a bell.

"Sacagawea, huh?" Cash asked. "I had Sacagawea once, but it was nothing a little penicillin couldn't clear up. *Hey-oh!*"

"Told you," Topher whispered to the others.

Cash looked around the museum as if he had taken a wrong turn and wound up in the wrong place. He removed his sunglasses to get a better look at his surroundings.

"Why does this place look like the set of *Davy Crockett*? Where's all the Superman stuff?"

The others shared a confused glance—clearly there had been a miscommunication.

"This is the Lewis and Clark Museum," Topher said. "You know, the famous explorers from history?"

Cash was appalled. "I thought you said you were going to a *Lois and Clark* museum. You guys came here *intentionally*? Good God, someone save these kids from themselves."

For the first time, the others noticed his eyes were bright red and his pupils were the size of pinholes. He was also standing a bit more hunched over than before and his head wobbled back and forth like a toddler's.

"Are you feeling okay, Cash?" Joey asked. "You seem a little... *loopy*."

"Oh—it's just my allergy medication," he said, and quickly changed the subject. "Anyway, the doors for the concert open at seven and the band goes on at eight. We should probably get going so we have time for a drink when we get there—it's a couple miles down the road."

They looked at the tickets and spotted something crucial Cash had overlooked.

"The tickets say this is a twenty-one-and-over show," Topher pointed out. "They won't let us in."

"Oh, that won't be a problem—I almost forgot," he said, and pulled four cards from his pocket. "I got you guys fake IDs."

Cash presented the IDs like a winning poker hand, but the idea of using fake identification mortified his friends.

"We left you alone for barely an hour! How did you have time to get concert tickets and fake IDs?" Mo asked.

"The prop guy from *Wiz Kids* is from St. Louis and passed along a contact," Cash said, and handed them out. "Tonight you get to leave your square Downers Grove personas behind you. Topher will be

Boris, Joey will be Hemi, Sam will be Katarina, and Mo will be Sue Yong. See, nothing to worry about!"

"Nothing to worry about?" Sam disagreed. "Cash, this is super illegal! You could have been arrested for this! And how would we have bailed you out?"

The actor grunted. *"Puh-lease,* if I had a nickel for every time I *could have gotten arrested,* the bail would pay itself. If you're worried about getting caught, don't be. These IDs are premium stuff—they're duplicates from the St. Louis DMV. Cost me a grand each. The guy had a case with hundreds of them and I picked the ones that resembled you guys the most."

"As if!" Mo objected. "This girl could be a sumo wrestler! And *Sue Yong* isn't even a Japanese name!"

"Look, we appreciate you going to all the trouble, but this is just too much for us," Topher said. "Besides, we have our hearts set on watching the sunset from the Gateway Arch. We don't want to miss that for a concert."

Cash was thoroughly disappointed. They tried to give him the IDs back but he wouldn't accept them.

"You four are the worst teenagers in the world," he said. "I've got news for you—the sun and the Gateway Arch aren't going anywhere, but your youth is passing you by like a taxi in a bad neighborhood. Using fake IDs and sneaking into concerts is what being young is all about. Let yourselves have a little fun while you still can!"

Topher, Joey, Sam, and Mo collectively sighed. The potential consequences made them nervous but they were tempted by the idea of *having a little fun.*

"I suppose misbehaving *just once* wouldn't be so bad," Sam said.

"And we did want to make memories on this trip," Joey said.

"Strategically speaking, the odds are in our favor," Topher said. "I imagine the likelihood of getting caught the first time we break the rules is a very low percentage."

"Okay, I'm in," Mo decided. "But if we get caught, I'm telling the police you forced us at gunpoint."

Cash rubbed his hands together eagerly. "It's a deal," he said. "Now let's get out of here—I swear Sacagawea just winked at me."

The five thrill seekers left the museum with so much anxiety it was as if they had just planned to rob a bank. They loaded into the station wagon and Cash guided Topher to the concert venue across the city. The location was much farther than he had first advertised and in a very questionable part of town. All the buildings had thick bars over the windows and murals of graffiti, and shoes hung from every power line.

"There it is!" Cash said as they drove past the venue.

He pointed to a large warehouse with a banner that said ROSE-MARY'S ABORTION—ONE NIGHT ONLY in a ransom-style font. A long line was already formed at the door. The concertgoers wore leather, spiked collars, and chains, and were covered in piercings and tattoos.

Joey gulped. "It's an interesting crowd," he said.

"Aren't you worried you'll get recognized in there?" Sam asked Cash.

"Nah," he said. "They don't look like people who'd watch a show about a time-traveling port-a-potty. I should be okay."

"They remind me of those aliens from that *Wiz Kids* episode in season seven," Mo said. "Remember? When the port-a-potty traveled to planet Dominaxitron?"

"Boy do I," Cash recalled. "That was the first episode I took my shirt off. I lived on yams and sit-ups for three weeks leading up to filming it. To this day, I can't smell sweet potato fries without it triggering extreme phantom abdominal pains. *Quick, that guy's leaving! Take his spot!*"

Topher parked the car a few blocks from the warehouse. The 1994 station wagon was the nicest car on the street and the passengers were afraid to get out. Cash ate a couple gummy bears from his backpack before leading the way, but didn't offer any to the others.

"Come on," he teased them. "Don't chicken out now. We're almost there."

They courageously left the car and joined the line outside the warehouse. They were obviously out of their element, but not as much as an old man walking past the line. He seemed very confused by the event and held a sign behind his back.

"Thank goodness," Topher said, and pointed him out to his friends. "Someone who looks more misplaced than we do."

Joey's face fell flat when he saw him, like he recognized someone he didn't like.

"He's not here for the concert," he said. "*Excuse me, sir?* There aren't actual abortions going on here. It's just an ironic band name."

"Is this Fourteenth Street?" the man asked.

"No, I believe it's Fourth."

"Oh, thanks!" he said. "Enjoy the show. *God bless.*"

The old man turned to leave and they saw that his sign read ABOR-TION KILLS! JESUS SAVES!

"How'd you know he was a protestor?" Cash asked.

"I recognized the lost but judgmental look in his eyes," Joey said. "My family used to protest outside Planned Parenthoods every Sunday after church. There's nothing more awkward than asking for directions with a picket sign in your hand."

"Interesting," Cash said. "My family just went to the movies."

They edged closer and closer to the door, which was monitored by a bald mountain of a man. The bouncer's disgruntled attitude made two things very clear: he wasn't easily fooled and he did *not* want to be working on a Sunday night.

"IDs?" he growled.

The bouncer checked Cash's first without a problem, but paused as he inspected the others', especially Mo's.

"I was going through a really tough time," she said.

The bouncer glared at their group suspiciously. "I've got a feeling these aren't real," he said.

Topher, Joey, Sam, and Mo all began to panic internally. *Was he going to call the cops? Were they going to get arrested? Should they make a run for it? Was he as fast as he was big?*

"Seriously, dude?" Cash said. "If we had fake IDs, do you think we'd be using them to see Rosemary's Abortion in Bumblefuck, Missouri? There are casinos down the street."

The bouncer shrugged—he had a point. "Go ahead."

The gang followed Cash through the door, shocked they had

actually pulled it off. Their anxiety was replaced with a strong burst of adrenaline.

"*What a rush!*" Mo said. "I get why people break the rules so much. I feel so naughty and alive!"

"Easy, Lizzie Borden," Cash said. "Don't get addicted to the dark side now."

The warehouse was packed with more tough-looking people. The Downers Grove natives stuck out like a hand of sore thumbs and worried that at any moment someone would ask them to leave. There were no seats but a large standing area in front of a small stage flooded with purple light. Cash led his group to a crowded bar at the side of the warehouse.

"I'm gonna get a drink. You guys want anything?"

"We don't drink," Topher said.

"Like *never*?"

"I had a sip of communion wine once," Joey said.

"Jesus, I'm traveling with the Brady Bunch," Cash said. "I'm starting to think I was sent to you by a higher power. You guys need someone to teach you how to have fun, how to let loose, and—"

"How to destroy a national landmark?" Sam said. "Because you can check that one off the list."

Cash smiled. "Exactly," he said, and faced the bar. "Bartender? I'll take a shot of Johnnie Walker Black!"

"All we have is Jim Beam," the bartender said.

"Sold," Cash said.

"Oh sure, he knows who *those* guys are but not Lewis and Clark," Mo whispered to the others.

The actor slammed a ten-dollar bill on the countertop and threw his head back to take the shot. *"I said goddamn,"* Cash hollered as he recovered from the burn in his throat.

"Are you supposed to drink on your allergy medication?" Topher asked.

"No, but it makes drinking a lot more fun," Cash said. "Gosh— I'm so ready to dance. Hope this band doesn't suck."

A trio of tattooed thirtysomethings in skinny jeans appeared onstage with their instruments. The crowd cheered and gathered around the front of the stage like a school of fish. Cash and the others were crammed among them like they were in a can of punk rock anchovies.

"Hello, St. Louis!" the lead singer greeted the crowd, which was impressive with the number of lip piercings he had. "We are Rosemary's Abortion. We're pro-choice and pro-rock-and-roll! Now let's get this party started! *One…two…three…four!"*

The opening notes of their first song blasted through the speakers and the crowd went wild. Topher, Joey, Sam, and Mo had to cover their ears while their eardrums adjusted to the volume. They couldn't make out a single lyric since the singer mostly yelled the song, but the fast-paced beat was hypnotic.

Everyone throughout the warehouse bobbed up and down excitedly to the beat of the song, but no one was more energetic than Cash. The others figured his whiskey was kicking in because the actor shimmied and shook like Jell-O in an earthquake. The crowd worried he was having a seizure and gave him space, but Cash just boogied his heart out even harder.

"I want whatever that dude is on," said a spectator.

Cash's erratic dance moves started gaining an audience of their own, and his friends worried they were about to have another McCarthy's incident on their hands.

"What do we do?" Topher asked his friends. "He might get recognized if he causes a scene! If people start asking for pictures, we'll be here until next week!"

"I've got an idea," Sam said. "We'll take the attention away from him."

"How?"

"Like this!"

Sam jumped next to Cash and began dancing even crazier than he was. He moved like a go-go dancer undergoing electroshock therapy. His plan was effective, because all eyes quickly moved from the actor to the psycho dancing beside him.

"It's working!" Joey said. "I'm going to help, too!"

Joey threw himself into the mix, impressing the onlookers with the zaniest moves he had learned from the Hip-Hop Dance Team. Sam cheered him on and tried mimicking his moves. Mo's mouth dropped open at the sight and she turned to Topher in shock.

"Oh my God, those are our friends!" She laughed. "I'm gonna dance, too. When in Rome, right?"

Mo sashayed toward her friends and bounced her backside like she was trying to shake off a spider. Sam and Joey laughed hysterically at her and tried to copy it.

As the song played on, it was less and less about creating a distraction from Cash, and more a full-blown competition of who could look like the biggest buffoon. Their eccentricity was contagious and all the people surrounding them began showcasing their own quirky moves, too. Like an airborne epidemic, the ridiculousness spread through the crowd until the entire warehouse was dancing wildly, and Cash was Patient Zero.

"Come on, Topher!" Sam said as he danced toward him. "Let your freak flag fly!"

"I'm good," he said. "I'm not much of a mover or a shaker. I'm just gonna go hang out by the bar until there's a slower song—"

"Topher," Sam said, and forcefully pulled him closer. *"Shut up and dance with me."*

All it took was a tug on his arm and a twinkle in Sam's eye, and Topher lost all sense of himself. He moved his body like an orangutan on speed, like an intoxicated father of the bride, like an inflatable at a car sale. He made Sam laugh so hard tears filled his eyes. Sam was so beside himself he had to stop and catch his breath. Topher had never seen him so happy before—he would have danced all night if it meant more time with Sam's smile and laugh.

That's when it dawned on him. *Oh no...,* Topher thought, unable to deny it anymore. *I've got a crush on Samantha Gibson.*

Sam caught his breath and continued dancing, twirling in a circle around Topher like an orbiting planet. Sam was so free, so loose, and so carefree, he was practically another person altogether, certainly not the girl Topher had grown up with.

Oh fuuuuuck..., Topher thought. *This is more than a crush. I might be in love with Samantha Gibson!*

Mo and Joey popped up on either side of them and started freak dancing like small dogs marking their territory. Apparently

Sam wasn't the only one in rare form—it was almost impossible not to let go.

There were no parents holding them back, no younger siblings needing to be cared for, no one telling them they were going to burn in hell, and no one telling them they had an illness. There were no *limits*, no *responsibilities*, no *religion*, and no *misunderstandings*. In that moment, there was just the music vibrating through their bodies. The worst part was knowing the music and the moment would eventually end.

After four or five songs' worth of intense dancing, Cash began to slow down. He looked at the dancing fools around him with pride, but then froze like he was about to be sick.

"Are you okay, bud?" Topher asked. "Need some water?"

As if it were happening in slow motion, Topher watched the light fade from his eyes, the smile fade from his lips, and the color drain from his face. The actor fell backward and collapsed on the floor.

"*CAAAASH!*" Topher screamed.

Chapter Eleven

STREAMSIDE STREAMING

Monday morning at eight o'clock, Topher gingerly approached cabin 8 of the Paul Bunyan Hotel and knocked on the door with his good hand. His whole right side was sore from carrying Cash out of the warehouse the night before. Luckily, the actor had regained consciousness once he had some fresh air, and had blamed the episode on low blood sugar. The others were so relieved he hadn't dropped dead that they didn't question him, but privately they had their doubts.

"Hey, Cash? Are you awake?" Topher said. "We're ready to go when you are."

When they arrived at the Paul Bunyan Hotel after the concert, Topher and his friends decided to give Cash one of the two cabins they'd reserved all to himself. After hearing the demonic noises he made in his sleep, no one wanted to bunk with the actor.

"Cash, can you hear me?" Topher said, and knocked again. "Are you even in there?"

The door opened a crack and Topher saw that Cash was still in a hotel bathrobe. The actor shielded his eyes from the sunlight like a vampire and moaned. He cradled a small trash can like it was a newborn baby.

"Good morning, Cash!" Topher said cheerfully.

Just the sound of his voice was agonizing for the actor.

"Sorry, I slept in." He groaned. "Is it time to leave already?"

"Yeah, but there's no rush," Topher said. "We're spending the whole day at the Mark Twain National Forest, so we can leave whenever you're ready."

"About that," Cash said. "Look, I woke up with a *terrible* headache. I feel like someone's hammering a pickax into my skull. I'm not sure hiking through the wilderness is a good idea."

"Can we get you some aspirin or anything?"

"No, I just gotta sleep it off. You guys should go ahead without me. I don't want to hold you back, so I'll just meet you in Oklahoma City tonight."

"Cash, that's like a six-hour drive," Topher said.

"It's fine—I'll call a car," Cash said. "Don't worry, I'm not ditching you. I'll see you guys later at the Vacation Suites."

Cash quickly slammed the door and Topher heard him vomiting behind it. The situation clearly wasn't up for discussion, so Topher returned to his friends in the car.

"Well?" Joey asked from the driver's seat. "Where is he?"

"The dude's hungover as fuck," Topher informed them. "He wants us to go on without him and meet us in Oklahoma City later tonight."

"What?" Mo said. "That's insane! Why don't we just leave the forest early and come back for him?"

"It wasn't exactly up for debate," Topher said. "He's in really bad shape."

Joey shook his head. "Low blood sugar my ass," he said. "That's what he gets for mixing medication with alcohol. And it's probably why he's developing a bad reputation in Hollywood—he's got to be more careful."

"Hopefully last night will be a wake-up call for him, then," Sam said. "How's your shoulder, Topher? Any better?"

"It feels like I've been drawn and quartered, but I'll be okay to hike today," Topher said. "I gotta say, passing-out incident aside, I had a *lot* of fun last night."

Everyone in the car smiled, completely in agreement.

"Oh my God, *soooo much* fun!" Mo said. "Definitely in my top ten favorite nights of all time—who am I kidding, top five. I know I had issues at first, but having Cash around might be kind of nice."

"It was a blast!" Sam said. "I haven't danced like that since I was a kid, and even then it wasn't as fun."

"Who knew Sam could move like that?" Joey said. "And who knew Topher could move at all?"

They laughed at him and playfully pushed his good shoulder.

"It was special," Topher said, then glanced at Sam when he wasn't looking. "*Really* special."

With Joey at the wheel, the station wagon left the enormous statues of Paul Bunyan and Babe the Blue Ox behind and ventured farther into Missouri. At the four hundred and thirtieth mile of their journey, they arrived at the Mark Twain National Forest. The gang changed into comfortable shoes and selected a hiking trail from the options on a large map posted at the ranger's station.

The sights and sounds of the forest were beautiful, the smells were transcendent, but all anyone could think about was the night before. They relived every moment of their night with Rosemary's Abortion, from sneaking past the bouncer to cutting loose on the dance floor, and even picking Cash up *off* the dance floor. It had been a day of frustrations but a night of firsts, and they would cherish it forever.

None of them had cell service as they hiked through the forest, which was a good exercise for a group of millennials. They enjoyed spending a few hours disconnected from the rest of the world—or at least that's what they said while checking for service every hundred feet. Only when their trail wound downhill to a small stream did the first bars of reception appear. Suddenly, everyone's phones started going off like winning slot machines.

"That doesn't sound good," Sam said. "I hope something bad didn't happen."

They checked their phones and found that their in-boxes were filled with hundreds of Google Alerts. Mo read the subject of the first one and screamed.

"Someone posted a video of Cash passing out in the warehouse last night!" Mo said. "It's all over the Internet! All the Wizzers are freaking out!"

"Oh my God, it's everywhere!" Topher said. "*Television Actor Blacks Out in St. Louis*—headline from CNN!"

"*Wiz Kid 'Wizzes' Out of Control*—Yahoo! News," Sam read.

"*Meet Me in St. Louis, Floor Says to Cash Carter*—TMZ!" Joey read.

"*Liberal Goes Down in Red State*—Fox News!" Mo read. "It's also on WizzerNet and the *Wiz Kids* forum page!"

"Guys, I have the video loaded on my phone!" Sam said. "It's got over ten million views and *we're all in it*!"

Topher, Joey, and Mo huddled around Sam's phone and he pressed Play. They'd never have to relive the experience in their memories again because the whole night had been immortalized by a shaky iPhone. Everything from Cash dancing like a madman to fainting and being carried off was on YouTube for the whole world to see.

"This is horrible!" Topher said.

"A disaster!" Joey said.

"I can't believe we didn't see anyone recording us!" Sam said.

"I'm so glad I was wearing a cute outfit," Mo said. "Look at the video recommendations—*Kylie Trig has already uploaded a video about it!*"

Sam clicked on it and the video loaded on his phone. After a thirty-second commercial for a lip gloss called PornStar, and Kylie's obnoxious theme song, the video finally played.

"*The president has to do something about Cash Carter,*" Kylie said right off the bat. "*Look, we all know fame and success change people. Other fandoms have survived the personality changes, the bad decisions, and the scandals of their show's star—and I know we'll get through this, too. But Cash Carter, what da fuck is going on with you, boy? I know you've been going through a* phase *lately, but I never expected to wake up to* this*!"*

Kylie played the footage from the warehouse in the corner of her video. The distressed YouTube host rubbed the sides of her temples as she watched.

"There are so many questions, I don't know where to start! First off, why is Cash in St. Louis? Why is he at a punk rock concert when we all know he listens to alternative *music? Why is he dancing like an epileptic on roller skates? But one question no one has yet to ask is* who the hell are these four deplorables with him*?"*

The footage paused and zoomed in on Topher, Joey, Sam, and Mo's faces. Their collective gasp was so loud it scared off all the woodland creatures within a mile radius.

"We're in Kylie Trig's video!" Joey yelled in disbelief. *"And she just called us deplorables!"*

"If you ask me, these fuckers *are who's to blame,"* Kylie declared passionately. *"I don't know if they're just an entourage sucking him dry of everything decent, if they've been paid by another network to sabotage the show, or if they were planted by the* Doctor Who *fandom so they could laugh at us as we watch him self-destruct. I just know these people* want him to fail*! And I'm hopeful Edward Snowden and/or WikiLeaks will answer my request and help us get to the bottom of this."*

"She thinks WE'RE the bad influence?" Mo asked in outrage.

"I'm sure the Wiz Kids *publicists will release some statement in the next hour claiming it was* dehydration*, but just in case the four leeches involved are watching this, just know the Wizzers are onto you! If you don't leave Cash alone, stop corrupting him, and stop fucking with his*

career—this fandom will hunt you down, we will find you, and we will kill you!"

"Holy shit! Kylie Trig just threatened our lives!" Sam exclaimed.

The video finished but was instantly followed by another.

"Hey, Wizzer sluts," Kylie said in a kind and casual tone. *"So, right after I posted my last video my lawyers called me and told me I needed to retract what I said. I used some pretty strong words but I was not serious about the threats I made, nor do I condone or encourage violence of any kind. Make sure you subscribe and I'll see you next time!"*

The second video ended, but Topher, Joey, Sam, and Mo stared at the screen for a few moments in absolute terror.

"Holy shit! Kylie Trig just threatened our lives and then took it back!" Sam clarified.

"Every Wizzer in the world is going to hate us now!" Mo said. "What do we do? Should we go into hiding?"

Topher decided to downplay the situation as much as possible— not to comfort his friends, but to comfort himself. This was more than he knew how to handle.

"Guys, I don't think we have to be worried about this," he said. "Everyone knows half of everything Kylie says is bullshit anyway. No one would be dumb enough to believe—"

Everyone's phones stared to buzz. They looked at their screens and saw video messages coming in from Huda and Davi. According to the tally beside their names, it was the forty-fifth time the international Wizzers had tried calling them that day. Joey was the first to answer.

"Hi, guys—"

"Excuuuuuuuuuuuuuuse me?" Huda shouted. *"Did something happen on your trip that you forgot to share with us?"*

"What the bitch are you guys doing with Cash Carter?" Davi demanded.

"Oh boy." Topher sighed. "I'm assuming you saw the video?"

"Seventy-four times!" Huda said. *"Now spill!"*

"Long story short, the night before we left I wrote Cash a letter and asked him to join us. The next morning he actually showed up."

"Hold on! You're saying Cash Carter joined your road trip *yesterday* and we had to find out about it from *Kylie Trig*?" Huda asked.

Topher shrugged guiltily. "Um...yeah," he confessed.

Their international friends screamed so loud Huda woke up everyone in her house and Davi scared everyone at the cybercafe.

"And you repay him by trying to kill him at a concert?" Davi asked.

"He's not dead, he just had low blood sugar," Sam said. "Kylie Trig was just being dramatic. He's only been with us for a day!"

"Is he with you right now?" Davi asked.

"He's back at the hotel," Mo said. "We've been hiking in the forest all day. That's why we haven't gotten your calls until now."

"What's he like?" Huda asked dreamily. *"Is he just as amazing as Dr. Bumfuzzle?"*

Topher, Joey, Sam, and Mo went quiet—afraid to answer.

"We'll have him call you and you can see for yourself," Joey said.

The images of Huda and Davi on their phones suddenly froze. It wasn't from bad service—the idea of communicating with the actor was so shocking they both went still as a rock.

"Huda? Davi?" Joey asked but didn't get a response. "Must be a bad connection—oh well."

They ended the call and paced around the streamside in silence. They scrolled through the comments section on every *Wiz Kids* blog and website, reading thousands of witty, rude, and nasty remarks that total strangers made about them.

"I can't believe we're *Internet* famous," Mo said. "Would it be unethical to use this to get people to read my fanfiction?"

"Yes," the others answered at once.

"Poor Cash," Joey said. "How does he live with this every day? I feel like I'm being pecked alive by a million invisible birds."

"And they don't even know our real names!" Sam added. "Most of them are calling us Huey, Dewey, Louie, and Kung Fu Panda."

"Wait—which one am I?" Mo asked.

"I hope this story doesn't upset Cash," Topher said. "He's the one it's going to impact the most. Everyone will forget about us by tomorrow. Maybe we should get back on the road and head to Oklahoma City so we can comfort him when he gets there. He might need a friend after this."

They all agreed, but just as they turned to leave, Mo's phone chimed with a new Google Alert.

"Whoa," she said. "It's not a good day for the *Wiz Kids* fandom. A naked photo of Amy Evans just leaked."

"Did she get hacked?" Joey asked.

"I don't think so—looks like it came from *her* Twitter account," Mo said. "She was probably just jealous Cash was getting so much attention. But in good news, all the Wizzers are talking about that now! You were right, Topher—*we're already in the clear*!"

The gang had never been so grateful to be part of a generation with such a short attention span. They followed the trail back to the station wagon, hopeful the afternoon would be their first and only involvement with breaking news.

Mo seemed a little disappointed their moment in the spotlight had finished so quickly. She replayed the video from the warehouse over and over again, giggling as she watched herself dance like a maniac. Sam peeked over Mo's shoulder but cringed at the sight of himself.

"Are you okay, Sam?" Topher asked.

"I'm fine—I just really hate seeing myself on camera," Sam said.

"You shouldn't be. You looked really pretty last night."

Topher smiled at Sam, and he could tell there was more than just the compliment behind his eyes.

"Oh—thanks, Topher," he said.

Sam always resented being called *pretty*, but that's not what bothered him. What weighed on his heart the most was seeing the heart on Topher's sleeve become more and more visible each day. The longer it went on, the guiltier Sam felt—like he was leading a horse with a false carrot. Before their trip was over, he had to tell Topher the truth, no matter how painful it'd be to say or to hear.

But how much truth did Sam want to give Topher? Was he even ready to tell a friend he was trans? Would it be easier to just tell Topher he wasn't interested in being more than friends, to stop his crush from growing? But then again, was *that* the truth?

After all, there was a reason Sam wanted to dance with Topher the night of Rosemary's Abortion, there was a reason Sam stayed up late on so many summer nights chatting with Topher online, and there was a reason Sam cared so much about how Topher would handle the truth.

Perhaps they had both wanted the same thing all along, and Sam was just scared Topher wouldn't want it with the *real* Sam. Perhaps he had been hiding the truth to spare *himself* the disappointment. Whatever the case may be, Sam was about to find out.

From that moment on, the trip was more bittersweet than before. By the time it was over they would head home with a dozen new memories, but maybe a couple of broken hearts, too.

Chapter Twelve

SINNERS AND SAINTS

The Downers Grove troop pulled into the parking lot of the Oklahoma City Vacation Suites at seven fifteen on Monday evening, but Cash was nowhere to be found.

"Did a man come in this afternoon, saying he was traveling with a group?" Topher asked the woman at the check-in counter.

"I don't believe so," she said. "What does he look like?"

"Never mind, he would have left an impression," Topher said. "We'd like to put one of our rooms under his name for when he arrives."

By the time they'd settled into their room, Topher, Sam, and Mo were exhausted—not just from hiking through the hills of the Mark Twain National Forest, but also from their emotional fifteen minutes of fame. They decided to grab a quick bite at Noodles Galore, the pasta house across the street from the hotel, and then head straight to bed.

"Are you going to eat before your registration meeting?" Sam asked Joey.

"I'll just grab dinner on my way back," he said.

"Have fun!" Mo said. "Don't party too hard without us."

"Yeah, right," Joey said. "A Monday night in Oklahoma City with a bunch of Baptists—*don't wait up!*"

As soon as the door closed behind them, Joey got ready for his "registration meeting" like it was a fire drill. He put together a nice outfit and Googled what the appropriate number of buttons was to leave open for a hookup date (four, apparently).

Joey followed the advice of a shirtless and energetic gay YouTuber on how to have a safe and pleasurable sexual experience. He dashed to the pharmacy down the street, taking the long way around the hotel so his friends wouldn't see him from Noodles Galore, and purchased the essentials to groom, clean, and protect himself.

By eight fifteen that night, Joey was feeling as fresh as humanly possible and prepared for anything the night had in store. There was only one problem: he still hadn't heard from the guy he was meeting.

He paced around the small hotel room, continuously refreshing his ManNip app in case it wasn't working properly. At eight thirty Joey worried his friends would return from dinner so he left the hotel and wandered aimlessly around downtown Oklahoma City while he waited to hear from Brian K.

At nine thirty, Joey figured he had been stood up, so he headed back to the hotel with his tail between his legs.

"*Yeah, Daddy!*" His phone rang three times.

Joey's heart fluttered. *Maybe the night wasn't a total waste?* He almost dropped his phone as he hurried to read the new ManNip messages.

Hey sexy!

Sorry, I just got off work.

Still in the mood to meet up?

XO Brian

Joey didn't want to seem desperate so he played it cool, waiting a good twenty seconds before responding.

Absolutely!!!

Just name the time and place.

There was no reply for a couple of minutes. Joey worried he might have scared Brian off by using too many exclamation points. To his relief, his phone chimed with a game plan.

Let's meet for a drink first.

There's a bar called Sinners and Saints.

It's on the corner of Robinson and Park Ave.

Meet me there at 10 ☺

The name couldn't have been more ironic and Joey took it as a sign their date was meant to be. He looked up directions and saw that the bar was only a few blocks away from where he stood. Joey strolled through town with a spring in his step and arrived twenty minutes early.

Sinners and Saints was in the basement of a tall bank building that doubled as a tornado shelter when needed. It had red carpet, big red booths, and red stools at the bar. It was decorated in framed portraits of Catholic saints and framed mug shots of notorious criminals. There were only two other customers, but the bar was completely empty, so Joey had a seat at one of the stools.

"Can I get you a drink?" a gruff bartender asked.

"Just water, thanks," Joey said.

The bartender refilled his water four times as Joey waited for his ManNip date to show up. Joey was so nervous his hands were shaky and he almost spilled his glass after every sip. His heart was beating out of control and every minute seemed much longer than the one before—it felt more like running on a treadmill than meeting a guy for a drink.

Finally, at five past ten, a tall, handsome, and muscular man walked into the bar and tapped Joey on the shoulder.

"Jay?" the man asked.

At first Joey forgot his own alias and didn't know who the man was talking to. He looked over his shoulder and instantly recognized him from his profile.

"Hi! You must be Brian."

Joey awkwardly shook Brian's hand. *How else were you supposed to greet a stranger you were about to have sex with?* Once he had confirmation, Brian took a seat next to him.

"Thanks for getting a drink with me," Brian said. "Whenever I meet someone from an app, I always like to see them in public first.

You can never be too careful. There are a lot of phonies out there, am I right?"

"Totally," Joey said with a nervous laugh. "Do you use the app often?"

He regretted the question as soon as it came out of his mouth. He might as well have asked *So, how big of a whore are you?* Luckily, Brian seemed to like his straightforwardness.

"I *try* to meet people the old-fashioned way, but that's hard to do when you're stuck in a place like Oklahoma City for a couple weeks," Brian said. "You're a breath of fresh air, believe me. You actually look even *younger* than you do on your profile—that's rare."

Brian actually looked slightly older than the pictures on his profile, but Joey wasn't about to tell him that.

"What can I say?" he said with shrug. "I've got good genes."

"I can see *that.*"

Brian flirtatiously looked him up and down. Joey's face filled with a warm rush of blood sent straight from his heart. *This was going to be a good night.*

"So, how was work? You're an architect, right?"

"Indeed, but it's not as glamorous as it sounds," Brian said. "My company's putting in an office building on Third Street. I was just arguing with the owner about the best location to put a freight elevator. What about you? What brings you to Oklahoma City?"

"I'm on a road trip with some friends," Joey said. "It's our last chance to hang out before we split up for college."

"College? Didn't you say you were in college?"

Joey was forgetting the lines to his own script. "Oh—I meant before they go off to graduate school," he lied. "They're all a little older than me. We met in the Anthropology program at Northwestern."

"How's Anthropology treating you?"

"Great," Joey said. "I sit around staring at artifacts all day—and those are just my professors."

Brian laughed, flashing his bright smile. Joey had nothing to compare their date to, but so far they seemed to be enjoying each other's company.

"Can I get you fellas a drink?" the bartender asked.

"I'll take a Manhattan on the rocks," Brian said.

Joey had no idea what the hell a Manhattan was, but it sounded refreshing. "I'll take the same," he said.

"Can I see your ID?" the bartender asked.

Sheer panic hit Joey's face like a deer in front of a semitruck. It only lasted a moment though as Joey remembered he still had the fake ID Cash had given him in his pocket. He took it out and handed it to the bartender.

"I'll be right back with your Manhattans," he said, and went to the other side of the bar to make them.

"Is that a Missouri driver's license?" Brian asked.

"Oh...yeah," Joey said. "That's where I'm from originally."

"You look different in your photo," Brian pointed out. "Can I see it?"

Before Joey could slip it back into his pocket or come up with an excuse as to why he didn't want to show it to him, Brian had already taken the ID and given it a better look than the bartender had. All Joey's high hopes for the night suddenly came crashing down.

"Hemi?" Brian asked. "Why are you carrying a fake ID?"

"I—I—I can explain."

"Did you *lie* about your age?" Brian said, and then looked around the bar in panic. "Wait—am I about to be arrested? Is Chris Hansen about to jump out somewhere with a camera crew?"

"No—relax, I'm eighteen!" Joey said.

"Eighteen?" Brian said. "Oh my God—I've been flirting with an eighteen-year-old! I feel like one of those dirty old predators. I need to go."

Brian was visibly shaken and stood to leave, but Joey grabbed his arm before he could walk away.

"Wait—please don't go," he pleaded. "I'm sorry I lied, but I'm not a deceitful person. I was just desperate to meet someone and didn't want anyone I know to find my profile, so I exaggerated some things."

The bartender placed their Manhattans on the counter and then hurried away to avoid whatever uncomfortable exchange was happening between them.

"Can we just have a drink and get back to where we were before you saw my ID? I don't know when I'll get another chance to do this. *Please?"*

The tense expression in Brian's eyes faded into sympathy. He wasn't looking down at a guy from an app anymore, but at a memory.

"You're still in the closet, aren't you?" he asked.

For the first time in his life, Joey's superior deflecting skills abandoned him. It was a lot harder to lie to someone when his honesty didn't come with a major consequence.

"Yeah," Joey confessed.

"And I'm guessing you're still a virgin, too?"

Joey couldn't bring himself to say it, so he just nodded. Brian glanced around the bar, as if trying to find Joey's chaperone. *Someone needed to talk to this kid.*

"You know what, let's have a chat," Brian said, and took a seat. "You probably don't want to get a lecture from the guy you were hoping to sleep with, but I wish I had someone to talk to me about this when I was your age. Tell me, why would you want to lose your virginity to a total stranger? Wouldn't you rather wait for someone special?"

"I'd rather just get it out of the way so I don't have to think about it anymore," Joey said.

"*That's* your hormones talking," Brian said. "Those little bastards will do anything to get you to spread your seed—that's a biological fact—but you can't let them overpower your common sense. It's practically impossible not to when you're young, horny, and live in an oversexualized society. Hell, even Instagram turns into a digital red light district after a certain hour—how can you not be tempted?"

"Dude, we just met on a hookup app," Joey reminded him. "Are you seriously giving me an abstinence talk right now?"

"Not the point I'm trying to make," Brian said. "Look, sex is the fucking best, but it can also be the fucking worst if you're not careful. Your first time could potentially set the tone of your sex life. If you don't start off with a *decent* experience or don't go into it respecting yourself, it could lead to some really bad habits. You don't want to become one of those guys with fulfillment issues who jumps into bed with every guy they meet—*believe me.*"

Brian downed his Manhattan in one gulp like he was washing away a bad memory.

"We're not hooking up tonight, are we?" Joey asked.

"Absolutely not," Brian said. "You're going to be talking about your first for the rest of your life. The last thing you want to do is look back with regrets or feel like someone unworthy is walking around with a piece of your soul. Trust me, I learned that the hard way. If I could do it all over again, I would lose it to a friend I knew I could trust, someone I could be safe with and laugh about it with later."

"I *think* I appreciate what you're saying," Joey said. "But it's more complicated than that. My dad's a well-known pastor and I'm going to a Baptist college next year. It's hard to think of a scenario that wouldn't get back to him aside from doing it with a stranger—and I'm not ready for my family to know."

"Now, *that's* rough," Brian said. "I've got an uncle that's refused to acknowledge me since I came out, but it's not an excuse to shortcut the most important parts of our lives. I know this is hard to understand when you're young, but if your dad would rather lose a son than accept you for who you are, that's *his* loss. Remember, for every person that doesn't accept you, you'll find a dozen who will. It's a gay law."

"Are you like a motivational speaker or something? You can't be making all this stuff up on the spot."

"Tuesdays and Thursdays at the San Diego LGBT Community Center," he said.

Joey couldn't believe his luck. Of all the people to meet online, he had found a person who *wouldn't* take advantage of him. Brian put some cash on the counter and stood to leave.

"Drinks are on me," he said. "Take care of yourself, Jay."

"Actually, it's Joey," he said. "And are you *sure* you don't want to take me back to your place? You'd make an awfully decent memory."

Brian laughed. When no one was looking, he quickly leaned down and kissed Joey on the lips.

"There," he said. "At least you got *something* out of the way. Good night."

Joey watched Brian go in total silence as he came down from the high of his first kiss. Sure, he didn't get what he wanted, but at least he'd leave the bar a little more of a *sinner* than a *saint*.

"Hey, Romeo! How was your date?"

Joey turned toward the voice and saw Cash Carter sitting in a booth in the very back. The actor had a huge grin and gave him a thumbs-up.

"Oh no." Joey gasped. "How long have you been sitting there?"

"The whole time," Cash said.

Joey had never been more mortified in his life. All the blood in his body rushed to the pit of his stomach. He covered his face with his hands, but nothing could shield him from the intense overexposure. The night he had been dreaming about since yesterday morning had quickly turned into a nightmare.

"He seemed like a nice guy. Too bad he wouldn't put out."

Joey hurried to his table and slid into the seat across from him.

"Please don't tell the others about this," he begged. "I know I lied to you in the car, and I'm sure there might be some satisfaction in calling me out on it, but I'm not ready for anyone to know."

Joey acted like he was begging for his life instead of asking someone to keep a secret.

"It's all good, man," Cash said. "I'm not going to tell anyone. I understand why you want to keep it from your family, but why not tell your friends? They seem open-minded enough to handle it."

"I just don't want to risk it, okay?" Joey said. "If word ever got back to my parents—well, I don't know what would happen. They'd probably disown me or ship me off to some facility where they shock the gay out of you. It's just better for everyone if I keep it to myself."

"Mm-hmm." Cash grunted. "Is that also why you're going to Oklahoma Baptist University for performing arts? Because it's better for *everyone?*"

"What are you getting at, Cash?"

"Dude, you're bending over backward to please the people you're *never* going to get approval from," Cash said. "I know because I'm guilty of it, too, and it's a total waste of time. It's like when I spend my days off doing favors for television critics. No matter how many head shots I sign or videos I record for their bratty kids, it isn't going to make them review my projects any better or write good things about me in their recaps."

"No offense, but I think pleasing *my family* and pleasing a bunch of critics is totally different," Joey said.

"Sorry—it was just the first example I could come up with," Cash said. "Your whole world is going to open up once you get out from under your dad's thumb. Don't you remember that whole It Gets Better thing the *Wiz Kids* cast participated in?"

Cash was trying to help, but it was only making Joey angrier by the second.

"You Hollywood people are so full of shit," Joey said. "You act like all our problems can be solved with a catchphrase or a hashtag—like our lives actually get easier if we see a bunch of celebrities with matching T-shirts in a PSA."

"Dude, I'm just trying to sympathize with you," Cash said. "I know what it's like to—"

"No you don't, Cash!" Joey yelled. *"You don't know what it's like to feel ashamed every time you have a physical attraction! You don't know what it's like to have most of the planet think you're a pervert, a demon, or mentally ill! You don't know what it's like to live in a country with judges and cabinet members that think you belong in jail! You don't know what it's like to know the people you love the most would never love the real you! You'll never know any of those things, so don't pretend you do!"*

Joey had to catch his breath and recover from the outburst like he'd just run a marathon. He had been so successful at hiding his anger, he didn't realize there was so much inside him. Once it started pouring out, Joey couldn't stop it, as if Cash had put the final crack in the dam around his heart.

"Feel better?" Cash asked.

"I'm so sorry," he said. "I've—I've—I've never said those things to anyone before. I don't think I've even said them to myself."

"I was worried the furniture was going to start levitating," Cash said. "You're right, though. I don't know what any of that is like. But I do know what it's like to feel trapped and too afraid to do anything about it."

"How so?" Joey asked.

"Agoraphobia," Cash said.

"Agoraphobia?"

"It's the fear of leaving your house," Cash said. "Remember the Christmas episode in season five? The one that implied the Virgin Mary was an alien abductee and Jesus Christ was an extraterrestrial/human hybrid?"

"Of course," Joey said. "People were not happy about that—my parents almost forbid me to watch the show."

"It was the worst backlash *Wiz Kids* had ever received," Cash said. "And even though I didn't write it, since I was the face of the show, people took their anger out on me. I got death threats from five different radical religious groups."

"What?"

Joey assumed it was another one of Cash's exaggerated stories, but he was being dead serious.

"Oh yeah," he said. "They threated to shoot me, to mail me poison, to put a bomb in my car—you name it! For a good year, I was terrified to leave my house. The only other places I went were the studio to shoot the show and WizCon to promote it."

"What did you do? How did you get over it?" Joey said.

"One day I woke up and decided I had had enough," Cash explained. "I realized it didn't matter what *might* happen to me outside, because the damage was already done. Those maniacs had already taken my life away by making me live in fear; it just took me a while to recognize it. So I finally built up the courage to step outside, and you want to know what I learned?"

"What?"

Cash smiled serenely. "I learned why they call it *fresh air*," he said. "And one day, you will, too."

Joey was stunned, not so much by the story, but that so much insight had come out of the man who passed out at a Rosemary's Abortion concert.

"Wow, none of us had any idea you went through something like that," he said. "That must have taken a lot of courage."

"It took strength I didn't even know I had," Cash said. "Also, the police traced all the death threats back to a forty-seven-year-old loser living in his mother's basement. That helped, too."

Joey shook his head and gave the actor a dirty look—he had *almost* fallen for it. There was definitely a thin line between a story-teller and a bullshitter, and it was becoming clearer and clearer which side of the line Cash was on.

"What are you even doing here, anyway?" Joey asked.

"I'm meeting up with someone, too, and there aren't many places to choose from on a Monday night in Oklahoma City," Cash said.

"Who are *you* meeting?"

"You're not the only one who uses the Internet to hook up," Cash said. "Now scram before you scare my strange away like you did yours. There's not enough cold water at the hotel for both of us."

Joey left Sinners and Saints and headed back to the Vacation Suites down the street. He didn't get the physical release he was hoping for, but after a night of honesty, it was *much* easier to breathe. He didn't want to give Cash any credit, but maybe there was some truth to his bullshit after all.

Chapter Thirteen

HIGH TIMES AT HIGH TYDES

At nine o'clock on Tuesday morning, the Downers Grove gang of four gathered around the door of room 406 at the Oklahoma City Vacation Suites. They were ready to depart for the next destination and hoped the fifth passenger would be joining them this time around.

"Are we positive Cash made it to his room?" Mo asked.

"I saw him on my way in last night," Joey said, stretching the truth. "He's definitely in the city, but I can't guarantee he's in his room."

"How'd he look?" Sam asked.

"Pretty good for someone hungover and in the middle of a scandal," Joey said.

Topher lightly knocked on the door and prayed today's wake-up call would be easier than the previous morning's. To their surprise, Cash answered the door almost immediately. He was completely naked expect for a bath towel wrapped around his waist. Topher shrieked and covered his eyes while the others stared in awe at the actor's unexpectedly toned physique.

"Good morning," Cash said happily. "Is it time to leave?"

"Morning!" Topher said awkwardly. "Glad you found your room last night. We were just about to head out. Do you need a few minutes?"

"A couple *seconds*, actually," Cash said. "I didn't exactly get a chance to unpack."

The actor moved through the room searching for his clothes. They were scattered across the floor like he had undressed in a hurry. He found his pants under the table, his shirt was over the lampshade, and his underwear was hanging from the handle of the minibar. Cash also found a red bra and a cheetah-print thong among his things, which confused the hell out of the others.

"Are you leaving already?" said a sleepy second voice in the room.

Topher, Joey, Sam, and Mo leaned into the doorway and saw a naked woman lying in the bed. They were as surprised to see her as she was to see four teenage strangers. The woman screamed and covered herself with the sheets.

"Sorry!" Topher said on behalf of his friends. "We didn't realize you had *company*!"

"Oh yeah, guys this is…." Cash paused as he made the introduction. "What was your name again?"

"It's *Brenda*," she said angrily.

"Right, *Brenda*," Cash recalled. "For some reason I almost called you Vicky—"

The pile of pillows next to Brenda started to move and *another* woman peeked out from under the sheets.

"*I'm* Vicky," she said.

"I completely forgot you were there, too!" Cash said. "I should really start writing names down before I fall asleep."

He gathered the rest of his clothes and popped into the bathroom to change. Topher, Joey, Sam, and Mo waited for him in the hall and looked at one another with open mouths and huge eyes. They didn't know how to feel about what they'd just seen; they just knew it could never be *unseen*.

"Ladies, thanks for showing me a good time last night," Cash said as he reemerged from the bathroom. "Checkout isn't until noon, so enjoy the room!"

He promptly shut the door of room 406 behind him and led the others down the hall to the elevators.

"Looks like you had a good night," Topher said.

"You can say that again," Cash said.

"I hope you weren't disrespectful to those women," Sam said.

"Please, if anyone was disrespected last night it was me—but I'll spare you the details," Cash said with a smirk. "I never thought I'd say this, but *God bless Oklahoma*."

They left the Vacation Suites and climbed into the station wagon. It was Sam's turn to drive so he had a seat behind the steering wheel. Topher sat in the front with him, Mo and Joey shared the backseat, and Cash took his usual spot lying on top of the luggage in the very back.

"So, where are we off to next, Captain Janeway?" Cash asked.

"Amarillo, Texas," Sam said. "We should get there in about four hours."

"More like five and a half if Sam is driving." Joey laughed.

"Not true!" Sam said, and hit his leg.

"How was Ernest Hemingway yesterday?" Cash asked.

Had the actor asked this question two days ago, the others wouldn't have known what he was talking about, but the more they spent time with Cash, the more they started speaking his language.

"The Mark Twain National Forest was great," Topher said. "We got a great hike in, saw some cool animals—"

"And we became the number one enemy of the *Wiz Kids* fandom," Mo added. "Don't forget that part."

Cash made a noise like he was guilty of breaking something valuable.

"I heard about that on the radio on my way into Oklahoma City," he said. "I'm guessing you guys were in the video, too, huh? Sorry about roping you into it."

"We were just worried about *you*," Topher said. "How are *you* handling it?"

"Oh, you don't have to worry about me," he said. "I'm so used to people making mountains out of molehills. This isn't the first time I've been in the news, and it won't be the last. Besides, the studio publicists already released a statement saying I was *dehydrated*, so that should clear it up."

The others shared a look—*Kylie Trig's prediction had come true.*

"The funny thing is no one actually checked in to make sure I was even still alive before announcing I was fine." Cash laughed. "Wishful thinking on the studio's part, if you ask me."

The actor yawned like a lion and stretched out his arms.

"This might be *shocking*, but I didn't get much sleep last night," he said. "Mind if I take a little snooze back here?"

No one objected—but they all put in earphones in preparation.

The station wagon reached the edge of town, and they drove onto Interstate 40 and headed west toward Texas. Once the city disappeared behind them, there was nothing to look at for miles and miles but the wide-open fields of the Oklahoma plains. It was an easy environment to notice something peculiar or out of place.

About two hours into their drive, Sam tapped Topher's leg with a suspicious look in his eyes. Topher took his earphones out to see what was bothering him.

"What is it?" he asked. "Did Cash say something offensive in his sleep?"

"No, check out the car behind us," Sam said.

Topher looked into the side-view mirror outside his window. Driving considerably close to the station wagon was a black Toyota Prius with a California license plate.

"They've been following us since the hotel," Sam said. "I've switched lanes a couple times but they won't pass me. You think we should be worried?"

Topher had a second look at the car. The windows were so tinted he couldn't even see who was driving the vehicle. It gave him a bad feeling, too, but it seemed unlikely to be a threat.

"I don't think so," he said. "We're just both on edge right now because of that whole video thing. There are only so many routes out of Oklahoma and this is a popular time to be on the road—they're probably headed back home."

"You're right," Sam said. "Thanks for talking me down."

He wasn't paying complete attention to the road and drove right over a massive pothole. The whole car shook like it was hitting a speed bump. Cash's body slammed against the roof the car, waking him up from a deep sleep.

"*Ouch!*" he moaned.

"*Sorry!*" Sam said. "Accident!"

Cash rubbed his head. "Are we there yet?"

"We're about halfway to Amarillo," Topher said. "But we'll be crossing the state line into Texas soon—so get your boots ready!"

Cash looked between the other passengers' heads at the road in front of them. They passed a sign that made the actor smile from ear to ear and point like a child seeing Elmo.

"We're going to pass highway 283! I had no idea we were *this* close to Kansas!"

"What's so special about highway 283?" Joey asked.

"*High Tydes!*" Cash announced as if they would all reciprocate his excitement.

"What are you talking about?" Mo asked. "Is that a city?"

"No, High Tydes is only the best amusement-slash-water park in middle America!" he said. "I used to go there all the time when I was a kid. My favorite childhood memories were spent in that park. Have you guys seriously never heard of it?"

"Why were you going to an amusement park in Kansas when you were a kid?" Joey said. "Aren't you originally from Orange County in California? *Don't look at me like I'm a stalker, Cash.* You know we were fans first."

"I grew up in Colorado Springs and moved to the OC when I was eleven," Cash said. "I've just never told the whole story publicly, because it's like *none of your fucking business*, Star Magazine, you know what I mean?"

"So *High Tides* was your favorite place as a kid?" Mo asked.

"It's the best!" he raved. "It's got incredible roller coasters, amazing waterslides, and an awesome racetrack. I'm not sure Sam is tall enough to ride all the rides, but you guys would love it."

"I'm five two!"

"You know what," Cash said, "I don't want to be controversial, but I'm just going to say what's on my mind: *I think we should ditch Texas and go ride rides at High Tydes!* It's just a couple hours north on the 283 highway. What do you guys say?"

Just as they did when Cash tried to change their plans before, Sam, Joey, and Mo turned to Topher like he was their unofficial chaperone.

"Er...I'm not sure that works with the schedule," he said. "We're supposed to see the Bundy and Claire Jailhouse Museum when we get into Amarillo this afternoon. We don't have time to do both."

Cash whimpered like Topher was making a catastrophic mistake.

"So let's ditch the dusty old museum and go to the amusement park," the actor pitched. "I don't mean to brag, but so far my trip suggestions have been a total hit. None of us know if we'll even like the jailhouse, but I know for a *fact* we'll have a blast at High Tydes!"

Everyone in the car absolutely wanted to go to the amusement park instead of the museum, but none of them wanted to be the first one to say it out loud.

"Well...I suppose if it's *just* a couple hours north we could still get to the Teepee Inn at a reasonable hour tonight," Topher said. "And if we wake up a little early tomorrow, we could potentially see the museum before we leave for Albuquerque...."

"Exactly!" Cash said. "One small detour for shitloads of fun!"

The interchange to highway 283 was fast approaching. They needed to make a decision quickly if they were going to amend their itinerary.

"It's up to Sam," Topher said.

"What? Why me?"

"Because you're driving," he said.

"We're gonna miss the exit!" Cash said. "Come on, Sam! Outlaws or outlandish fun! What will it be?"

The pressure was on. At the very last second, Sam made a rapid, daring, and slightly *illegal* right turn onto highway 283—nearly giving a heart attack to the driver of the Prius behind them. The whole car cheered him on as the station wagon rerouted north toward Kanas.

"You aren't going to regret this!" Cash told them. "High Tydes has a pirate theme and all its attractions are based on ocean folklore. There's this roller coaster called Poseidon's Revenge that will blow your mind! Make sure we ride that on empty stomachs. And if you guys are in the mood to get wet, the Kraken is the longest waterslide east of the Rocky Mountains—I knew someone that started reading *War and Peace* at the top and was finished by the bottom. Not to mention, High Tydes has the best fried seafood in Kansas—and I'm not being sarcastic!"

The actor went on and on, praising his childhood paradise. He animatedly recalled all his most cherished memories from the park, described all his favorite attractions at great length and detail, and listed all the reasons why High Tydes was the best amusement park in the world. He was so descriptive the others felt like they had already been there and were very eager to authenticate the images and expectations in their minds.

After two hours of traveling up the 283, Cash was still raving about his favorite theme park, but he hadn't indicated where it was located or when they'd arrive. The others kept their eyes open for any advertisements along the highway but never saw anything pointing it out.

"Are you sure we haven't passed it?" Sam asked.

"Don't worry, you'll see a huge billboard with Captain Tydes, the park's mascot," Cash said. "Just take the exit after it."

After another hour, there still was no billboard in sight. The impatient passengers were beginning to worry the actor was directionally challenged.

"How come there's nothing on the Internet about High Tides?" Mo asked. "I'm trying to look up an address, but there's nothing here—not even a photo."

"It's probably under new ownership and they changed the name," Cash said. "I can't wait to see what they've done with it! Hopefully they're cool updates and nothing shitty."

"We're about twenty miles away from Dodge City," Sam said. "Are we getting close to the park?"

Cash scrunched up his face. "That can't be right. Dodge City is *way* east of High Tydes. It's just outside Garden City."

"My phone says Garden City is an hour *west* of here," Topher said. "Are you sure you know where you're going?"

"Oh shit," the actor said. "High Tydes isn't off the 283, it's off the 83! But no one panic, we're not far. Once we get into Dodge City, take the 400 west, and that'll spit us out on the 83 north. I'll guide you from there."

Topher, Sam, Joey, and Mo were starting to feel like Spanish explorers in search of the Fountain of Youth. The longer they followed Cash's guidance, the more restless they became. They eventually made it to the 83 but they still had no proof they were going in the right direction. Soon they started to doubt the amusement park even existed.

"I don't have a good feeling about this anymore," Topher said. "We won't even have much time in the park before it gets dark. Maybe we should turn around and head to Amarillo—"

"There it is!" Cash energetically announced. "There's the billboard! Take the next exit and make a left!"

After five hours and three hundred miles off course, the station wagon drove past the Captain Tydes billboard and the passengers finally had confirmation that High Tydes wasn't just a figment of Cash's childhood imagination. From that moment on, Cash seemed to know the area like the back of his hand. He guided the car through miles of fields, pointing out every boulder and tree on the side of the road as if they were old friends. Then like a mirage in a blistering desert, High Tydes appeared in the distance.

"That's it! That's it! That's it!" Cash said, and bounced up and down like a giddy child. "I can't believe I'm back after all these years! It's like I'm returning to my homeland!"

The theme park was surrounded by a tall brick fence and

evergreen trees, making it impossible to see anything but a few roller coasters peeking over the treetops. The station wagon turned into an enormous parking lot but it was completely empty.

"I'm having déjà vu to the world's biggest rubber-band ball," Joey said.

"Don't worry, the off-season is always less crowded," Cash said.

"*Summer* is the off-season for a water park?" Mo asked. "Something tells me it's closed and we've made a huge mistake."

"Guys, I don't mean to seem high on my own stash, but I'm a famous actor from television," Cash reminded them. "Even if it's closed—*they'll open it.*"

The car pulled up to the entrance on the south side of the park and the passengers discovered they should have trusted their instincts. The front gate was boarded up and wrapped in thick chains, and a large sign posted across it said HIGH TYDES CLOSED INDEFINITELY AS OF 9/26/07. Everyone in the car turned to Cash with the dirtiest looks physically possible.

"*You jackass!*" Joey yelled.

"*This park has been closed for a decade!*" Sam hollered.

"*We could have gotten to Amarillo five hours ago!*" Topher shouted.

"*Why didn't you tell me Tydes was spelled with a y!*" Mo roared. "*I could have saved us the trip if I knew what I was searching for!*"

Cash was so devastated he wasn't paying any attention to the anger directed his way. He stared at the bolted gates like he had just seen a small animal run over by a car. He shook his head in disbelief and looked like he was about to cry.

"I can't believe it," he said softly. "What happened? Why would they close it?"

"According to Google, High Tydes was shut down by Elkader Township officials after a series of sexual harassment complaints," Mo read from her phone. "Apparently the characters were inappropriately groping the guests when they had their pictures taken. Also, they were caught serving alcohol to minors."

"Explains why he liked it so much," Joey said.

"I can't believe we just drove three hundred miles for *nothing*!" Sam said.

"Let's just get back on the road before we waste any more time," Topher said. "As it is, we won't get to Amarillo until midnight!"

As Sam put the gearshift into drive, the station wagon began making noises like a chain-smoker after a long jog. The engine rumbled like a robot taking its final breath and then came to an involuntary stop. Sam turned the ignition a number of times but the car wouldn't restart.

"What's happening?" Joey asked. "Are we out of gas?"

"No, it says we still have a quarter of a tank left," Sam said.

Topher quickly checked the dashboard. *"Fuck!"* he yelled. "The gas gauge doesn't always work! I forgot to reset the trip meter when we last filled up!"

"I'd offer to walk to a gas station, but I haven't seen one for miles," Joey said.

"Wait—so we're *stranded* here?" Mo asked.

"Only temporarily," Topher said. "I'm going to call Triple A, they'll come fill us up, and we'll be back on the road in no time."

Topher took the Triple A card out of his wallet and called the number on the back. After a few minutes of cheesy and unhelpful mood music, an operator answered.

"Yes, hi—hello!" Topher said. "My friends and I are on a road trip and our car just ran out of gas. . . . Yes, my membership number is 199052712-1. . . . What's that? Hold on one second. . . . *Cash, what's the address to this place?*"

"It's 1005 High Tydes Boulevard," Cash said somberly. "It's on the corner of Broken Dreams and Ruined Childhood Memories."

"I think you mean on the corner of Karma and Serves You Right," Mo said. "It sucks when something you adored as a child is ruined, doesn't it?"

"It's 1005 High Tydes Boulevard," Topher repeated into his phone. "Yes, in Kansas. . . . I agree, the middle of nowhere. . . . It's a long story. . . . I'm sorry, please repeat that. . . . *What?*"

His eyes suddenly filled with dread, and the anxiety in the car automatically doubled.

"Is that seriously the best you can do? No, we're not in any immediate danger. . . . How many cars were involved? I suppose that makes sense. . . . Okay then. . . . Bye."

Topher clicked off the phone and looked at the others like he had just gotten the worst news of his life.

"What is it, dude?" Joey asked.

"They say there was a huge accident on the 160 and their roadside service cars are backed up. The earliest they can send someone out is tomorrow morning at seven."

Everyone in the car moaned like a herd of cows in heat. Topher took a deep breath to calm down—even *he* was unprepared for a situation like this.

"So we're stuck here until *tomorrow morning*?" Joey asked.

"We're going to have to sleep in the car like struggling musicians!" Mo declared.

"But we haven't eaten since breakfast! How are we supposed to get through the night?" Sam asked.

"Actually, I put together an earthquake kit before we left home," Topher said. "It's got enough granola bars and bottles of water to last us three days. We'll be fine for one night."

"Why do you have an earthquake kit?" Cash asked.

"Because we're going to *California*—duh!" Topher said as if it was as obvious as carrying sunscreen into the desert.

"Cash, can't you call someone to helicopter us out of here?" Mo asked. "I mean, it's *your fault* we're here in the first place. Surely there's something you can do."

"I would but I don't have my phone," he said.

Joey groaned. "Who goes on a road trip and doesn't bring his phone with him?"

"Gee, I don't know, maybe *everyone* before 1999," Cash snipped at him. "Besides, the only person I know with a helicopter is Harrison Ford, and we're not speaking anymore."

With nothing to do and nothing to say to make the situation any better, they all crossed their arms and sat in silence like frustrated kindergartners. Cash looked out the window at the locked gate of High Tydes again—and it gave him an idea. The actor crawled over the backseat, climbed across Mo's lap, and stepped out of the station wagon.

"Where are you going?" Sam asked.

"He's going *nowhere*," Mo answered for him. "There's literally *nowhere* to go!"

"Actually there is somewhere to go," Cash said. "You guys can stay in the car and pout all night if you'd like, but I'm going to go explore the park."

The others thought he was joking but he walked to the park's entrance and tried climbing the gate.

"He can't do that—it's trespassing," Mo said.

"It's only trespassing if someone claims ownership," Joey said. "I doubt there are any working security cameras on the property. Should we go with him?"

"*Joey!*"

"We're already stranded in the middle of nowhere. You really think things will get worse if we explore an abandoned theme park?" he asked.

"Are you *hearing* the words coming out of your mouth?" Mo asked. "You just described the beginning of a *Stephen King novel*! The park is probably home to cannibals! I wouldn't be surprised if some homicidal maniacs are just waiting for a group of naive teenagers to stumble into their territory so they can feast on our flesh!"

"Sounds cool," Joey said, and got out of the car.

"I agree," Sam said. "Sure beats spending the whole night in a station wagon."

"Me too," Topher said. "Come on, Kung Fu Panda."

Mo was furious with her friends for ignoring her warning, but knew her chances of getting murdered would be greatly increased if she stayed by herself. She begrudgingly left the station wagon and joined her friends and the actor at the theme park's entrance.

"I think I can unlock the gate from the other side," Cash said. "One of you guys give me a boost and I'll climb over."

Topher and Joey joined hands and launched the actor upward. Cash grabbed the top of the gate and pulled himself over it—years of Hollywood stunt work had finally paid off. He swung his legs over the edge and the rest of his body went with them. The others heard the actor land with a heavy *thud* on the other side.

"Are you all right, Cash?" Sam called over the gate. "Please tell us you didn't break anything."

The gate opened with a terrible *screech* and Cash welcomed them into the abandoned amusement park like a deranged Willy Wonka.

"You guys have got to see this," he said with large, frightened eyes. "This place makes Chernobyl look like Legoland."

Topher, Joey, Sam, and Mo followed him through the gate and immediately saw what he meant. What was once a colorful, adventurous, and family-friendly amusement park was now a decaying, smelly, pest-ridden apocalyptic wasteland. There was peeling paint, mold, and cobwebs everywhere they looked. Plant life had taken over the park and there were weeds taller than Topher and grass growing between the slabs of concrete.

The front of the park was called Portville. The row of gift shops and arcades designed to look like a charming seaside village now resembled a ghost town. In the center of the park was Captain's Cove, where a pirate ship the size of the Disneyland castle floated in a pool of green algae and dead pigeons. To the ship's east was Hurricane Hideaway, an area of thrill rides populated by dueling families of raccoons and possums. To the ship's west was Siren Sea, where the state's longest waterslides emptied into the world's largest petri dish. To the ship's north was Buccaneer Bay, an area of kiddie rides and cartoonish statues, which after so much exposure to the elements could have been renamed Satan's Nursery.

It was unsettling while there was still light, but the farther the sun descended, the creepier the empty park became.

"It's getting dark," Cash said. "Let's make a campfire!"

They dragged a wooden statue of Captain Tydes from the base of the giant pirate ship and lit it on fire. It was a macabre move, but after it had suffered years of neglect from everything but termites, using the mascot as firewood felt strangely like a mercy killing.

"Should we tell ghost stories?" Cash asked the group.

"*No!*" they all said at once.

"How about a game?" Cash said. "I know! Let's play never have I ever."

"How do you play?" Sam asked.

"Hold up all ten of your fingers," Cash explained. "We'll go around in a circle and say something we've *never* done before. If you've done the thing someone mentions, you put one of your fingers down. The last person to have fingers up wins."

Everybody shrugged and raised their fingers. *What else was there to do?*

"Let's start with an example," Cash decided. "Never have I ever done a line of cocaine off a CW star's ass. Now, if I was playing with my *Wiz Kids* costars, that's something I would say because I'm the only one who *hasn't* done a line of cocaine off a CW star's ass—does that make sense?"

It was hard to follow a remark like that. The others were already disturbed and they hadn't even started the game.

"Go ahead, Topher. Give it a shot."

"Oh geez," he said. "Never have I ever...um, *murdered someone?* Is that good?"

"Nice try—but the idea is to eliminate everyone else," Cash said. "Think of things everyone's done *but* you. Joey, you're next."

"Never have I ever been in trouble with the law," Joey said.

Cash was the only one to put a finger down.

"Good one," the actor said. "And to put those judgmental looks to rest, I was *lightly arrested* once in 2014 for protesting this pipeline thing, but I was just trying to impress this actress I was sleeping with. Sam, now it's your turn."

"Never have I ever starred in a television show," he said.

"Well, that was pointed," Cash said, and lowered another finger. "Mo, you're next. And let's try to be more original, like my CW reference."

"Never have I ever ruined a landmark," Mo said.

Cash sighed and dropped his hands. "Okay—new game, guys," he said. "Why don't we just cut to the chase? Let's go in a circle and tell a secret we've never shared before. Why don't *you* start, Joey? I've got a feeling you have a secret you want to share."

The actor gave him a playful wink. Joey glared at him like his days were numbered.

"Sure...," he said. "This one time when I was ten, I took a twenty-dollar bill out of the offering basket at church so I could go see the new *X-Men* movie. My parents wouldn't give me money to see it.

They said any form of evolution, even fictional mutants, was a mark of *the beast*. I felt so guilty about it, I tithed all the money from my next birthday to the church."

His confession made his friends laugh and feel sad at the same time.

"Solid secret," Cash said. "Let's go to Topher next."

"Oh gosh," he said. "The night we were all watching the season six finale of *Wiz Kids* at Joey's house, I was actually supposed to be watching Billy while my mom was at a Bunco party. I gave him some cold medicine so he would sleep and ran home to check on him every commercial break."

His friends were flabbergasted—amused, but flabbergasted.

"I remember that!" Mo laughed. "We all thought you had diarrhea and just didn't want to poop at Joey's house!"

"Nice one, Topher," Cash said. "Sam, it's your turn to spill a secret!"

"I've got it," he said. "This one time, I got so mad at my mom, I threw her pageant tiara out of the window of our apartment. It shattered into eight pieces. Thankfully, I was able to put most of it back together, but a good chunk of it was irreparable. So I replaced it using a wire hanger and Skittles dipped in glitter. To this day, my mom still hasn't noticed the difference. I almost included it in the portfolio I sent to the Rhode Island School of Design."

"*Sam, you didn't!*" Joey said.

"*Girl, that's hilarious!*" Mo said.

"*I can't even imagine what your mom would do if she found out!*" Topher said.

The gang burst into laughter as they imagined what Candy Rae Gibson's face would look like if she learned the truth.

"Mo, think you can top that one?" Cash asked.

"Well, I did go through this *trolling* phase once," she confessed. "There's this girl named WizKidLiz01 who also writes fanfiction. She was getting a lot of attention so I checked out her stuff—*more than half of it had been plagiarized from my fanfiction!* Needless to say, I was furious. I tried calling her out on it in the comments section, but no one ever acknowledged it—in fact, they only showered WizKidLiz01 with even more praise. I didn't know how to handle my emotions, so I created a fake user name, HydeBitch666, and spammed her comment section with the foulest things I could find on the Internet. Then one day, as I was posting a GIF of a decapitated giraffe on her profile, I learned WizKidLiz01 was a little girl with Down syndrome."

Everyone else gasped so deeply they made the fire flicker. They were so appalled it took a few moments before their shock settled into uncomfortable laughter.

"Mo, that's awful!" Sam said.

"And I thought *I* was going to hell!" Joey teased.

"I've made up for it," Mo said in her defense. "Every time Wiz-KidLiz01 posts something new I leave her at least ten positive comments from my real account, and I always send her an e-card on her birthday."

"Okay, I guess it's my turn next," Cash said.

"I doubt there's anything we don't already know about you," Topher said. "And *nothing* that would shock us at this point."

The actor was up for the challenge. "Let me think of something really good," he said, and went quiet until he thought of the perfect confession. "I bet none of you knew my real name isn't Cash Carter."

"No way!" Joey said.

"You're joking!" Mo said.

"It's true," he said. "After I was cast in *Wiz Kids*, I had to turn in some paperwork to the Screen Actors Guild to get my SAG card. Well, if your real name is already taken, you have to come up with something else. "Jackson" by Johnny Cash and June Carter happened to be playing in the lobby of the SAG headquarters, so I came up with Cash Carter."

"That's insane!" Sam said.

"So what's your real name?" Topher asked.

"Now, *that* you're not going to believe," Cash said. "It's Tom Hanks."

The others laughed harder than they had all night.

"I don't believe you!" Mo said.

"We're not falling for that one!" Joey said.

"I'll prove it," Cash said, and showed them his driver's license. "See, my legal name is Thomas Anthony Hanks."

The Downers Grove quartet were amazed. Three days ago they thought they knew everything there was to know about their favorite actor, but he had more surprises in him than a *Game of Thrones* episode.

"Why didn't you go by Anthony?" Sam asked.

"Because that's my dad's name," Cash said. "And he's not really in my life anymore—neither of my parents are."

"Where are your parents?" Joey asked.

Cash stared into the fire, deeply hesitant to answer. But since they were sharing such personal stories with him, he wanted to share something personal, too. There was something between him and the teenagers he hadn't felt with other people in a very long time—*trust*.

"Last I heard, my mom was still in prison and my dad was just getting out," he said. "They're not good people. They used to beat each other up and sometimes I'd get caught in the middle of it. Child Protective Services eventually removed me from their custody and sent me to live with my great-aunt Peggy in Orange County. That's why I loved this place so much as a kid—it was the only escape I ever got."

The others weren't expecting a story like that to come from him, but they were glad it did. For the first time since Cash came into their lives, they didn't see him as their favorite character on television or the pain-in-the-ass celebrity beneath a facade; Cash was just another soul sharing his secrets and scars around a makeshift campfire.

"I'm so sorry to hear that, man," Topher said.

"Don't be," he said. "It worked out for me in the end. If I hadn't been sent to my aunt Peggy's house, I would never have auditioned for *Wiz Kids*. She was a wannabe actress in her early days and pushed me into the business to live vicariously through me. *Wiz Kids* was only my fourth audition, so imagine her surprise when we got the call that I had booked the job!"

"I can't imagine how excited she must have been," Mo said.

Cash laughed at the thought. "I've still never seen a smile fill a face so much," he said. "Peggy was diagnosed with Alzheimer's a couple years ago. She doesn't remember a thing about Thomas Anthony Hanks or Cash Carter anymore."

The vibe among the group had definitely changed, but the actor was keen to get them back on a positive note.

"Okay, no more secrets!" he said. "I've got something that will lighten our spirits."

The actor removed a joint from his pocket and waved it through the air like it was a magic wand. The others exchanged a troubled glance and tensed up like he was holding a deadly weapon.

"I'm willing to bet some serious money none of you guys have ever smoked pot before," Cash said.

"Correct," Topher said. "And we're not going to start now."

"No way," Mo said, and shook her head like a toddler refusing to eat her vegetables. "That stuff kills brain cells."

"You shouldn't have that stuff here! It's illegal in Kansas," Sam said.

Cash raised his hands defensively to calm them.

"Easy, GOP youth," he said. "Do I look like I've got a black cape and a twirly mustache? I'm not going to force it on you. I just thought it might be something you'd want to try before heading to college."

"I wanna do it!" Joey said.

Of all the absurd and shocking things they had heard tonight, Joey's eagerness to smoke marijuana was the most shocking of all.

"Joseph Davis!" Mo said. "What if we get caught?"

Cash looked around the park to make sure she was in the same place the rest of them were.

"Who's going to catch us?" he asked. "You think the police are going to sniff it out and storm through the gates? Good! Maybe they'll give us a ride back into civilization."

"And it seems like we have more fun when we step outside our comfort zones," Joey said. "If I'm going to do it, I'd rather make the memory with you guys than with some strangers in college. Besides, I doubt there'll be many chances for new experiences where I'm going."

His reasoning must have resonated with the others, because after Joey took the first hit, he passed the joint around to his friends and they *all* gave it a try. The smoke burned their throats and lungs as they inhaled, and they coughed and wheezed as they exhaled. Topher passed out bottles of water and cough drops from his earthquake kit.

"How do you guys feel?" Cash asked.

"Not bad after I stopped coughing," Topher said.

"I guess I feel more relaxed," Sam said.

"My eyes feel heavy but other than that I'm fine," Mo said.

"Yeah, it's not as intense as I thought it would be," Joey said. "Should we hit it again?"

"Give it a couple minutes," Cash recommended. "This stuff is fresh off the Los Feliz streets, none of that medicinal pussy shit. It may take a moment to kick in or it might not even work at all your first time."

A half hour later, Topher was sitting as still as a statue, Joey was staring at the starry sky in wonder, Sam was trying desperately not to laugh at everything he saw, and Mo was rubbing herself like she was covered in bugs. The three-day supply of granola bars in the earth-quake kit had also been consumed in a matter of minutes.

"Looks like it's kicking in," Cash observed. "How are you guys feeling now?"

"*Clouds,*" Topher said slowly. "There are *clouds* in my head."

"Congratulations, you're *a traditional stoner,*" Cash said. "What about you, Sam?"

With the attention suddenly placed on him, Sam couldn't contain his laughter anymore. He rolled onto his back and rocked back and forth like a roly-poly that couldn't get up.

"Everything tickles!" he peeped as happy tears streamed down his face.

"Sam's in a good place—we call that *a comedian*," Cash said. "Joey? How you feeling, bro?"

Joey never looked down from the stars. "I feel like parts of my brain are working that I've never used before," he explained with prolonged blinks. "It's like, I sense this deep connection with the stars and stuff. It's like, they always had names, colors, and feelings before, but I'm only just noticing it. I can't tell if this is like, a *forever-and-always-from-this-day-forward* sort of thing, or an *only-right-now-today-in-this-moment-because-I'm-high-in-the-state-of-Kansas* thing, you know?"

"Joey's a *professor*," Cash declared. "How's the Mary Jane treating you, Mo?"

"I hate to say it, but I actually don't feel any different than before," she said. "I'm a little jealous it's not working on me the way it is on—HOLY SHIT, WHAT THE HELL WAS THAT?"

Mo jerked her head toward a small noise in the distance.

"Relax, Mo," Cash said softly, like he was talking to a toddler. "It was probably just a raccoon—"

"A RACCOON?" Mo shouted in terror. "HOW AM I SUPPOSED TO RELAX WHEN THERE ARE RACCOONS? HOW CAN ANYONE SLEEP AT NIGHT WHEN THOSE THINGS ARE CRAWLING AROUND THE WORLD? OH MY GOD, THEY HAVE DIGITS! WHY WOULD GOD MAKE AN ANIMAL YOU CAN HIGH-FIVE—WHY WOULD HE DO IT?"

"Mo, the pot's making you *paranoid*. Don't worry, it happens to a lot of people. Just remember, the raccoons are more afraid of you than you are of them, I promise."

"The raccoons are afraid of Mo!" Sam giggled. *"They read her fanfiction and now they're scared!"*

"Raaaaccoooooon," Topher slowly sounded out. "Huh, strange word."

"It makes you wonder why any of us are what we are, doesn't it?" Joey said as if he was speaking directly to the stars. "I mean, what separates us from raccoons? Like, *really* though? We're born, we fight, we eat, we mate, we raise our young, and we die just like them. So why aren't *we* the raccoons? We don't dig through the trash like they do, but we're still scavengers."

"I dig through the trash!" Sam squealed. *"Does that make me a raccoon? I'd be such a cute raccoon!"*

"CAN WE STOP SAYING THE WORD *RACCOON*?" Mo begged, and rubbed her body like one was crawling under her skin. "THEY'RE GOING TO THINK WE'RE CALLING THEM OVER HERE! IF THEY TEAM UP WITH THE POSSUMS, THEY'LL OUTNUMBER US!"

"Poooooossuuuuum," Topher said slowly. "That's a funny one, too."

"You know, before there were rodents, there were just stars," Joey said. "That's how people got all their information originally. The night sky was the very first Bible. But what's the difference between religion and mythology? What's the difference between men and monkeys? Or moths and butterflies? Or frogs and toads? Or muffins and cupcakes? Why are there are so many questions in this world?"

Their reactions intensified as the night went on. They were the most eccentric group of stoners Cash had ever seen and he couldn't take his eyes off them, like they were the subjects of a fascinating nature documentary.

"GUYS!" Mo shrieked. "CAPTAIN TYDES JUST MOVED! I SAW IT! I THINK HE'S COMING TO LIFE!"

"*No—he's just a little toasty!*" Sam laughed. "*Get it? Because he's on fire!*"

"OH GOD, WE KILLED CAPTAIN TYDES! WE'RE MUR-DERERS! WE'LL NEVER BE ABLE TO PLAY NEVER HAVE I EVER AGAIN BECAUSE WE'VE DONE IT ALL! WE'VE BRO-KEN ALL THE LAWS AND DONE ALL THE CRIMES! OH GOD, I JUST WANT MY NORMAL LIFE BACK!"

Cash had had his fill for one night. The actor got to his feet and stretched his whole body.

"Well, my damage here is done," he said. "I'm going to go sleep in the car."

"You aren't going to get high with us?" Topher asked.

"No way," Cash said. "That shit's clearly been laced with some-thing. You can't trust the stuff you buy off the street anymore—*there's a lesson you won't learn in college.*"

The actor yawned and headed for the gate. The others tried to join him, but none of them could remember how to stand.

"Don't stay up too much longer," Cash called behind him. "*The coyotes come out at midnight!*"

"COYOTES?" Mo screamed.

"*Good night!*"

Chapter Fourteen

RADIO HOSTS AND RACISTS

As Topher awoke on Wednesday morning, the first thing he noticed was a warm sensation on his face. The second thing he felt was a very solid and rough surface under his body. As he opened his eyes, Topher saw the sun blazing in a corner of the sky and found himself lying on the ground in the middle of Captain's Cove. He quickly sat up and discovered Joey, Sam, and Mo passed out on the ground nearby.

"What the hell?" he asked.

Topher looked around the abandoned theme park and saw a family of possums staring at him with judgment beaming from their beady little eyes. He recalled the bad decisions from the night before, he and his friends were suddenly splashed with water.

"Good morning, Guns N' Roses," Cash said as he poured water on their faces to wake them up. "Rise and shine!"

Joey, Sam, and Mo jolted to life and looked at their surroundings in disbelief. Their memory of the previous night was hazy like a bad dream.

"We slept *outside* last night?" Sam asked.

"How could you leave us out here, Cash?" Mo asked angrily. "A rodent probably had its way with me while I was asleep!"

"I'd say that's a little presumptuous given all the choices," Cash said. "Also, you were so rowdy last night I doubt an animal would approach you. How do you guys feel?"

"Surprisingly well for sleeping on cracked concrete all night," Topher said.

"What was in that stuff?" Joey asked.

Cash shrugged. "We'll never know," he said. "I caught a raccoon eating the rest of the joint this morning. All concerns aside, you guys are doing much better than he is."

The actor nodded to a dead raccoon nearby. The creature was stretched out on its back like a starfish and had bulging eyes and a slight smile on his muzzle—like he had seen God but didn't live to tell the tale.

"I can't believe we did *drugs* last night!" Sam said. "And in an abandoned theme park no less!"

"Then why are you smiling?" Mo asked.

"Because I still feel them!"

The newly christened delinquents couldn't believe the sharp turn their lives had taken. They started their trip as outstanding citizens with great reputations and zero record of any criminal activity. However, in just three days' time they had used false identification, trespassed, done illegal drugs, and passed out outside. *How did they fall from grace so quickly? What kind of people had they become?*

"I think the words you're looking for are *Thank you for another fun night, Cash* or *Thanks for pulling the sticks out of our asses, Cash,*" the actor teased.

"You call that *fun*?" Mo asked. "I was tripping balls all night waiting for those coyotes to show up! I thought I was going to have a heart attack!"

Cash chuckled and gazed at the group like a proud father.

"You'll laugh about it one day," he said. "Now we should get going. The Triple A guy showed up about fifteen minutes ago. There isn't a gas station for miles, so he has to tow the car to the nearest one. Friendly warning—*he smells like cheese.*"

The gang helped one another to their feet and said good-bye to High Tydes. They sluggishly emerged from the gates looking and feeling like the cannibals Mo had warned them about the day before.

A very heavy and hairy Triple A serviceman hooked the station wagon up to his tow truck and hauled their vehicle southward to the nearest gas station. Topher, Joey, Sam, and Mo shared the backseat of the truck while Cash braved their driver's fumes in the front. Once High Tydes was a good distance behind them, the seriousness and guilt of their recent choices faded away, too, and the Downers Grove quartet couldn't look at one another without laughing.

"How much did our detour derail our trip?" Joey asked. "Are we *totally* screwed or *lightly* screwed?"

"Actually, it doesn't ruin anything," Topher said. "We left our first day in California open just in case we ran into any problems on the road. I got insurance on all the tickets and hotel rooms, so we can just push everything back a day."

Of them all, Cash was most relieved to hear it. "Sorry I'm what caused the push," he said. "From now on, I'm not recommending anything else. I got my two stops out of the way, so let's just stick to the plan you guys created."

It was the first time the actor had shown any remorse—*ever*—but it was hard blaming him. Sure, they didn't get to ride any of the attractions they had hoped, but they hadn't left the park shy of a thrill.

"I mean, it wasn't *all* terrible," Mo confessed—fighting off a smile.

"We're definitely going to get stories out of this trip," Sam said.

"Yeah, just not the ones we were planning," Topher said.

The tow truck ventured through Kansas, but there wasn't a building in sight, let alone a gas station. The serviceman listened to a crude and conservative radio host the entire way, which was easy for the others to tune out until he started a particular segment.

"That's enough about how Democrats are destroying our democracy," the host said. *"Let's move on to a topic people tragically care about more in our society—*Hollywood gossip! *I'm not sure any of my listeners watch the show* Wiz Kids, *I think it's the dumbest thing to hit television since* Cop Rock, *but apparently it's been a huge hit for nine seasons now."*

Topher, Joey, Sam, and Mo sat straight up in their seats and leaned closer to the radio—worried where this was going. Cash just turned his head to the radio like he was casually listening to a weather report. The serviceman noticed their interest and turned up the volume.

"Well, there's this video circulating on the Internet of the lead actor, twenty-two-year-old Cash Carter, passing out at a concert in St. Louis on Sunday night. In case you've missed the video, it's up on our website, but it's been getting so much attention I don't know how you've managed

to not see it somewhere. A representative of the actor released a statement yesterday claiming he was experiencing dehydration *and is feeling much better. Which, I'm sorry, is* complete *bull! Watch the video and you'll see the guy is clearly wasted or on drugs!"*

The four in the backseat were so uncomfortable they held their breath as if the radio speakers were spewing toxic chemicals.

"Can we change the station?" Topher asked.

"Not yet," Cash said. "I want to hear what he says."

"With the amount of money Cash Carter makes and the kind of fame he has, you'd think he would try really hard *not to do anything to jeopardize his public image. You'd think he would try* really hard *to never make a fool of himself and embarrass all the young people looking up to him. Unfortunately, we all know none of these Hollywood types think that way. I mean, why take responsibility when you have a dozen publicists lying for you? Why change your lifestyle when everything is handed to you? Why take anything into consideration when it's more fun to be a careless and spoiled little brat? Cash Carter is another example of someone with too much wealth, too much attention, and not enough intelligence to appreciate it. He should be ashamed of himself, but we should be ashamed of ourselves for sensationalizing this kind of behavior. We'll be right back with more after this—stay tuned."*

The host's defamatory rant was replaced with a commercial for the local county fair. The others were ready to defend Cash's honor, but the actor never gave them any indication he wanted them to.

"Those are some strong opinions about a guy he's never met," Cash said.

"Gotta say I agree with him, though," the serviceman said.

"Privileged little prick. All those Hollywood actors are just alike. I wouldn't be surprised if he'll be part of that twenty-seven club."

Obviously, the serviceman had no idea the *privileged little prick* was sitting right next to him.

"I think you're giving him too much credit," Cash said. "He'll be long gone by then."

The actor dug through his backpack and took three white pills from a prescription bottle inside. He looked out the window and was silent for the rest of the drive.

After an hour of nothing but open fields outside their windows, the tow truck finally pulled into a small gas station. Cash insisted on paying for the towing expenses and a new tank of gas since it was his fault they were in the predicament. The station's pumps were outdated so he had to go inside to use his credit card. Joey had had to use the restroom for the past twenty miles, so he followed Cash to get the key to the station's bathroom. Along the way, he came to a halt when something disturbing caught his eye.

"What is it?" Cash asked.

Joey nodded to a large Confederate flag displayed in the gas station's window. All his father's advice about avoiding trouble rushed to the forefront of his mind.

"I shouldn't go in there," he said. "I'll just wait until our next stop."

"Don't be ridiculous," Cash said. "The owner's probably just a big *Dukes of Hazzard* fan. You've got nothing to worry about—I'm with you."

"Actually, that means I should have *more* to worry about."

The actor grabbed the timid teenager by the arm and forced him inside against his will. They approached an old man who was sitting behind the checkout counter reading a newspaper. He wore a cowboy hat and sported a thick mustache that was a few weeks overdue for a trim.

"Good morning, sir," Cash said. "I'd like to pay for gas on pump number four and my friend needs the key to the bathroom."

The old man stood to greet him but his entire demeanor changed as soon as he laid eyes on Joey. He stared at him with such disdain Joey felt like an invisible hand was pushing him backward.

"I'll sell you gas, but your friend is out of luck," he said. "We don't serve his kind around here."

"Why? Because he's black or because he's gay?"

"Cash!" Joey said like he was out of his mind. *"What the hell?"*

"Relax, I'm just joking." Cash laughed. "And he was, too. *Weren't you, sir?* Because only one of those old bigots who give the human race a bad name would say something like that. Right?"

The old man's hateful scowl extended to both of them and he pointed to the door.

"Get your asses out of here!" he commanded.

"Cash, we need to go back to the car," Joey said.

"WAIT!" Cash ordered.

As if he were being controlled by Cash through telekinesis, Joey stayed exactly where he was. He had never seen Cash look so angry before. The actor glared at the old man with as much hatred as they were being shown. Joey didn't know which of them to be more afraid of.

"I don't know what year you think it is, but it's 2017 for the rest of us," Cash said. "What you're doing is illegal. Unless you change your attitude, I'm calling the police and telling them what's going on."

"And you can tell them Johnny at the gas station says hello," the old man said. "The police and I are like-minded folk, you see. So unless you want to be thrown in jail for a week, I would shut my goddamn mouth. I don't know who the hell you think you are, *boy*, but no one gets to come into our town and tell us how to live."

Cash glanced at the man's newspaper on the counter. As fate would have it, he saw a picture of himself next to a headline that read *Loose Cannon Cash Carter: Actor Loses Consciousness at Concert.*

"Actually, you do know who I am," the actor said, and pointed to the article. "I'm that loose cannon you were just reading about. They could have printed a better picture, but at least it's a recent one."

The old man looked back and forth between Cash and the newspaper, like it was some kind of magic trick.

"Since we're better acquainted now, allow me to put *my* dick on the table, *Johnny*," the actor said. "You might be friends with the local police, but I'm friends with the police of the world—they're called *fangirls*, and I've got about thirty million of them watching my every move right now. So you're going to apologize to my friend and then you're going to give him the key to the bathroom. Because if you don't, I'm going to tell the fangirls about the treatment we've received today and *unleash them upon your establishment like a plague of locusts! They'll harass you, humiliate you, and chase your wrinkled, old, racist ass into hiding for the rest of your miserable existence!* Do I make myself clear?"

The old man gulped. He retrieved the bathroom key from underneath the counter and tossed it to Joey.

"I'm sorry," he said while looking at the ground.

Cash and Joey headed for the door, but Cash paused in the doorway to look back at the old man.

"By the way, the gas is on the house," he said with conviction. "Also, I'm taking this bag of Funyuns."

The actor slammed the door behind them and immediately got out his cigarettes once they were outside.

"Cash, what were you thinking?" Joey asked. "That was so stupid of you! Don't you watch the news? Do you have any idea what could have happened to us? *What could have happened to me?*"

The actor was much more rattled than Joey predicted. He must have known the danger he had put them in because his hands were trembling as he smoked.

"I know, I know," he said. "I'm so sorry—I don't know what got into me back there. We walked in and as soon as he said what he did something snapped inside me. It was like I lost control of myself—I just couldn't let him get away with saying that shit to you. I never get a chance to stand up for myself, but I needed to stand up for *someone*, you know?"

It made more sense the longer Joey thought about it; he just wished Cash wouldn't risk *his* safety to work out his issues.

"I get needing to be a hero—just don't be a dumb ass about it," Joey said. "It could have gotten really nasty back there. With that said, it was pretty cool seeing the look on that guy's face when you told him off."

"Yeah," Cash agreed. "It felt good saying it, too. Let's keep this between us, though. It might give Mo an aneurysm."

Chapter Fifteen

THE DRIVER'S SEAT

By ten o'clock on Wednesday morning, the station wagon was refueled and reunited with highway 83. The car cruised southbound with its sights set on Amarillo, Texas—but whether or not they'd make it this time was anyone's guess. With Topher back behind the wheel, the roadies were making good time and were expected to arrive at two o'clock that afternoon. Cash kept the group entertained with stories from behind the scenes at awards shows—not that they asked.

"So while the Golden Globe for Best Original Song was being announced, Tobey and I went to use the restroom," Cash said. "And that's when we saw him—*Leonardo DiCaprio at a urinal!* All the dudes in the men's room couldn't believe their eyes. It was like we had caught a demigod committing a mortal act."

"Did you say anything to him?" Sam asked.

"No, Tobey and I were both *paralyzed* in his presence," Cash said. "Then, when Leo was finished, everyone sort of lined the hall and bowed as he left—like he was royalty. I'll never forget it as long as I live. I also remember he used the only eco-friendly toilet in the restroom, but I could be making that detail up."

"Did he recognize you?" Joey asked.

"Of course not!" Cash said. "When you're a television star walking among movie stars, it's like being a freshman at a senior prom; you can't expect anyone to recognize you. This one time, after the Katzenberg Night Before the Oscars party in 2013, I was standing outside and *Helen Mirren* mistook me for a valet."

"What did you do?" Mo asked.

"I took the ticket and brought her the fucking car—*that's* what I did!" Cash said. "I mean, anyone should be so lucky. She tipped me twenty bucks. I've got it framed in my house next to my Teen Choice Award."

As the car crossed the Texas state line, Cash became more and more animated about the stories he told. He spoke with much larger gestures, kept getting louder and louder, and rocked back and forth as he recalled the events. His behavior made the others nervous—it reminded everyone of how he'd acted the night of Rosemary's Abortion.

"Let me give you some tips in case you ever find yourself on a red carpet," the actor said. "Always start with a small smile, because your expression grows the longer you hold it, and you don't want to look like Pennywise the clown in the premiere photos of *Frozen*. Nothing is creepier than an adult who's super excited to be at a children's movie. Flex the muscles under your tongue and stretch your neck to avoid a double chin, make sure to exhale so you're photographed at your slimmest, and for God's sake, find something natural to do with your hands."

"Thanks for the advice." Topher laughed. "I can't imagine we'll be needing it anytime soon—"

"I'm not finished," Cash said. "Don't try to look sexy—because it doesn't work when you try. Instead, just think of the punch line of your favorite dirty joke—that'll translate better. And if you ever find yourself in front of photographers you weren't expecting, like paparazzi, go into the bathroom and blot your face with one of those paper toilet seat covers. It's gross, but it'll take the shine off, and if you're shiny under bright flashes, you'll look drunk. And if you *are* drunk, never look directly at the camera—you'll look more candid and less sloppy that way."

"You've really got it down to a science," Joey said.

"Can we talk about something else?" Mo asked.

"Yeah—I think we get it," Sam said.

Despite their requests, Cash wouldn't change the topic. He was like an old man recalling the era he grew up in.

"Also, always be cautious around reporters on red carpets. You have to triple-think every answer you give like you're running for president. They'll take whatever you say and run with it as far as they possibly can. If you casually mention how hot it is outside, they'll post a story with the headline *Actor Breaks Silence About Global Warming Views.* If you say you like Batman, they'll write *Shocking Revelation: What Cash Carter Has to Say About the DC Universe.* If you imply you like potato chips, they'll write *Wiz Kid Speaks Out About Americans' Addiction to Processed Foods.* And the worst part is reporters never mention the questions they asked—they act like you just randomly decided to declare something to the world—*STOP THE CAR!*"

Topher slammed on the brakes and the station wagon came to a screeching halt.

"*What the hell was that about?*" Topher asked.

Cash was pressing his hands and face against the window in the back as if he had just seen a long-lost family member on the side of the road. The other passengers looked, too, but all they saw was a junkyard with a bunch of banged-up old cars.

"Are you guys seeing what I'm seeing?" the actor asked.

"A staph infection waiting to happen?" Mo asked.

"Look at that car in the corner!" Cash pointed out. "It looks just like *a Porsche 550 Spyder!*"

He was referring to a small convertible sports car. The vehicle was so banged up it looked like it had been recovered from the bottom of the ocean. It was missing its headlights, none of its tires matched, and it had either a coat of faded brown paint or a layer of rust.

"How can you even tell it's a Porsche?" Joey asked.

"Any actor would spot that—it's a Hollywood icon," he explained, but they didn't understand. "A 550 Spyder is the kind of car James Dean famously drove around town. He called it his *Little Bastard*! I've got to get out and see if I'm right."

Before the others had a chance to object, the actor swiftly hopped over the backseat, crawled over Joey, and stepped out of the car.

"Didn't he *just* say he wasn't going to make us stop again?" Topher said.

"I think we all knew that wasn't going to last long," Sam said.

Cash crossed the highway and walked along the junkyard's fence. A massive bullmastiff and a small pug came out of nowhere and barked ferociously at him. It got the owner's attention and he came to the front to see what all the noise was about.

"*Doc! Marty! Heel!*" the owner said, and approached Cash. "Can I help you?"

"Hi! My friends and I were driving down the highway and I couldn't help but notice your Porsche. That doesn't happen to be a 550 Spyder, does it?"

"It *was* a 550 Spyder." The owner laughed. "Just like I *was* a quarterback once."

Once his hunch had been validated, Cash gazed at the car like King Arthur observing the Holy Grail.

"Does the engine still run?" he asked.

"Everything but reverse and uphill," the owner said. "Are you interested in buying this piece of junk? Because I've got much better options in the—"

"I'll give you a thousand bucks if you let me take it for a test-drive."

The next thing the others knew, the junkyard owner led Cash through the fence and up close to the car of his dreams. The actor petted the hood of the Porsche like it was an animal and whispered sweet nothings into its side-view mirror.

"He's not actually going to drive that thing, is he?" Topher asked.

"Is he even okay to drive?" Sam pointed out.

Cash slid into the driver's seat and gripped the steering wheel like a ship captain clutching the helm on his maiden voyage. A cloud of dust erupted from the back of the Porsche as its engine roared to life for the first time in a very long while. It was a shaky start and the engine didn't seem like it would last long, but Cash willed it to work.

He drove the Porsche out of the junkyard and pulled up alongside the station wagon.

"I'm going to take this thing out for a quick spin," he announced. "You guys stay here—I'm using you as collateral."

"Cash, we're all really anxious to get to Amarillo and take a shower," Topher said.

"I'll only be a couple minutes. Sorry, but I have to do this or I'll regret it forever. It's on my bucket list."

The actor hit the accelerator and zoomed down highway 83, leaving a trail of smog behind him like a snail. The others could hear him cheering all the way down the road until he disappeared in the distance. Twenty minutes later, Cash returned with an enormous smile stretched across his rosy, wind-beaten cheeks.

"You guys gotta try this!" he said. "There's only room for one passenger but you can take turns. Somebody hop in!"

"We're not getting in that thing," Joey said.

"It looks like it's one speed bump away from imploding," Sam said.

"Don't judge a book by its cover," Cash said. "Cars were built to last in the old days. You gotta hear the engine when it gets going—it purrs like a kitten."

Mo raised an eyebrow. "A kitten with *bronchitis*, maybe."

"Come hear it for yourself, Mo!" Cash egged her on. "I promise when the wind hits your hair you'll feel just like a Bond girl!"

Mo had the strongest reservations out of all her friends—but Cash knew the exact button to push. Her hesitation crumbled at the thought of feeling like a Hollywood starlet.

"Weeeeeeeell, I suppose just a mile or two wouldn't hurt," she said, to her friends' amazement. "Don't look at me like that—you all smoked pot last night!"

Mo sat in the passenger seat beside Cash and they rocketed down the highway. The Porsche rattled more and more as it gained speed. The open air hit Mo's face and her dark hair flickered behind her ears like a flag in a tropical storm. The ride felt like a roller coaster compared to the station wagon they'd grown accustomed to.

"Isn't this great?" Cash called out—but it was hard to hear each other with all the wind in their faces.

"It's fantastic!" Mo said. "I feel like Marilyn Monroe!"

"What?" Cash asked. "You want to see how fast this thing can go?"

"No!" Mo said. "I said I feel like Marilyn Monroe!"

"Okay, let's see how fast this baby can go!" he said.

Cash punched the gas even harder and the Porsche flew down the highway at a reckless pace. They were moving so fast Mo could barely breathe let alone tell him to slow down.

"Cash, that's fast enough!" she said.

The actor tapped the brake but nothing happened. He turned to his concerned passenger with unmistakable terror in his eyes.

"The brakes aren't working!" he said.

"WHAT?" she said. *"What about the emergency brake?"*

"There is no emergency brake!" Cash said. *"The accelerator is stuck, too! I can't get the car to slow down!"*

Mo couldn't believe she had been so easily lured into a death trap. She had a panic attack and images of everything she held dear—her cat, her father, her friends, the positive comments on her fanfiction—flashed before her eyes.

"Do something!" she yelled. *"I can't die in a car crash with you! I don't want my death to get second billing!"*

"Don't worry—I promise you'll live to see the halls of Stanford!"

"Fuck Stanford!" she cried, and the truth spilled out of her like lava from a volcano. *"I'm only going there because my dad is making me! I don't want to study economics, I want to study creative writing! But none of that matters now because I'm about to be roadkill!"*

Cash abruptly hit the brakes and the Porsche came to a stop. Mo's crying turned into laughter once she realized they were safe. She hugged the actor in celebration.

"The brakes worked!" she said. *"It's a miracle!"*

"Of course the brakes worked, I was just fucking with you," Cash said.

"YOU WHAT?" Mo yelled, and punched him in the shoulder as hard as she could. *"You son of a bitch! I thought we were about to die! What's wrong with you? How could you do that to someone?"*

"Doesn't seem like it would have mattered that much if I wasn't," Cash said. "Clearly I would have just saved you from a life you don't want. Why the hell are you going to Stanford if it's not where you want to go?"

"I would never have said that if I didn't think I was about to die!" she said. "Please don't tell the others about this—I don't want them to know."

"Why not?" Cash asked. "They'd only encourage you to follow your passion."

"I know—and that would make it worse!" Mo said. "It's hard enough knowing I'll be stuck going to a school I don't want to go to and forced to study a subject I have no interest in. Having my friends encouraging me and making me feel like I have a say in the matter would only make it more painful."

Cash sighed and shook his head. "What is wrong with you kids?" he said. "Of course you have a say in the matter! The only reason you're letting your parents control you is because you're too scared to take responsibility for yourself."

"Says the rich and famous actor," Mo said. "No offense, but I don't think you're exactly the voice of reason on this matter. I don't have a bottomless bank account like you—my dad is in control of my college fund. He thinks writing isn't a real profession and won't pay for me to pursue it. I don't want to be paying off student loans my whole life so I've got no choice!"

"Oh, boo fucking hoo," Cash said. "Is that really worse than being miserable for the rest of your life?"

Mo looked away and crossed her arms. There wasn't a single thing he could say that she hadn't thought of a million times.

"Look, you're right, I don't know what it's like to be in your shoes," he said. "I've had people telling me what to do my whole life, too, so I sympathize with you. But you aren't under *a studio contract*! You don't have *legal obligations* to a network! No one is going to sue you for everything you have if you don't follow their orders! Your world is as open and free as this road—you just don't see it!"

It was a convenient perspective given their location, but Mo didn't know what he expected from her.

"So what should I do?"

"You need to claim the driver's seat," Cash said. "Never take a backseat to your own life! You gotta take that bitch by the steering wheel with all your might—even if the road is bumpy, even if there's blood under your fingernails, even if you lose passengers along the way. Only *you* can steer your life in the direction that's best for you."

"That's a nice metaphor—but real life isn't always that simple."

"You want something real?" Cash asked. "Fine, I'll give you something real. Your lesson starts right now—come on, *Chinese fire drill*!"

"I'm Japanese!"

"That means we're switching places!"

Cash ran around the car, slid into the passenger seat, and pushed Mo in front of the steering wheel.

"Drive us back to the junkyard," he instructed. "And if this car doesn't prove it's better to live life in the driver's seat, then nothing will."

"I don't have my driver's license," she said.

"*I don't have my driver's license,*" Cash mocked her. "*I don't have a college fund! I don't have a daddy who understands me! I don't want to be inconvenienced in exchange for happiness!* Do you know how many people would slap you in the face right now? *Shut up and drive!*"

Once again, Cash knew the exact button to push. Mo looked at the open highway in an entirely new light. She wrapped her fingers around the steering wheel and stepped on the gas, and the sports car roared down the road. It was fun to be a passenger in the Porsche, but it was a completely different experience behind the wheel. Cash controlled the stick shift, but knowing she was in complete control of the speed and the direction gave Mo a sensation she had never felt before: she was in charge—*and it was addictive*!

"This is awesome!" Mo said.

"I told you!" Cash said. "This is how your life should feel!"

"Fuck you, Stanford!" Mo yelled toward the open sky.

"Yeah, that's it!" Cash said.

They raced down the road until it became another highway altogether. Mo turned back around and only slowed when she saw her friends and the junkyard in the distance.

"Wow!" she said. "This is exhilarating! No wonder everyone in Hollywood loves James Dean so much—I can only imagine the freedom a car like this gave him."

Cash knew very well that the icon was actually killed in 1955 after crashing his Porsche 550 Spyder, but he didn't have the heart to tell her.

"Dream as if you'll live forever. Live as if you'll die today. That was his motto."

Chapter Sixteen
THE JAILHOUSE

"Over here, you'll find the last photo Bundy and Claire Carmichael ever took," the tour guide said. "The photograph was taken in 1933 at a secret location organized by the *Chicago Daily Tribune*. The pair had caused a media sensation during their time on the run and agreed to an interview if the *Tribune* paid them the costly fee of one hundred dollars. The newspaper was later criticized for aiding wanted criminals and their business suffered greatly until the attack on Pearl Harbor in 1941."

The Bundy and Claire Jailhouse Museum in Old Town, Amarillo, Texas, was barely big enough for Cash and the Downers Grove gang to stand comfortably inside. However, at five o'clock on Wednesday afternoon, the small brick building was crammed with them, three large families, and their tour guide.

"Here, we have a wanted poster from 1929, where the reward for capturing the dangerous duo was set at a whopping three hundred dollars," the tour guide said. "Beside it are some examples of how Bundy and Claire have impacted our pop culture. This barrette is one of many pieces they inspired for Marc Jacobs's 2008 fall collection, Bad Marc. Here's a photo from the set of the 1965 film *Jailbirds*, where Jack Nicholson and Ann-Margret famously portrayed the Carmichaels. Next to it is a picture of the 2001 television remake starring Frankie Muniz and Hilary Duff. As you may have noticed, the couple were not as attractive in real life as they're often depicted."

"That's putting it nicely," Joey whispered to Topher.

"Right?" he whispered back. "I thought they were bulldogs in people clothes."

The tour guide squeezed through the center of the group to show the items on the other wall.

"Moving along," she said. "This map shows all the locations of Bundy and Claire Carmichael's crimes throughout the late 1920s and early 1930s. As you can see, it reads like a timeline. They were teenage lovebirds from southern Illinois who eloped in 1926 to avoid the arranged marriages planned by their families. Then in 1927, they met notorious gangster Baby Face Bucky and joined his band of Chicago mobsters. He introduced them to a world of crime, and they became the infamous criminals we know today."

"Sounds familiar," Mo whispered, and eyed Cash.

"Eventually the Carmichaels had a falling out with Baby Face Bucky—and by *falling out* I mean they shot him in the face. In 1929, they fled to Missouri and started their own gang. From 1929 to 1935, the couple committed twenty-seven robberies and thirty-six homicides across the southwestern United States. Law enforcement officials of eight different states joined forces to track down the pair. After a grueling six-month manhunt, they captured the Carmichaels in the desert just a few miles away and brought them back to *this jailhouse*. But the rambunctious couple's story is not over yet. *Right this way.*"

The tour guide stepped into a jail cell the size of a broom closet.

"This is where Bundy and Claire Carmichael awaited trial for two whole months. While incarcerated, they befriended the jailer, Officer Clancy Jones. The officer was fascinated with their criminal history and the manipulative couple took full advantage of him. They filled his head with grandiose stories from their time as outlaws. Slowly but surely, Bundy and Claire convinced Officer Jones to help them escape and join them on the run. On November 3, 1935, the jailer brought them weapons, but as soon as he opened the cell door, they shot poor Clancy dead. Other police officers nearby heard the gunshot and rushed to the jailhouse—and so began the most infamous shootout in American history. The Carmichaels were outnumbered, outarmed, and out of time. With no possible way for them both to get out alive, Bundy made the famous decision to sacrifice himself for his wife. He shielded Claire from the police's gunfire long enough for her to escape into the Texas desert. They spent weeks looking for Claire Carmichael, but the woman was never seen or heard from again."

All the women in the room sighed and held a hand over their heart. The tour guide pointed to one of a thousand bullet holes in the brick walls.

"As you look around the jailhouse, you can still see the damage that resulted," the guide said. "That concludes this afternoon's tour of the Bundy and Claire Jailhouse Museum. Are there any questions?"

Sam raised his hand.

"Yes?" the tour guide asked.

"I've read numerous reports that Bundy and Claire actually *seduced* Officer Clancy Jones and were caught in a devil's threesome when the shootout began," he said. "Can you confirm or deny?"

The tour guide gulped and side-eyed the families in the jailhouse.

"That I can't," she said. "The Bundy and Claire Jailhouse Museum only shares history that's appropriate for Texan families. Are there any *other* questions?"

A little girl raised her hand. "I've got one!"

"What's that, pumpkin?"

The girl looked up at Cash. "Are you the guy from TV that everyone's talking about?"

Everyone in the jailhouse turned to Cash like he was the most exciting exhibit on display. Topher, Joey, Sam, and Mo cringed.

"Nope!" Topher said. "Definitely not him."

"He gets that all the time, though," Sam said.

"That guy is *way* cuter than he is," Mo added.

"Hey, I've got a question!" Joey announced. "Can we take pictures in the cell?"

It was the perfect diversion and all the families immediately whipped out their cameras. While they eagerly awaited the tour guide's answer, Topher, Joey, Sam, Mo, and Cash made their own Claire Carmichael–esque escape and quickly dashed into the gift shop next door.

The museum shop was five times the size of the jailhouse itself. They hid the actor behind a towering shelf of tacky merchandise while the other visitors took pictures and eventually headed out.

"Okay, they're all gone," Topher said from the lookout. "I thought the family in the matching T-shirts would never leave."

"I'm starving, can we get some food?" Joey asked.

"Oooo! Let's do Tex-Mex!" Sam said.

"We aren't going anywhere until I buy these Bundy and Claire salt and pepper shakers!" Mo said and pulled a pair off the shelf. "These are too good to pass up."

The others waited in the front of the shop while Mo paid at the checkout counter. Topher and Joey browsed a magazine section and were disheartened to see Cash on the cover of all the tabloids. Apparently his fainting episode in St. Louis was the biggest story of the week. The boys blocked the magazines so Cash didn't see them—but they couldn't shield him from *everything* in the shop.

A television in the corner of the store was showing an episode of *The Panel*, a daily talk show cohosted by four well-known women: a comedian, a trophy wife, a corporate tycoon, and a retired athlete. No one was paying it the slightest attention until Cash became the topic of their discussion.

"Since everyone else in the world is talking about him, we might as well, too," the comedian said. *"By now I'm sure all our viewers have seen the video of actor Cash Carter passing out at a St. Louis concert or the hilarious video remix that's recently gone viral. The actor's representation released a statement on Monday saying he was simply* dehydrated *and is now feeling much better—but not everyone is convinced. Ladies, what do you think? Is this incident the actor's one-night stand with scandal, or is it the overture to something far worse?"*

"This breaks my heart because my kids and I love Wiz Kids *so much,"*

the trophy wife said, and placed a hand over the golden cross of her necklace. *"I know a lot of people have been quick to judge the actor, but I'm not going to make a big deal out of this. We all make mistakes. He probably had too much to drink and is learning a lesson the hard way."*

"Unfortunately, this is not the actor's first episode of questionable behavior," the corporate tycoon said. *"Since this story broke on Monday, numerous reports have come out of the actor getting drunk at bars, partying at clubs, breaking and entering, receiving various noise complaints at his home, and driving around Hollywood with strippers. All of these incidents have happened within the last three months, by the way. I think it's very clear Cash Carter isn't making mistakes but is having some kind of mental breakdown."*

"I agree," the retired athlete said. *"Personally, I've been dehydrated many times over my career. The way Mr. Carter was dancing just before losing consciousness is not how someone would be acting if they just needed water. He's been juiced up with the wrong flavor of sauce, as we used to say on the field. I'll be interested to see if this affects viewership for his show when it returns in the fall. I imagine he's disappointed a lot of fans."*

"You see, I disagree with all of you," the comedian said, and swiveled her head. *"I did a lot of drugs back in my day and I know how thirsty it can make you. I believe the statement his reps released—I just think they left off a couple details."*

The Panel's studio audience roared with laughter. A stagehand ran onto the set, handed the comedian a cue card, and then hurried off camera.

"Well, it seems things are only about to get worse for the Wiz Kids

star," she said as she looked over the cue card. *"According to news that broke during our last commercial break, sources close to the show say the actor didn't show up for work today. Stunt training for season ten of* Wiz Kids *began this morning, but Cash Carter was nowhere to be found."*

The studio audience booed and hissed. The trophy wife fanned invisible tears forming in her eyes.

"I just don't understand why he's doing all this," she said. *"As a parent, it leads to some very uncomfortable conversations when your children see their heroes acting so poorly. The world has been watching Cash Carter since he was just twelve years old—this is not the Dr. Bumfuzzle we all know and love."*

"But isn't that the real problem?*"* the corporate tycoon asked. *"I've never seen the show but even I recognize him as that character. And when you're that recognizable from something, it can damage an actor's longevity. I'm going to be frank—the kid's probably never going to work again after* Wiz Kids *is over. I bet he's starting to realize that and* that's *what's at the core of this bad behavior. It's got to be a tough pill to swallow knowing you'll spend the rest of your career at conventions, especially when his lesser-known costars are booking jobs like* Moth-Man.*"*

The audience agreed with her analysis and applauded.

"Well, we want to hear what our viewers think," the retired athlete said directly into the camera. *"Is Cash Carter the next Bieber, Britney, or Bynes? Is this a breakdown, a meltdown, or just a letdown? How many strikes does he have left before he should be taken out of the game? Go to thepanel.com to share your thoughts and enter to win a prize vacation to Puerto Rico, courtesy of American Airlines. We'll be right back after this."*

The Panel went to a commercial break, ending the hypnotic trance the program had placed over Topher, Joey, Sam, and Mo. As much as it infuriated them to watch, they couldn't take their eyes off it. They all turned to Cash with the deepest sympathy on their faces, but once again they were more affected than the actor himself. Cash just let out a heavy sigh and rubbed his eyes, as if he had been assigned homework instead of criticized on national television.

"I've been avoiding reality for long enough," he said. "You guys go to dinner without me. I have to go back to the hotel and make some calls before this thing gets any bigger."

Cash headed out of the gift shop but Topher was compelled to ask him something before he left.

"Hey, Cash?" he said. "It's not true, is it? Are you really missing work to be on this trip with us?"

The actor paused for a moment before responding, which wasn't reassuring.

"Of course not," he said. "It's all a bunch of bullshit to keep the story going. I'll see you guys tomorrow morning."

Cash exited through the gift shop and walked across Old Town, Amarillo, to the Teepee Inn at the end of the street. The others searched the area for a Tex-Mex restaurant and found one nearby called the Armadillo Kitchen. They ordered a mountain of guacamole and entrees drenched in cheese, but they barely spoke to one another during the meal. They were on their phones checking the *Wiz Kids* blogs and fan forums. Unfortunately, the latest gossip about Cash was all the rage in the Wizzer universe, too.

"I'm amazed this story is still going," Sam said. "It's one thing to have all the Wizzers focused on Cash—but the *whole world* is talking about how he didn't show up for work today! Is there really nothing else going on?"

"And people are actually *believing* this crap," Mo said. "A tabloid in the UK called *The Beast* said Cash missed work because he's *in hiding* from a Russian drug lord he owes money to—and now a Wizzer in Florida has started a GoFundMe page to help him pay it off!"

Joey shrugged. "We've fallen for some pretty stupid things written about Cash before. Remember that rumor about him leaving *Wiz Kids* to join NASA's mission to Mars? We obsessed over that and it wasn't even from a reliable source. Who knows what we'd believe right now if we weren't actually with the dude."

Topher clicked off his phone and sat back in his chair. A strong suspicion had been eating at him for a while, but until now there'd been no real reason to voice it to the group.

"Are we sure Cash is being honest with us?" he asked.

"Yeah, *to a fault*," Mo said.

Sam and Joey nodded in agreement, but they weren't getting Topher's point.

"I know we want to defend and protect Cash because we've had a lot of fun with him, but do we have any proof that the media isn't *right* about him?" he asked. "What if he was on drugs that night at the concert? What if those pills he's always taking aren't for his sinuses? What if joining our road trip is just part of this big breakdown he's having? Maybe he's always stretching the truth to *cover up* the truth?"

From the concerned looks on his friends' faces, Topher could tell it had crossed their minds, too, but just like him, no one wanted to doubt the actor just yet.

"Topher, you read too many John Grisham books," Joey said. "I think Cash was getting some bad press in Los Angeles and wanted to clear his head, so he took the first opportunity he got to get away. Unfortunately, the whole thing has totally backfired on him. Sure, he drinks like a fish, probably smokes like a chimney, and he isn't careful about mixing them both with medication, but I think we'd know it if he was mentally unbalanced or an addict of some kind."

"I agree," Mo said. "With all the other shit that comes out of his mouth, I doubt he'd be able to keep some deep dark secret from us. On the contrary, I bet he'd *love* bringing it up just to see the terror in our eyes—he seems to get off on that."

They all laughed but Topher felt guilty for bringing it up and went quiet.

"I get what you're saying, Topher," Sam said. "But remember what you said at McCarthy's? About letting Cash be human because he rarely gets a chance? Well, you were right. He let his human side show too much and now the whole world is painting him as some kind of scoundrel. So the least we can do is give him the benefit of the doubt. No one else seems to be."

Topher smiled sweetly at him. Only Sam could tell Topher he was wrong about something but make him feel good about it at the same time. In fact, Sam was the only person in the world who made Topher feel a lot of unique feelings—and the longer he smiled at him, the stronger Topher felt them.

"I *can't even* with Kylie Trig right now," Mo said, and dramatically put her phone away.

"What'd she do now?" Joey asked.

"Apparently she's trying to organize a Wizzer protest to march outside Cash's house in Los Angeles," Mo said. "She thinks it'll persuade him to go back to work. I couldn't bring myself to watch her newest video. Can we *please* change the subject? Let's talk about anything else!"

"I really enjoyed the museum today," Sam said.

"Oh yeah, it was awesome," Joey said. "Such an incredible story."

"I know, right?" Mo said. "It was like something straight off the pages of my fanfiction. Could you imagine loving someone so much you'd be willing to *die* for them? Be still my heart!"

"I'm beginning to," Topher said.

Although Sam purposely didn't look up at him, he could feel Topher's telling gaze aimed in his direction. As if Topher's eyes lit a fuse inside him, a powerful surge of guilt exploded in Sam's core. It burned so strongly he worried it would give him an ulcer if he didn't do something. Sam couldn't keep the truth from Topher any longer. The next moment they were alone, he was going to tell him—and since there was no way of knowing how Topher would react, Sam dreaded the moment like an approaching plague.

Later at the Teepee Inn, Sam couldn't sleep a wink with the looming confession on his mind. At midnight, he decided to go for a walk and clear his head. He gathered his things and quietly snuck out of teepee number 3 without waking his friends.

Old Town, Amarillo, was completely deserted this late at night. Sam kept a watchful eye for anyone or anything lurking in the shadows, but he was completely alone with his thoughts. He wandered up and down the street for a couple of hours, but the Old Western part of town didn't offer any new solutions.

Sam had a seat on a bench just outside the Bundy and Claire Jailhouse Museum and hoped the ghost of Claire Carmichael might show up and give him advice on how to escape his own troublesome situation.

"Hey, Captain Janeway!"

Sam jumped at the unexpected voice. It echoed through the vacant street but he couldn't find a source anywhere.

"Up here!"

He looked up and saw Cash sitting on the roof of the jailhouse museum. The actor held an open bottle of Johnnie Walker Black in one hand and sipped from a Dixie cup he held in the other. He had a crooked smile and glossy eyes, obviously intoxicated. Sam could smell the whiskey on Cash's breath from where he sat.

"What the hell are you doing up there?" he asked.

"Gettin' *krunk*." Cash laughed. "You couldn't sleep, either?"

"I've got a lot of college stuff on my mind," Sam lied. "Nothing like what you're dealing with, though. It's no mystery why you're still up."

"Yeah, it's been a fist-fuck of a day," Cash said. "That and my teepee smelled like cat piss and mistakes. Want to come up and join me? No point in being insomniacs by ourselves."

Sam shrugged—he didn't have anything better to do.

"How do I get up there?"

"There's a ladder in the back next to the trash cans," Cash said.

Sam found the ladder and climbed onto the roof. The view wasn't much different from the bench below but they could see some of the lights from downtown Amarillo and the neighborhoods in the distance.

"Care for a drink?" Cash asked.

Sam's initial instinct was to deny the offer, but given his current state of mind, he thought he could use one.

"I've never had a drink before," Sam said. "Will it help me sleep?"

"Like mother's milk," Cash said.

The actor poured whiskey into another Dixie cup for Sam and topped off his own. Cash threw his head back and drank his in one gulp and Sam copied him. Once it was swallowed, Sam coughed and gagged as if the actor had poisoned him.

"That tastes like battery acid!" Sam gasped. "How do you drink this stuff?"

"It burns at first but then numbs everything else," Cash said. "And I could use a little numbing after today."

The actor refilled their cups and they each took another shot. The second one was easier than the first, but still very unpleasant. Sam felt his cheeks getting warm and his mind started to slow down like he had taken too much cold medicine—it was a nice change. Also, words began spilling out of his mouth before he had a chance to think about them.

"I'm sorry the world won't leave you alone," Sam said. "It's just *cruel* for everyone to analyze you like they are. It's like everyone forgets you're a human being because you're on a television show."

"I'm used to it," Cash said. "You lose the right to humanity when you become famous. It's just the way it is, but I'm not going to whine about it. It's similar to how people treated monarchy back in the olden days; it's all fun and games until a revolution comes, then they want your head. This week it's my turn to be Marie-Antoinette, next week it'll be someone else's."

"But that doesn't make it right," Sam insisted. "And for the record, I don't care what the women of *The Panel* say. You're absolutely going to work again. Any director or studio would be lucky to have someone as talented and popular as you in a project. It's ridiculous for anyone to think otherwise."

"Oh no, they're right about that." Cash laughed. "But it wasn't a recent revelation—I've known that since season two. I'll never forget the time a director wouldn't let me audition for his reboot of *Beverly Hills Chihuahua*. If that's not humbling, I don't know what is. It doesn't bother me, though. I mean, *c'est la vie*, right?"

The actor took a chug straight from the whiskey bottle and stared out at the city lights ahead. Sam didn't understand how he could be so carefree about it.

"What *does* bother you, then?" he asked. "I don't mean to pry, but if the world was saying or thinking *half* the same things about me, I'd be a wreck."

Cash had to think about it and nodded when the answer came to him.

"I suppose being compared to something that isn't real is what bothers me the most," the actor said. "It's a real mind fuck when you're held to *fictional* standards. People have thought of me as a quantum physics expert since I was twelve, and every time I prove I'm not, they act like I'm doing something wrong—like I'm offending them by stepping outside the parameters of the character I play on TV. Does that make sense?"

Sam nodded, too. It resonated with him a lot more than Cash would ever have thought it could.

"I think so," Sam said. "Because they've seen you doing it for so long, they don't realize how much of a performance it is. So anytime they're reminded it isn't real—it's a *betrayal* or an *attack* on something they love."

"Right," Cash said. "People get addicted to the fantasy you provide them, and then they turn on you the second you can't give it to them anymore. You know, if I were a rock star, no one would be talking about me right now. The only reason it's making such a splash is because my behavior is so unlike Dr. Bumfuzzle's. You get what I'm saying?"

"Completely," Sam said softly. "People give you the wrong expectations and then blame *you* when you can't meet them. It's *your* fault for not being the person they want you to be. *You're* the freak. *You're* the monster. When in reality, you're just trying to be ... *yourself*."

He couldn't tell if it was the whiskey or the conversation, but Sam was becoming emotional. He looked toward the city lights to hide his glistening eyes.

Cash was shocked by how much Sam understood. "Exactly," he said. "Truthfully, that's been the hardest part about being on *Wiz Kids*. Nothing is worse than having the whole world think you're something that you're not. It's *lonely*, it's *frustrating*, and more *painful* than anyone could ever—"

Sam suddenly burst into tears like a broken sprinkler system. They poured down his face so forcefully he couldn't keep up with wiping them away. He sobbed so hard he could barely catch his breath and made little yelping noises like a small dog. The emotional release took Cash completely by surprise and he stared at Sam like he was a vase he had accidentally knocked over in his drunken state.

"Um . . . what's the matter, Sam?" Cash asked.

"*Nothing!*" Sam sniffled. "*I'll be f-f-f-f-fine!*"

"Was it something I said?"

"*N-n-n-no,*" Sam cried. "*I just understand m-m-m-more than you know.*"

Sam used his whole shirt to wipe away his tears, but they kept coming.

"Do you wanna talk about it?" Cash asked.

"*I can't,*" he said. "*I'm not ready to talk to someone about it yet.*"

"Lucky for you I'm not a person—I'm a *celebrity*, remember?" Cash joked but it didn't help. "No offense, but you should probably get it off your chest before you flood the city. It'll feel better if you just let it out."

As if he'd been struck by emotional food poisoning, Sam couldn't hold the secret inside any longer.

"I'm *transgender!*" Sam declared. "I know what it's like to have everyone treat you like something you're not because people have been doing it to me my whole life. I've never met someone who could relate—but it's like everything you just said! We're both trapped! We're both prisoners of unfair expectations!"

The confession took Cash a moment to process. He had thought it would be about affording college, trouble with his friends, or something to do with his mother—but he never expected Sam's dilemma would be so personal. The actor looked around the roof to see if there was someone more qualified to handle the situation, but he was all Sam had.

"Wow," Cash said. "I just thought you were rocking an Anne Hathaway look. Are you positive you're *transgender?*"

"Of course I'm positive," Sam said. "It's not something someone says just for the hell of it—I've never once identified with being female. Every time I see myself in the mirror or in a photograph, I feel like I'm looking at someone else. I know I'm trans like I know we're breaking several state laws by drinking on this roof."

"Have you talked to anyone else about this?" Cash asked

"I went to a psychologist in Downers Grove," Sam said. "He basically told me I was mentally ill. Other than him, you're the only person I've ever told."

"Well, it's hard for some people to understand—"

"But it shouldn't be!" Sam said. "I have the heart and mind of a man, and I want the rest to match—it's that simple."

"So you haven't told your friends or family?" Cash asked.

"My mom probably thinks *transgender* means a rare tiger species," he said. "When I was younger I was afraid to tell my friends because I was afraid of how they'd react. Now I know they'd accept me. I'm just afraid my honesty might hurt someone."

"You're preaching to the choir on that one," Cash said. "I'm guessing you're talking about Topher, huh?"

Sam glanced at him like the actor had read his mind. *"How did you know that?"*

"Please, that kid is easier to read than *Dick and Jane*," Cash said. "I've seen how he glances at you in the car and across the table at lunch. It's adorable and pathetic at the same time."

"Well, that pendulum swings both ways," Sam said.

"*What?*" Cash asked. "You mean, you've got the hots for Topher? Well, you certainly hide it better than he does."

Sam nodded. "It was a recent discovery," he explained. "I used to think I was hiding the truth from Topher to protect *his* feelings—I didn't want him to get hurt when he realized the girl of his dreams was actually a guy. Now I realize I've been hiding the truth from myself to protect *my* feelings—I'm scared he isn't going to like the real me or that he'll be upset when he learns I've been lying to him. I'll understand if our relationship doesn't go beyond friendship, but I can't think of anything worse than losing him completely."

"Jesus," Cash said. "There isn't a Taylor Swift song to get you through that one."

"Nope," Sam said.

Cash poured another round of whiskey shots, and neither of them felt the burn in their throats this time.

"Forgive my ignorance, but is all of this going to change?" the actor asked. "Will you start liking girls after you transition?"

"No, gender identity and sexual orientation are completely different," Sam explained. "Most people don't understand that it's a separate issue and different for every trans person. There are a number of ways someone can transition, but it rarely changes their sexual orientation."

"Really?" Cash said. "I didn't know there were options."

"Of course," Sam said. "Some trans people are *gender fluid* and switch from female to male over time. Some are *genderqueer* and may relate to neither or form a combination of the two. Others are *transsexual* and emotionally and psychologically relate to the opposite sex, like me. You can change a body, but you can't change a soul. The heart wants what it wants."

"Wow," Cash said. "That's incredible."

"Oh come on, it's not like we're magical creatures," Sam said.

"No, I meant *you're* incredible," Cash said. "Most people spend their twenties and thirties finding themselves, but you know exactly who you are before college. It's really inspiring."

Sam had spent so much time focusing on his disadvantages that he never realized there might be an advantage hidden among them.

"Thanks, I guess," he said. "I've never thought of it like that, though. It's a tough world to find yourself in, but an even tougher one to be yourself in."

"The world's never been a great place, but that shouldn't stop you from being your greatest self," Cash said. "It's not going to be easy, but is anything worse than living life as someone else? Look at me. I've pissed off every prepubescent science fiction nerd in the world by being myself, but I wouldn't take it back. You might be scared now, but you've got to imagine how good you'll feel once you cross the finish line. Let *that* encourage you, not your fears."

Sam agreed and tried to put on a brave face, but it was the first time he'd ever felt like someone was actually listening, instead of diagnosing. A couple more tears spilled down his face and Cash wiped them with his sleeve. Sam couldn't believe he was still talking to the same man they had met on Sunday.

"Where did all this insightful knowledge come from?" Sam asked. "Where was *this* guy while the other Cash was getting us stoned and giving us fake IDs?"

Cash laughed. "A lot of knowledge comes with transitioning, and you aren't the only one going through that," he said. "I'm turning into a big old has-been, remember?"

Sam smiled for the first time that night. The actor poured them one final round of whiskey shots before they headed back to the Tee-pee Inn. Cash held up his Dixie cup to toast him.

"To transitioning," Cash said.

"To transitioning," Sam repeated.

Chapter Seventeen
THE TRUTH IS OUT THERE

The Downers Grove gang allowed themselves to sleep in on Thursday morning since it was one of the lighter days in their schedule. The extra hours in bed were very much needed after spending the previous night on the concrete of an abandoned theme park. Sam didn't get to bed until three thirty after his rooftop talk with Cash, so he was especially grateful for the additional rest. He woke up with a slight headache from the whiskey but also with an enormous sense of relief. His problems weren't over by any means, but getting a chance to talk to someone made his spirits soar higher than they had in years.

At ten o'clock Topher, Joey, Sam, and Mo gathered outside the door of teepee number 5 to let Cash know they were headed to the car for their trek to Albuquerque, New Mexico. They could hear him talking on the phone through the door and the actor didn't sound happy.

"Hi, Carl, this is Cash," he said. "Yeah, I lost my phone. . . . I'm calling from Amarillo.... Listen, I just got your message.... Is this something we need to respond to right away or can we wait until I'm back in Los Angeles? I should be back by Monday."

"We should wait by the car," Topher told his friends. "It's really messed up to eavesdrop on him like—"

"A fucking *lawsuit*?" Cash yelled.

With that, Topher, Joey, Sam, and Mo abandoned all their moralities and leaned closer to the door to hear the actor better. Mo even emptied her Starbucks in the grass and held the cup against the door like a stethoscope.

"That's completely fucked up!" Cash went on. "We've never begun stunt training this early before a shoot.... If they wanted to send a message they could have done it over the phone, not legal documents.... Damien *wants* it to leak and embarrass me.... Yeah, I know they don't have all the information but I don't want them to have it yet.... Because they'll find a way to use it to their advantage.... Fine, if it'll prevent a lawsuit from becoming breaking news, send them whatever you have to.... They can do whatever they want, but I don't want anything announced until after, well, you know...

Cash hung up the phone and emerged from teepee number 5 so fast the others only had a split second to reassemble themselves in a non-eavesdropping position.

"Good morning," they said in unison.

Cash didn't respond and didn't look anyone in the eye.

"Where are we going now?" he asked, disgruntled.

"Albuquerque," Topher said. "But we're making stops at the UFO Observation Tower and Dinoworld along the way."

"Gotcha," he said. "Well, let's quit standing around and get to it, then."

The actor put on his sunglasses, pulled his backpack over his shoulder, and led the charge toward the station wagon in the parking lot. The Downers Grove gang shared a moment of uneasiness before following him. They had seen many sides to Cash Carter in the past week, but he was acting totally different today. He was groggy and grumpy, like the wind had been taken out of his sails. They knew something was wrong but didn't want to ask.

What do you think is going on? Mo mouthed to the others.

I think it's all starting to hit him, Joey mouthed back. *Hopefully the observation tower will cheer him up.*

The station wagon pulled onto Interstate 40 with Joey behind the wheel and began its westward haul to Albuquerque, New Mexico. Cash didn't seem like he was in the mood to talk, so everyone stayed silent and listened to the radio along the way. Cash could tell they were giving him space and appreciated it.

"Sorry I'm so quiet," Cash said. "I just woke up on the wrong side of the bed this morning."

"That's okay," Topher said. "Especially after the week you've had."

"I suppose so," he said. "What's this UFO Observation Tower thing, anyway? Why are we stopping for it?"

"It's the site of the famous UFO crash in 1948," Joey said, but it didn't register with the actor. "You've never heard of it?"

Cash shook his head. "Guess I was too busy losing my virginity," he said. "Sorry, that was rude. I should probably explain myself so you guys know my attitude isn't personal."

Everyone else sat a little taller in their seats, anxious to know what his phone conversation had been about. The actor took a deep breath and rubbed his eyelids under his sunglasses before he explained.

"I found out this morning that stunt training *did* begin yesterday. It always starts three weeks before production begins on a new season, and we aren't scheduled to shoot until the middle of August. I think the St. Louis thing made the producers nervous and they moved training up a month to reel me in before I cause another scene. They threatened to sue me if I didn't go back, but my contract clearly states I need two weeks' notice before training begins, so my lawyer is taking care of it. Needless to say, my Black Swan is *out* today. So I'm going to keep my mouth shut until it all rolls off my back."

"No worries," Topher said.

"Yeah—take all the time you need," Sam said.

Three and a half hours later, on the one-thousand-and-two-hundredth mile of their initial two-thousand-mile journey, the car pulled into the parking lot of the UFO Observation Tower, a few miles beyond the small town of Santa Rosa, New Mexico. The tower resembled the Seattle Space Needle, but was about five hundred feet shorter, a quarter of the size, and made out of cheap tin. It was shaped like a flying saucer and suspended off the ground by five concrete pillars.

The roadies parked the car and walked up a steep spiral staircase that ascended into the tower above. The inside of the UFO Observation Tower was one large, round room with a glass ceiling. The walls were covered in charts of various alien spacecraft and different types of alien species, and photographs of the most famous UFO sightings from around the world. Most of the unidentified flying objects were shaped like saucers, but some were triangular, and others were just orbs of multicolored light.

The merchandise was just as cheesy (if not more so) as the stuff on sale at the jailhouse museum. There were THE TRUTH IS OUT THERE bumper stickers, EXTRATERRESTRIAL CROSSING road signs, and alien head antenna ornaments. There were tacky T-shirts that said WE COME IN PEACE, I WAS ABDUCTED AND ALL I GOT WAS THIS LOUSY T-SHIRT, and PROBE ME, I'M IRISH. There were also plush alien dolls, posters of Sigourney Weaver, novels written by Shirley MacLaine, and the complete series of *The X-Files* on DVD.

Topher, Joey, Sam, and Mo were very amused by the items on sale, but Cash just rolled his eyes and sighed at everything he saw.

There was only one employee working and she was sitting behind the checkout counter reading a book on her Kindle. Topher and the others were halfway through the store before she realized she had customers.

"Hi," Topher said. "Are you open?"

"Well, hello, *bonjour, hola, guten tag, buenos días*, and *kon'nichi-wa*," she said, and stood to greet them. "Welcome to the UFO Observation Tower, where you can find all your extraterrestrial essentials and exhibits at no extra price. We're open every day except for holidays or unless I have jury duty. I'm Dr. Darla Plemons, owner and deep believer that *the truth is out there*. What brings you to the shop today?"

Darla spoke with the energy and enthusiasm of a camp counselor on crystal meth. She was tall and thin and wore a vest with hundreds of alien-related badges and pins. The gang was instantly exhausted just by being in her presence. Cash even took a couple steps backward when she introduced herself.

"We're on a road trip from Illinois to Santa Monica," Joey explained. "We've all read about the UFO crash that allegedly took place here in 1948 and saw on your Facebook page you had some exhibits about it."

"The UFO crash that *allegedly* took place?" Darla asked like she was speaking in front of a giant crowd. "My friend, if you think it's all just a bunch of allegations, then the government has already won. I bet you believe we actually went to the moon and Lee Harvey Oswald shot JFK, too."

"So the crash actually happened?" Sam asked.

"Were George Washington's teeth made of wood? Was Walt Disney cryogenically frozen moments before death? Was Beyoncé created in a Houston laboratory as an instrument for world peace?"

This only confused them more, and they stared at her blankly.

"Beats me, too," Darla said with a shrug. "There's absolutely no evidence to prove or disprove any of the theories I just mentioned."

"There's a theory Beyoncé was created in a lab?" Mo asked.

"When it comes to solving conspiracies, you should never look at the information they give you, only the information they *don't*," Darla said, and winked like a broken baby doll. "And when it comes to the UFO crash of 1948, the government sure spends an awful lot of time and effort telling us it *didn't happen*."

"I can't tell if that's brilliant or just bonkers," Topher whispered to his friends.

"It's 150 percent bonkers," Cash answered.

Darla clapped her hands. "So you guys want to see some cool alien crap or what?"

She led them to the far side of the room to a square case that was covered in a black cloth. She put her hands over the top as if an exotic animal might jump out at any second.

"Before these objects are revealed I think it's important to give you a little history lesson," Darla explained. "Picture it—New Mexico in 1948. Truman was president and there wasn't a damn thing to do but reproduce, raise cattle, and die. Two lonely farmers named Elmer and Essie Fitzpatrick awoke one summer night to the sounds of their livestock going berserk. They ran outside to see what the problem was and they saw smoke in the distance. They hurried toward it as fast as Elmer's clubfoot would allow. In the exact spot where this tower stands, the farmers discovered *a crashed flying saucer and four dead bodies of extraterrestrial beings!*"

"Neat," Joey said.

"Whatever," Cash said.

"What did the farmers do?" Sam asked.

"What any respectable couple would do upon such a discovery—they called the sheriff," Darla said. "However, Elmer and Essie didn't realize at first what they had discovered. Being simple country folk during the time of World War II—and *blatant racists*—the couple assumed the four little green men among the debris were Japanese fighter pilots. So the sheriff immediately called the military when he got off the phone with the Fitzpatricks. They drove up from a base in southern New Mexico and were at the scene of the crash within three hours—but it only took a matter of seconds before they realized what they were looking at. The military had the whole scene cleared in under an hour and they shipped the wreckage and the bodies off to some secret government facility. The Fitzpatricks were told the crash was just a weather balloon and the bodies were seasick little people who had stolen it. But luckily for us, that wasn't before Elmer Fitzpatrick took a piece of the wreckage for himself!"

Darla uncovered the display case with gusto, revealing a very thin piece of scrap metal.

"That's a piece of aluminum foil," Cash said.

"I see there's a *skeptic* in our midst," Darla said, and zeroed in on him. "If you think it's a piece of foil, then answer me this: How could the Fitzpatricks get their hands on a piece of aluminum foil if there was an aluminum shortage in New Mexico during the late 1940s due to World War II?"

"Fuck the Fitzpatricks—*you* could have stuck that in there this morning for all we know," Cash said. "You can still see some chicken grease on the corner of it."

"You'd be surprised how similar chicken grease looks and smells to extraterrestrial DNA," she said. "Trust me, I have my doctorate in Ufology from the William Shatner Online Institute. Now, please follow me to exhibit number two."

Darla led the group to the opposite side of the store, where another square case was covered by a black cloth. She removed it at once and the others stared inside at a tray of oddly shaped pieces of metal.

"What are those?" Mo asked.

Darla looked around the room to make sure no one from the

government was listening. "*Those* are alien implants found in abductees," she whispered. "They've been removed from people from all over the world who have been experimented on by the tall grays, the short grays, the Nordic blonds, the mantis, and the Reptoids. As you can see, each alien species leaves a differently shaped object in their victims."

"What do the implants do?" Sam said.

"No one knows," Darla said. "The technology is so advanced we may never comprehend their purpose. Our best bet is that they're some kind of tracking device—meaning the aliens could be listening to us right now!"

"Those look like metal pieces from old board games," Cash said. "Wait—that's *exactly* what they are. That one in the corner is the candlestick from Clue, and the one in the center is the dog from Monopoly."

Darla shrugged. "I didn't say all abductees are honest," she said. "Some people will do anything for attention."

"Just abductees?" Cash said, and glared at her. "Because I'm pretty sure you're full of shit, too."

The others were appalled by the actor's rudeness.

"*Cash,*" Topher said.

"I'm sorry, but all of this is bullshit and anyone who believes this woman is an absolute moron," the actor said.

"Dude, chill out," Joey said. "We're just here to have a good laugh. Don't take this too seriously."

"Sorry but I'm not laughing," Cash said. "I don't think it's funny because people *do* take this stuff seriously—even when they're told it's completely fake, people believe in it anyway. Then, instead of facing the truth, they dedicate their whole lives to making it a reality and don't give a fuck who it hurts in the process. Well, I deal with that enough already—I don't need to go to an observation tower to see it. I'll meet you guys outside."

Cash stormed out of the observation tower and stomped down the spiral staircase. The others were stunned by the actor's outburst. It was a complete and utter tantrum and they hadn't seen anything quite like it come out of him before.

"We apologize for our friend," Topher said. "He's going through a lot right now. I'll go talk to him."

Darla put out a hand to block Topher from following Cash.

"Let me handle this," she said confidently. "As part of my Ufology doctorate I was required to take several courses on counseling and crisis management. You guys enjoy the tower and I'll have a word with your friend."

Before the others could tell her it wasn't a good idea, Darla Plemons hurried down the spiral staircase after the upset actor. Cash was smoking in the shade of a concrete pillar when she found him.

"That was quite the scene back there," Darla said.

"Sorry, lady," Cash said. "I didn't mean to be rude, I've just had a really bad week."

"You're that actor from *Wiz Kids*, aren't you?" she asked. "*Cash Carter*, if memory serves me correctly."

"Let me guess, you watch *The Panel* or read *Star Magazine*?" he asked.

"No, I recognize you because we've met before," she said. "You don't remember me, do you?"

Cash shrugged. "Were we abducted together and I can't recall it because the aliens wiped my memory?"

Darla crossed her arms and looked him up and down with a grin. Her voice became deeper, she stood a little taller, and her wacky demeanor melted away.

"No, I used to be an entertainment lawyer at Weinstock Harrison Krueger," she said. "My name isn't Darla Plemons, it's Diane Feldgate. I helped negotiate your first *Wiz Kids* contract with Carl Weinstock. Does that ring a bell?"

Cash suddenly felt like he was having an out-of-body experience similar to an alien abduction. He recognized Diane from a meeting he had years ago, before *Wiz Kids* even started. Diane walked toward him with a much more confident stroll than she had inside and smelled his secondhand smoke like it was a bouquet of roses.

"Are those Marlboro Lights?" she asked. "Can I bum one off of you?"

The actor obliged and lit the cigarette for her. The crazy alien lady took an impressively long drag and blew it in his face.

"What in God's name happened to you?" Cash asked. "Did you get caught stealing from the firm or something? How did you end up in a place like this?"

"Typical," she said. "Whenever someone leaves the entertainment industry, everyone still in the entertainment industry sees it as a giant step backward—like some detrimental failure. Would you even believe me if I told you I left because I wanted to?"

"Of course I would," Cash said. "I just don't understand why."

"It's hard being a rule keeper in an industry that doesn't have any rules," Diane said. "It's enough to drive you crazy. So I left while I still had some of my sanity."

"So that's why you moved to the desert to work inside a flying saucer? Because you were *sane*?" he asked. "I get leaving the industry, but why sell tacky T-shirts instead of practicing a different kind of law?"

"I thought it'd be a hoot and a nice change of pace—and I was right," she said. "Elmer and Essie's son, Doug Fitzpatrick, sold it to me before he died. I bought it at a great price—practically stole it from him. And I've had a lot more fun here than I would behind a desk at another law firm. I actually wrote a book about all the crazy people I've encountered in this place. The television rights were just optioned by Bad Robot, you know, J.J.'s company."

"Yes, I'm aware," Cash said. "So the move worked out for you. But you still spend your life selling people a lie? Don't you get tired of it?"

"No, because I don't see it that way," Diane said. "People are going to believe whatever they want to—you know that more than anyone. All I'm doing is giving them a place to believe it *in*. It's very similar to what you do—you're just too wrapped up in yourself right now to see the bright side of it."

Cash grunted. "It's hard finding the bright side to being the subject of tabloid gossip and criticism on national television."

"It won't always be like that," she said. "Even presidents aren't criticized and talked about forever. Soon, they'll get bored with making things up about you and will want you to entertain them again. It's a vicious cycle of give and take—but that's show business. You're crazy to leave but even crazier to stay."

"It's still annoying as hell," Cash said. "I've always known people thought I was the character I play on TV—I just never expected to be punished when they figured out I wasn't."

"As annoying as it is, you still get to supply an audience with an escape from their troubles," Diane said. "Take Doug Fitzpatrick, for example. He spent his whole life and all his savings on a silly roadside attraction to celebrate a family legend. Doug knew the UFO crash was bullshit and sacrificed his reputation by telling people it wasn't— the whole state thought he was a madman. But do you think Doug died feeling like he was a fraud? Do you think he died thinking about all the people who thought he was crazy? No! Doug died thinking about all the *joy* he had brought to the world. One day, that's what you'll focus on, too, not the annoyances that come with it."

"So I guess it's safe to say you don't believe *the truth is out there*," Cash said.

"The truth *is* out there," Diane corrected him. "But who wants the truth when they have something *better* to believe in? And with the world in the shape that it's in, who could blame them?"

Cash tried really hard not to let the words of the crazy UFO lady resonate with him, but she was starting to make sense.

"I might agree with you, but I still think you're nuts," he said.

Diane laughed. "I sell shirts that say PROBE ME, I'M IRISH. Do you think I give a shit about what people think? Now come upstairs and get out of this heat. I'll treat you and your friends to Strawberry Probesicles—on the house."

Chapter Eighteen

CARNIVORES

At three thirty on Thursday afternoon, Cash's attitude still hadn't changed much since they had left the Teepee Inn—not that the others could blame him. As they walked around Dinoworld, all their moods took a turn for the worse. For one, it was so hot in the New Mexico desert they felt like they were being cooked alive. And just like with the world's biggest rubber-band ball, it was obvious Dinoworld's website was run by total liars.

After viewing the images on Dinoworld's home page, the Downers Grove gang was expecting a colorful and primitive biosphere like in *Jurassic Park*. Instead, the world's largest collection of proportionate dinosaur statues was a *trailer park*—literally. For just ten extra dollars with admission, travelers could park their RVs among the large reptiles for the night. The dinosaur statues were so worn-down it was hard to tell them apart from the motor homes parked throughout the site. Even the nicer ones looked more like weathered piñatas than the giant creatures that once dominated the earth.

"Oh look, it's a triceratops," Sam pointed out.

"That's just a Volkswagen with its hood popped up," Joey said.

"You know, none of us were here sixty-five million years ago," Topher said—always ready with a silver lining. "This could be exactly what the real dinosaurs looked like and Steven Spielberg's the one who got it wrong."

"Then no wonder God killed them all," Mo said.

Dinoworld was by far the biggest letdown of the trip thus far. They would have asked for their money back if the tickets hadn't been just two dollars apiece.

"This blows," Cash said. "I'm going to take a nap in the ptero-dactyl nest. Wake me up when it's time to leave the Land of the Lost Afternoon."

The nest he was referring to was actually just a pile of dinosaur limbs that had broken off over the years, but the actor made himself comfortable in it anyway.

"We should have gone to Santa Fe instead," Mo said. "How far away are we from Albuquerque?"

"About a half an hour," Joey said. "And our dinner reservation at the Aztec BBQ isn't until seven o'clock. So we've got some time to kill."

"Do you guys want to go watch those people at the Winnebago?" Sam suggested. "It looked like they were building a rocket."

Everyone shrugged and headed in that direction.

"While you guys are people watching, I'll go put gas in the sta-tion wagon," Topher said. "It'll be one less thing we have to do tomor-row morning."

Topher returned to the station wagon and drove a little ways down the road to a gas station that also had a dinosaur theme, called BrontosaurGas. He swiped his credit card at the pump and played a game on his phone while he waited for his tank to fill up.

A black Toyota Prius with tinted windows pulled in to the pump next to Topher. He glanced at it for a second and saw the vehicle had California license plates. It was identical to the one Sam had been paranoid about two days ago on their way out of Oklahoma City. Topher knew the odds it was the same vehicle were highly unlikely, but it didn't stop a suspicious feeling from forming in the pit of his stomach.

The driver got out and filled his Prius with gas. He was in his forties, wore a Hawaiian shirt and fedora, hadn't shaved in a week, and chewed on the end of a toothpick. As he waited for his gas tank to fill he kept glancing over at Topher and the station wagon. Topher got the feeling he wanted to start a conversation but he didn't look up from his phone.

"Is this your mom's car?" the man asked.

"Excuse me?" Topher replied, not sure who the man was talking to.

"I asked if this was your mom's car," he said. "I noticed the MY CHILD'S AN HONOR STUDENT sticker on the bumper. You seem a little young to be a father."

"I'm the honor student," Topher said. "Well, I was. I just graduated from high school."

"So I was right," the man said. "Are you going to college?"

The strange man was a little *too interested* in Topher for Topher's comfort.

"Um...yeah," he said awkwardly. "I start in the fall."

"And what about your friends? Are all of them going to school, too?" he asked.

Topher suddenly felt like the lead character in a stranger danger PSA. *Was he referring to the friends he was traveling with? If so, how did he even know he was traveling with friends?* He glanced at the man's pump and saw the numbers weren't even moving—he wasn't there to get gas, he was there for *him.*

"Dude, you're creeping me out," he said. "Why don't you leave me alone before I call the cops?"

"Forgive me—where are my manners?" the man said, and stepped forward to shake Topher's hand. "The name is Barry, Barry Reid."

Topher didn't shake his hand. "You were following us in Oklahoma, weren't you?"

"Ah...yes, as a matter of fact I was," he said. "I gotta tell you, you guys have covered some serious ground in the last couple days. I thought Jennifer Lawrence was hard to follow, but that tomboy in your crew put her driver to shame."

"I'm calling the cops," Topher said, and started dialing 911.

"Actually, there's nothing they can do," Barry said. "You see, you're traveling with a person of *special interest.* And when you're with a person of *special interest,* legally, guys like me are allowed to follow you."

"You're *paparazzi,*" Topher said.

"I prefer the term *freelance photographer,* but yes," he said. "Look, I didn't just appear like the grim reaper. Someone made the mistake of using Cash Carter's real name at the Vacation Suites in Oklahoma

City and the concierge tipped me off. The dude is causing quite the scandal—the first picture of him after he fainted would sell for a lot of money. I've got to eat, so here I am with my camera."

"I hate to disappoint you, but Cash left yesterday," Topher said, thinking on his feet.

"That's funny," Barry said. "My contact at LAX didn't mention he was traveling."

"I didn't say he went home or caught a flight, I just said he *left*."

Barry smiled at Topher like he could read his mind.

"Honor student indeed," the paparazzo said. "I get it, you're a struggling college student and see an opportunity to make some dough. I respect that. I'll give you five grand if you tell me where Cash went."

"What? I'm not trying to get money from you."

"All right, hotshot, *seven* grand," Barry negotiated. "But that's my final offer."

Topher didn't say a word, forcing Barry to try another tactic.

"I get it, I get it," he said. "You probably consider him a friend and don't want to sell him out. As far as I'm concerned, Cash sold himself out when he started acting like a fool. He's a smart guy—he knew exactly what would happen if he acted out. Now a lot of people are benefiting from the mess he's made—that's why they're all eager to keep this story going. The longer Cash is out and about making a total jackass of himself, the more hits, clicks, and views all the news sites get. So why don't *we* take our piece of the pie, too?"

"I don't like pie," Topher said. "I couldn't tell you where Cash went if I wanted to because he didn't tell us where he was going. Now piss off or I'll call the cops—there's no more *special interest* here."

The paparazzo seemed to have met his match. He was both disappointed and impressed with Topher. Barry pulled out his wallet and handed him a business card.

"That's my info in case you hear from him and change your mind," Barry said. "Think about it, kid. Seven grand would go a long way for a college student. Enjoy the rest of your trip."

The paparazzo unhooked his car from the pump and drove off. Topher was so shaken by their encounter he didn't get back into his car until the man was out of sight. He ripped Barry Reid's card in half, threw it in the trash, and then headed back to Dinoworld to pick up his friends.

Topher had woken up that morning expecting to see some pretty scary carnivores by the time the day was finished, but he wasn't expecting the scariest one would drive a Prius.

Chapter Nineteen

IMPACT

Cash had spent all of Thursday in a terrible mood, but on Friday morning the actor awoke as a different person altogether.

"Hey, Cash?" Topher said as he knocked on the door of the actor's hotel room.

"What do you want?" Cash yelled from inside.

His tone took Topher off guard. Cash wasn't raising his voice simply so his friend could hear him through the door, but *shouting* so his irritability was perfectly clear.

"I'm sorry," Topher said. "Is something wrong?"

"Just tell me what you want," the actor demanded.

"It's eight o'clock," he said. "We were supposed to meet in the lobby at seven forty-five, remember? We've got a lot of ground to cover today and want to get on the road as soon as possible."

"I'll be out in a minute," Cash yelled. "And please don't hover outside my door like you did yesterday—it won't make me move any faster."

"Oh…okay," he said. "We'll meet you in the car, then."

An hour later, the actor finally emerged from the Albuquerque Vacation Suites and joined the others at the station wagon. They could all tell something was wrong from his physicality alone. Cash walked very slowly, as if every muscle and every bone in his body ached. He was breathing heavily like a bulldog after a long walk. A dissatisfied expression was frozen on his face as he moved, as if absolutely everything in the world bothered him.

"I can't ride bitch today," Cash said when he got to the car. "Someone needs to switch places with me."

"I'll do it," Joey said, and climbed into the back of the station wagon with the luggage.

"Cash, no offense, but you look like shit," Mo said.

"Maybe that's because I *feel* like shit, genius," he said. "I'm out of sinus medication and I woke up with a *fucking* migraine."

"Do you need us to stop and get you something?" Sam asked from the driver's seat.

"All I need is *silence*," Cash snipped. "Can we all be quiet in the car today? Is that allowed?"

"Um…sure," Topher said. "We can do that."

"Good," the actor said.

The others stared at Cash in disbelief. It was like a demon living inside of him had taken the reins.

"What are we waiting for?" he griped. "Let's get this fucking show on the road."

They drove for three hours in total silence per the actor's request. Cash ferociously chain-smoked the entire way and popped gummy bears into his mouth every fifty miles or so. He kept his eyes shut most of the ride, too, and only opened them when he was lighting a cigarette or searching for gummies in his backpack.

At noon, the station wagon arrived at the Petrified Forest National Park. They exited Interstate 40 and drove down a long curvy road through the scarlet badlands of the Painted Desert and the indigo-striped hillsides of the Blue Mesa, and followed the signs leading to the Jasper Forest to see the petrified wood. The national park was so unique Topher, Joey, Sam, and Mo thought their car had taken a turn and wound up on another planet altogether. About twenty miles into the park, the car pulled into a viewpoint overlooking the Jasper Forest. It was a small canyon sprinkled with tree logs that had fossilized into multicolored stone over the course of several millennia. The Downers Grove gang got out to take pictures of the rare phenomenon while Cash stayed in the car so the park ranger wouldn't catch him smoking. Sam read the information on a stand set in the center of the viewpoint.

"The Jasper Forest is home to many pieces of petrified wood," he read. *"The petrification process most commonly occurs after wood is burned by volcanic ash and constrains the wood from decomposition due to lack of oxygen. Flowing water then deposits minerals in the plant's cells, forming a stony mold in its place. These are the fossilized remains of terrestrial vegetation stretching back to the Triassic period, approximately two hundred and thirty million years ago."*

The last bit of information must have struck a chord with Cash because the actor got out of the car to see the fossilized wood for himself. He climbed down into the canyon and fell to his knees at the first petrified log he found. The actor placed his hand on the log and began to weep uncontrollably. He cried so hard tears and snot dripped down his face, like he was kneeling at the tombstone of an old friend.

Topher, Joey, Sam, and Mo couldn't figure out what was causing his bizarre mood swings. Still, they all kneeled beside the actor to offer him their support.

"What's wrong, bud?" Topher asked.

"I just can't believe how long this has been here...," the actor cried. *"It's overwhelming when you think about it.... Somehow this wood has stood the test of time beyond anything else we know.... It was here hundreds of millions of years before us and it'll be here for hundreds of millions of years after us.... It's a little certainty in such an uncertain world.... None of us even know what tomorrow will bring.... None of us know what's next...."*

The actor rested his head on the petrified wood and continued crying. Although he wasn't making much sense, the Downers Grove natives realized where all the emotion was coming from. After a week of being criticized, analyzed, insulted, humiliated, and vilified by every news source, radio station, talk show, magazine, and gossip blog on the planet, Cash Carter was finally having the breakdown the media all wanted. It was possibly the most human moment the actor had ever experienced, and unfortunately for the tabloids, no one was there to catch him in the act.

Once they finished exploring the Petrified Forest, the Downers Grove gang journeyed farther west toward the Arizona Meteor Crater. At four o'clock they exited the interstate and ventured down another winding desert road to the site of the prehistoric impact.

From the parking lot the attraction just looked like a rocky hill, but once they climbed up to the observation deck surrounding the crater, they stared down at the enormous hole in awe. It was nearly a mile wide and several hundred feet deep.

"This is incredible!" Sam said. "I had no idea how big it would be!"

"That's what she said," Joey joked. "But I know, right? It's like God just scooped out a piece of the earth with a giant ice cream scooper."

"Finally, something on this road trip that doesn't disappoint," Mo said. "I was afraid this would just be a glorified pothole."

"Some scientists think this was the meteor that killed all the dinosaurs," Topher informed the group. "Can you imagine how hard the ground must have shaken on impact?"

Cash wasn't as interested in the attraction as the others. He skulked to the far end of the observation deck and lit another cigarette. Meanwhile, Topher, Joey, Sam, and Mo took selfies, group pictures, and panoramas of the crater. They posted their pictures on Twitter, Facebook, Instagram, and Snapchat—grateful to finally have something worth sharing.

All their phones began to buzz at the same time with an incoming video chat.

"Oh look, Huda and Davi are calling us," Mo said. "I bet they saw our pictures and are *jeeeeeeealous*! Let's answer our phones with the crater in the background to really rub it in."

They turned their backs to the crater and answered their friends' calls at the same time.

"Hey, guys!" Topher said. "Guess where we are!"

Huda and Davi were very distressed, like some kind of tragedy had occurred. Davi's face was bright red and he was panting like he had run all the way to the cybercafe. Huda's eyes were puffy like she had been crying.

"Is it *true?*" Huda sniffled. "We figured you guys would know since you're with him."

"Is what true?" Mo asked.

"You haven't heard?" Davi asked in shock. "It's been all over the news and the Wizzer blogs."

"We've been trying to avoid the Internet since St. Louis," Joey said.

"Are you talking about the rumors of Cash missing stunt training?" Sam asked. "Because if so, you guys don't need to worry about that. It was just a misunderstanding and Cash took care of it."

His words were anything but helpful. In fact, the international Wizzers started panicking a little more.

"Davi, they don't know what we're talking about!" Huda said. "How can they be in the dark when they're *with* him?"

"Sorry, our Google Alerts were becoming too much so we turned them off," Topher said. "What's going on?"

They could tell Davi was searching the Internet while talking to them because his eyes darted all over his screen. The Brazilian boy came across something that made him gasp and cover his face.

"Oh no!" Davi exclaimed. "Huda, it's true! Some site called Deadline just confirmed it!"

The Saudi Arabian girl burst into tears like she had learned a family member had been killed. She had to cover her mouth so she wouldn't wake up anyone in her house.

"You're scaring us!" Mo said. "Just spit it out! What happened?"

"*Guys...*," Huda whimpered. "*We didn't want to believe it at first....The network made the announcement this afternoon....*Wiz Kids *has been canceled! The show's not coming back! It's all over!*"

Topher, Joey, Sam, and Mo unanimously went into a state of shock.

Apparently the Arizona Meteor Crater was only the *second* biggest impact of their day.

Chapter Twenty

HEROES AND HAPPINESS

The drive from the Arizona Meteor Crater to the Grand Canyon was the quietest the station wagon had been the whole trip—but not by special request. The Downers Grove gang were too stunned to speak. As if they had magically been transported into a snow globe, their whole world had been turned upside down and violently shaken apart, and they didn't know where to begin picking up the pieces. The travelers didn't know what to say, what to do, or what to think. The only guidance they had was their itinerary, so they followed it and hoped some reassurance would be waiting at their next stop.

Cash stayed quiet, too, but his silence inspired a thousand questions. Did the actor know his show was getting canceled or was it news to him as well? If he was aware, how long had he known? Was his behavior the reason the network had pulled the plug? Why would he join fans on a road trip if he knew this news was coming? The car was driven over a hundred miles before anyone was brave enough to voice the taunting questions aloud.

"Did you know?" Mo asked.

Her stern gaze was aimed directly at Cash but the actor never looked away from the Arizona desert outside his window.

"I knew I wasn't returning for season ten," he said softly. "But I had no idea they were going to cancel the show over it."

"So you've been lying to us," Joey said.

"I never lied about anything," Cash said. "I just didn't tell you the whole truth—there's a difference."

"Why are you leaving the show?" Sam asked.

"Because it's just my time to go, okay?" he said. "God, I've spent all week telling you about what a nightmare it is—does it actually surprise you? Can you blame me for wanting it to end?"

"You should have told us," Mo said. "You should have prepared us for this—this—"

"Disappointment?" Cash finished her sentence. "Well, I'm sorry to disappoint you. Actually, I don't really give a shit. I've already disappointed the whole world—who cares if four more nerds are added to the list?"

"Cash, you knew how much the show meant to us," Topher said. "You knew we've been watching it since we were in elementary school. And you knew the show was going to keep us connected when we went away to college. How can we *not* be disappointed right now?"

The actor slowly shook his head at the notion.

"Dumb ass," Cash said under his breath.

"Excuse me?" Topher said.

"I'm not talking about you, I'm talking about me," he said. "You see, for once I thought I had found people that might care about *me* more than the show I was on. For once I thought I may have found a group of *friends*, but I guess I was wrong. There are only two types of people someone like me gets to have in their life: *fans* and *critics*. I'm stupid for expecting anything else."

"Now you're just being a drama queen," Mo said. "We can be your friends and fans of your show, too. As fans we're heartbroken our favorite show is over, but as your friends we're pissed off you didn't tell us sooner. Seems like *you're* the one who doesn't know how to be a real friend."

"So you're saying if I told you on day one that I was leaving the show, we could have *still* had fun together?" he asked the car. "Because today is *day six* and you guys are acting like I'm a murderer. Face it, you guys are *fans first*. All you really care about is the show and the fantasy it provides you—that's the only reason you put up with me this week. So don't lecture *me* about real friendship."

The others wanted to object but they couldn't prove him wrong. Despite how close they'd become to Cash, maybe he wasn't a real friend if their loyalties were still with *Wiz Kids*. After all, they'd only known the actor for less than a week, but they'd known his show for the majority of their lives.

"Don't worry, I won't be with you much longer," Cash said. "As soon as this car stops I'll happily leave the trip so you're free to crucify and vilify me just like all the other Wizzers in the world right now."

At seven o'clock on Friday evening, the station wagon pulled in to a lookout point on the edge of the Grand Canyon. Cash grabbed his things and hopped out of the car before it came to a complete stop. He stormed off into the forest beside the canyon without the slightest clue where he was going—he just wanted to get as far away as possible.

"Where do think you're going?" Topher said.

The actor ignored him and continued through the trees. Topher ran after him and the others followed, but Cash was moving at such a determined pace it was difficult to keep up. The breathtaking sight of the Grand Canyon was just a few feet away but none of them were paying any attention to it.

"There's nowhere to go for miles," Topher tried again. "You're going to get lost."

"Like you give a fuck," Cash said.

"What are you talking about?" Topher asked. "We've spent this whole trip giving fucks about you! When I carried you out of that warehouse, *that* was giving a fuck! When we delayed our plans to go to High Tydes, *that* was giving another fuck! When we stopped on the side of the road so you could drive a Porsche, *that* was giving a fuck, too! When we hid you from those tourists at the jailhouse, *that* was also giving a fuck! And now we're chasing your ass through a forest because, guess what, we give a fuck!"

"So what do you want? A medal?"

"No, we're just asking for a little consideration," he said. "This has been a terrible week for you, but it hasn't been easy for us, either! We learned secrets about our favorite television show, we found out our hero isn't who we thought he was, we found ourselves in the middle of a scandal, and we just found out we've lost everything that held our friendship together! Why don't you cut us some slack?"

The remark got under Cash's skin and he stopped to face Topher and the others.

"I'm sorry I ruined your favorite show. I'm sorry I ruined your little road trip. I'm sorry for dragging you into the dark side of my world. But I'm not sorry you lost a *hero*, because you're all *adults*. You should know by now that heroes don't exist. It's your own fault for thinking they do."

"That's not true!" Topher said. "I know heroes exist because I'm my little brother's hero. It isn't easy, it's not always fun, it's full of hard choices, and sometimes you have to put yourself second to help the people you love. But being a hero is a *choice* and you've chosen to disappoint millions of people by leaving your show! So don't tell me heroes don't exist when you're just too selfish to be one!"

Joey, Sam, and Mo were expecting this to infuriate Cash, but the actor didn't look upset at all. On the contrary, he stared at Topher with pity like he was a sad little boy.

"You're wrong, Topher," Cash said. "You could devote years to doing everything you just said and *still* disappoint people the second you put yourself first. You can't manage your brother's happiness any more than I can manage yours. The truth is you're only responsible for one person and that's yourself—believe me, I've learned that lesson the hard way."

The actor suddenly dropped to his knees and held his head in pain.

"FUCK, MY HEAD HURTS!" he moaned.

Cash opened the front pouch of his backpack but couldn't find what he was looking for.

"Shit, I'm out of gummies, too!" he said. "Maybe one fell to the bottom."

Cash dumped out his bag and frantically searched through his things. An empty prescription bottle rolled out of his bag and across the ground to Topher's feet. He picked it up and read the label.

"OxyContin?" he said. "Why are you traveling with narcotics?"

"Don't look at that!" Cash demanded. "Give it back."

"Is this what you've been taking?"

The actor's face filled with shame—it was the first time they'd seen him embarrassed about something.

"It's not what you think," he said. "Look, I got injured on the set of *Wiz Kids* a couple months ago and I've been trying to wean myself off—"

"You've been popping these like vitamins since our trip started! That's hardly weaning yourself off," Topher said, and came to a disturbing realization. "Holy shit—you're an *addict*! Everyone was right about you! We've been protecting you and defending you this whole time—and you've been *lying* to us!"

Cash let out a low and sinister laugh as he repacked his things.

"It sure is rich to be called a liar by *you* lot," he said. "I mean, *thou without their own secrets cast the first stone*. Oh that's right, you can't, because you've all been lying to each other, too!"

Topher couldn't see his friends behind him, but the comment made Joey, Sam, and Mo very tense.

"What the hell are you talking about?" Topher said. "We don't keep secrets from each other."

"Oh really?" Cash asked. "Shall I go down the list?"

"*Cash, no!*" Sam said.

"*Please stop,*" Mo said.

"*Don't do this, man,*" Joey said.

Topher was very confused by the pleading expressions on his friends' faces. It was like everyone knew something he didn't.

"Why is everyone freaking out?" he asked.

"Let's go in a circle," Cash said. *"Joey's gay*—I caught him on a date with a guy he met on a gay hookup app. *Mo's throwing her life away*—she's only going to Stanford to please her father. *Sam's transgender* and the only reason he's hiding it is because *Topher's in love with him* and *he's in love with Topher*. Did I miss anyone?"

Everyone froze as if Cash's words had turned them into stone. They had never in their lives felt more exposed, more violated, or more gutted. It was as if someone had ripped off all their clothes and chucked their hearts into the depths of the Grand Canyon. Cash knew what he had just said was horrible and inhumane, but it was too late to take it back. The damage was done.

"I can see a hiking party headed this way," he said. "I'm going to ask them if someone will give me a ride to the nearest town."

The actor struggled with how to say good-bye to the kids from Downers Grove, but the right sentiment never came. Instead of saying anything, Cash just hurried through the trees toward the hikers he saw and disappeared from sight. Topher, Joey, Sam, and Mo didn't follow him, though. In fact, they stayed exactly where they were, silent and still, until it was dark outside.

As the sun set over the Grand Canyon that evening, it didn't just mark the end of an emotional week or a terrible day for the four friends, but the end of an era for Wizzers all around the world.

Chapter Twenty-One

CALIFORNIA DREAMING

The seven-and-a-half hour drive to Santa Monica, California, the following day was the most uncomfortable ride of their lives. The four best friends felt like complete strangers as they traveled the last five hundred miles to their destination. Each passenger stayed quiet but their minds were rabid with their own unique blends of shock and shame. It wasn't until the station wagon crossed the state line of California that anyone said a word.

"So...we're just *not* going to talk about it?" Mo asked. "We're just going to sit here and pretend we don't know each other?"

"Do we?" Joey asked.

"*Yes*, we do," she said assertively. "Maybe it's easier for me because my secret was the least surprising, but I don't think this is as big of a deal as we're making it. I'm sure we all had good reasons for keeping the secrets we did—but it's not like we don't *trust* or *care* for one another."

Mo was eager for the healing to begin. She looked each of her friends in the eye and told them exactly how she felt about their situations.

"Joey, I have *always* wanted a gay best friend. I'm not mad because you hid your orientation from me; I'm just upset because of all the *Will & Grace* opportunities we've missed out on. Sam, it doesn't bother me for one second that you're transgender. I only wish you had told me sooner so I could have felt ahead of the times by smothering you with my love and support. And, Topher, I don't care that you have a crush on Sam. The only reason it bums me out is because I always thought you had a crush on me."

"Did you *want* me to?" Topher asked from the driver's seat.

"Of course not—you're like my brother," Mo said. "It was just a nice self-esteem boost from time to time. I'm gonna miss it."

The aspiring writer wasn't being as helpful as she thought. Mo could tell her friends wished she would just stop talking.

"What I'm trying to say is that this should only make us closer," Mo said. "Everyone has secrets, and now that ours are all out on the table, it should only make our friendship stronger. So can we just go back to being friends again? Are we really going to let this put a dent in our friendships?"

"Not all of us are processing it as easily as you, Mo," Topher said. "Let's just leave it alone for a bit."

Even though his eyes weren't aimed at him, Sam knew his words were. Topher was taking the news even worse than he feared.

"So what are we going to do when we get to Santa Monica?" Mo asked. "Are we going to avoid each other and do our own thing?"

"I think that's a good idea, actually," Topher said. "It'll give us some time to think. Besides, now that *Wiz Kids* is over, there's really no point in continuing a friendship that's not going to last."

It was upsetting, but Topher had a point. Staying connected in the years to come would be considerably more difficult without the show. Instead of gradually losing touch over time, maybe it was better just to nip it in the bud.

At five o'clock on Saturday evening, the station wagon arrived in Santa Monica. They checked into the Sea Glass Inn, the cheapest hotel that was walking distance to the famous Santa Monica Pier. Topher read online that the *Wiz Kids* sets at Sunshine Studios had already been torn down to make room for *NCIS: Boise*, so there was no point in taking the studio tour—not that they would have even if the sets were still up. The Downers Grove troop spent their first two days in Southern California wandering through the Los Angeles area on their own. The only time they saw each other was at the hotel and it was only for a few minutes at night before bed and in the morning.

On July 4, their third and final day in California, they still hadn't regrouped or reconciled. Sam spent the evening on the Santa Monica Pier watching the sun set over the Pacific Ocean. He thought he knew loneliness before, but now that he and his friends weren't speaking, Sam was learning the true definition of solitude. He prayed the journey back to Downers Grove would mend the group, but others weren't as patient.

"Hey."

Sam turned around and saw Topher standing on the pier behind him. He figured Topher must have been there for a while because he hadn't heard any footsteps.

"Hey," he said.

It was an awkward moment between the two. There was so much to say, but no easy way of saying it, so they just stared at each other.

"Rough week, huh?" Topher said.

"That's an understatement," Sam said. "You did say it would be a summer to remember."

"I did," Topher said with a laugh. "So, what have you been up to? Have you seen anything cool?"

"I've mostly just stayed in the area," Sam said. "I went to the promenade, the aquarium, saw a movie—nothing too exciting. How about you?"

"I've just been walking," Topher said. "I walked to Venice, to the Pacific Palisades, to Brentwood, and to some place called Century City. I never planned to go anywhere, they're just where I've wound up."

"Topher, there probably isn't anything I can say to make you feel better, but I never meant to hurt—"

"Sam, you have nothing to apologize for," Topher said. "I just needed some time to myself—to think about things, you know?"

Sam nodded. "I get it," he said. "Just like MIT, I'm the second thing that isn't going to work out the way you hoped."

"But why not?" Topher asked. "If we both want it, what's stopping us?"

The comment made Sam's head spin.

"You mean, this doesn't *complicate* things for you?"

"Sure, it complicates things, but is any relationship *not* complicated?" Topher asked.

Sam was speechless. Of all the things he imagined the truth might bring, *this* was last on the list.

"Sorry, I just don't know what to say," he said. "I thought for sure you were avoiding me the last couple days because you were upset—"

"I wasn't avoiding you because I was angry, I was avoiding you because I was confused. It was a surprise finding out you were trans, but an even bigger surprise when I realized I was okay with it. I've always been attracted to girls, but there's only one person I can say I've *loved* in that way...and that's *you*. The world isn't black and white, and the people who think it is are the ones who always screw things up. I don't want to be one of those people. I just want to be happy, and nothing makes me happier than you. So what do you say? Can we try being *gray* together?"

"But what if it doesn't work out?" Sam asked.

"Then it doesn't work out," Topher said with a shrug. "Even if we end up as just friends, I can't imagine anything worse than not having you in my life. So, I'll always be here for you, for whatever you need, whenever you need it. It's as simple as that."

Topher's words brought tears to Sam's eyes, but for the first time in as long as Sam could remember, they were tears of joy. Sam gave Topher the biggest hug physically possible.

"You have no idea how long I've been waiting to hear someone say that," he said.

"Was that okay?" Topher asked. "I've been practicing that in my head all freaking day. I hope it didn't come across as too cheesy or desperate because I really meant it."

"No, it was perfect." He laughed. "And nothing would make me happier than being *gray* with you."

Topher and Sam were so wrapped up in their conversation they didn't even notice Joey had snuck up beside them.

"Seems like you guys are in good spirits," he said. "Hope I'm not interrupting anything."

"Nope, we were just regrouping," Topher said. "Care to join in? I'm so bored of not speaking to each other."

"Absolutely," Joey said. "I've missed you guys. This city is beautiful but it's terrifying by yourself. Last night I went to see *The Rocky Horror Picture Show* and a transvestite drew Vs on my face and wrapped me in a boa."

"That's a lot more excitement than either of us have had," Sam said. "I say we find Mo and do something fun together—it *is* our last night on the West Coast. We should make the most of it."

"Does that mean we're going to be okay?" Joey asked. "Are we going to stay friends after all?"

Topher sighed. "Who the hell knows," he said. "But I'm willing to put as much effort into keeping us together as I possibly can. When we first started this trip, I was afraid it was the beginning of the end for us, but after all the shit we've been through this week, I'd say this trip has just cemented our friendship. Let's be honest, no one else is ever going to believe any of this happened to us. We need to stay friends for the stories alone!"

"I couldn't agree more." Joey laughed. "You know, I was furious when Cash put our lives on blast like he did—but I'm glad I don't have to lie to you guys anymore. I didn't realize how much it was killing me to be dishonest."

"Me too," Sam said. "It's nice not having barriers between us anymore. It sounds like we've all got long roads ahead, but at least we won't be walking them alone."

All three of their phones buzzed at the same exact time.

"It's Mo," Sam said. "She sent us a group text."

"Come to my room, there's been an emergency," Joey read. "Oh shit!"

The three left the pier at once and ran to the Sea Glass Inn as fast as their legs would carry them. Mo's hotel room door was ajar when they arrived and they found her inside sitting on the windowsill. Her face was bright red and tears were streaming down it.

"Oh my God," Topher said. "Mo, are you okay?"

"Do I look okay?" she cried.

"What happened? What's the emergency?" Sam asked.

"Our friendship is the emergency!" Mo declared. "We've never gone this long without speaking and I can't take it anymore! Our friendship is the only positive thing in my life! If we aren't going to be friends anymore then I might as well *jump out this window!"*

She dramatically opened the window behind her and an ocean breeze filled the room.

"Mo, we're on the first floor," Joey said.

"I'm using it figuratively!" Mo said. "Look, I know we were all going to use *Wiz Kids* to stay in touch, but let's be real—the show's sucked since season three! It might be the reason we *became* friends, but it's not the reason we *stayed* friends. We were just using it as an excuse to spend time together and I'm not going to let our friendship end just because the show is! You guys are more than just friends to me—*you're my real family*! Who cares if we'll be separated for college—I want to spend the rest of my life with you guys! I want us to be together for vacations, and holidays, and Zac Efron's birthday just like a real family!"

"Aw, thanks, Mo," Topher said.

"Yeah, that's really sweet," Joey said.

"We feel the same way about you," Sam said.

"Good—because my dad and my cat are *assholes*!" Mo said. "So we need to promise each other that no matter what, after graduation we're all going to move to the same city and keep this going! Topher won't have to take care of his brother anymore, Joey will be able to live openly away from his parents, Sam will probably have transitioned by then, and I'll be the only girl when we go out and will get all the attention—everybody wins! But it starts right here, right now! We need to make up and be friends again because I never want to live for another day without you guys in my life!"

Mo stopped to breathe for the first time since they arrived. None of her friends seemed overburdened by her requests. They shared a look and shrugged like it was perfectly reasonable.

"Sounds good to me," Topher said.

"Me too," Joey said.

"Can't wait," Sam said.

Mo was thrilled they were on board but their willingness was very confusing. It was so much easier than she had predicted.

"Did something happen that I'm not aware of?" she asked. "Did you guys already make up without me? Because an hour ago none of us were even speaking and you just agreed to stay friends forever."

"Yup," Topher said. "Just now on the pier, actually."

"We happened to be in the same place at the same time," Joey said.

"Yeah, we didn't exclude you or anything," Sam said.

Mo nodded approvingly and wiped away her tears. She had prepared an additional half-hour-long speech about why they needed to save their friendship, but she clearly didn't even need it.

"Well...*great*," she said. "I wish someone had mentioned that when I threatened to jump out a window, but I'm glad we're all back together again! Now come help me off this ledge and give me a hug!"

Her friends happily obeyed. Just as they concluded their obnoxious group hug, a series of explosions came from outside the window and took them completely by surprise.

"What's that?" Topher asked. "This is a good neighborhood, right?"

"It's the Fourth of July, dummy!" Sam reminded him. "They must be launching fireworks over the pier! Come on, let's go watch them together!"

The reunited friends joined a massive crowd on the Santa Monica Pier to watch the colorful show together. They had a lot more to celebrate than just their country's independence. Their new devotion to one another suddenly made the future seem brighter than it had ever been. No matter what life threw their way, they knew they'd have one another to help them through it.

Halfway through the fireworks Topher felt another buzz in his pocket. He looked down at his phone and saw a new notification from CashCarter.com:

> Wanted you to know I'm in Phoenix getting help. Hoping you guys can stop by on your way back. Said some things I really regret. 778 S. Grant Street. —CC

Chapter Twenty-Two
PROMISES

On Wednesday, July 5, the Downers Grove gang awoke early to begin their two-thousand-mile journey back home. After a very long and tiresome discussion, Topher persuaded his friends to add an extra hundred miles to their return route so they could visit Cash Carter in Phoenix, Arizona.

Seven hours later, the station wagon arrived in Phoenix and pulled into the parking lot of the Sunny Skies Care Center located at 778 S. Grant Street. Topher got out of the car and walked a few yards toward the care center when he realized he was alone.

"Are you guys coming?" Topher asked.

"We agreed to come to Phoenix, but we never said any of us were going to see him," Mo said.

"He wants to apologize," Topher said.

"Then he can send us a letter," Sam said. "I don't want to see him."

"But he broke down the barriers between us, remember?" Topher said.

"He still *betrayed* us," Joey said. "If you want to feel like a Good Samaritan, that's great, but none of us feel inclined to do him any favors."

Topher didn't argue any further. The only reason Topher was compelled to see the actor was because he, too, had said some things he regretted. Getting a chance to apologize would be a relief for them both.

"All right, all right," he said. "Here, take my keys and keep the engine running so you don't overheat. I'll try to make this quick."

Topher left his friends in the car and walked up a stone path to the Sunny Skies Care Center. The lobby was very clean and decorated in light, relaxing colors. Topher spoke to a nurse at the front desk.

"Hi, I'm here to see Cash Carter," Topher said.

The nurse typed a few words into her computer but nothing came up.

"I'm sorry, there are no patients here by that name," she said.

"My mistake, he's probably under Thomas Hanks," he said.

"Oh yes, he's in room 828," the nurse said. "I'll buzz you in."

She hit a button on the counter and a large glass door gradually opened behind her. Topher's eyes wandered around the lobby as he waited for the door. He noticed a large family sitting together in the corner with a priest. They were all crying about something and the priest seemed to be counseling them. On the other side of the lobby was another family who sat with a very old man in a wheelchair. They tried to talk with him, but the old man just stared off silently like he was stricken with Alzheimer's.

"Excuse me?" Topher asked the nurse. "What kind of rehab is this?"

"This isn't a rehab, it's a hospice facility," she said. "Now, you're going to go through this door and make a left at the end of the hall and the room will be on your right-hand side."

"Thanks," he said.

As Topher followed her directions, he wondered if his friends had been right to wait in the car. What on earth was Cash doing at a hospice center? Was he visiting a sick friend or fan? If so, why would Cash have tricked them into coming? Why did he lie and say he was getting help?

Topher stepped inside room 828 but there was no sign of Cash anywhere. A very thin and frail young man was asleep in the bed but he wasn't anyone Topher recognized. He had dark circles under his eyes and was hooked up to several machines and an IV drip. Whoever he was, he didn't appear to have much time left. Topher quietly paced around the room as he waited for Cash to appear. He was there for twenty minutes and the actor still hadn't shown up.

"You came."

Topher looked to the bed and saw the patient was awake. He was staring at Topher with a weak smile and his eyes were opened just barely enough to see. He clearly knew who Topher was, but Topher couldn't place him.

"I wasn't sure you got my message," the young man said softly. "I'm so glad to see you."

It suddenly dawned on Topher who the patient was—he was in such bad shape Topher hadn't recognized him.

"Cash?" he asked. "What the hell happened to you?"

"I took a turn for the worse last Saturday," the actor said. "The hikers drove me to Flagstaff the night I left you. I was looking for a pharmacy when I blacked out and woke up in some hospital. I was transferred here on Monday. It was the only hospice facility nearby that had room for me."

"But why?" Topher asked. "Are you sick?"

"I have glioblastoma," Cash said. "That's a fancy stage name for brain cancer."

Topher felt like the room was spinning and he slid into a chair at the foot of the bed. He was so dizzy he held on to the seat with all his might as if he was on a roller coaster with no seat belt.

"Brain cancer?" he said in shock.

"Sorry to spring the news on you like this," Cash said. "Shit just got real human, huh?"

"Are you just finding out about it?"

The sick actor looked away guiltily and slowly shook his head.

"In April I started getting these really bad migraines," Cash explained. "A doctor came to the set and recommended I get a scan. We were behind in production so the producers wouldn't give me time off to get it done. In May, after we wrapped season nine, I finally went in for an MRI. They found a tumor the size of a grape on my brain stem."

"And...and...and did you start treatment for it?"

"My options were limited," he said. "Surgery was risky and could have potentially damaged my verbal skills—and you know how much I like to talk, so that wasn't going to work for me. Other treatments might have left me paralyzed or impaired my memory and that didn't sound like any fun. The neurologist said I had a good three months left if I did nothing, so I decided to make those count instead."

"Hold on," Topher said, and waited a moment to ask him the question he didn't want the answer to. "Cash, are you saying that you're...you're...*dying*?"

The actor took a deep breath before confirming it.

"Yeah," he said.

Topher closed his eyes and went silent as he processed the news. He didn't want to believe it was real, but so many things from the week before began making sense and the dots practically connected themselves.

"So all that bad behavior...The partying, the drinking, the smoking, the dancing, the lawbreaking...All the stuff everyone was condemning you for...That was just..."

"Me squeezing life for every last drop," Cash said.

"And the night at the concert, the morning after the concert, the crazy mood swings, the migraine, the gummy bears, the OxyContin in your bag..."

"Just symptoms and remedies," he said. "I told you those pills weren't what you thought."

It all made sense, but that didn't make it any easier. Topher tried putting on a brave face for Cash but it was impossible to shield the devastation coursing through his body.

"How much time do you have left?" he asked.

"They said it's a matter of days," he said. "The MRI I had on Sunday showed the cancer is spreading and growing pretty fast. The tumors are like Starbucks—there's one on every corner now."

"If you were so sick, why did you come on our road trip?" Topher asked. "Why would you spend your last days with total strangers?

Surely there are much better things a dying man could do with his time."

The actor smiled—he was hoping Topher would ask.

"There's a black binder in my backpack," Cash said. "Open it."

Topher found the backpack on another chair by his bedside. He zipped it open and pulled out the binder. It was filled with dozens of letters addressed to Cash; some were handwritten and some had been printed off the Internet. Topher didn't understand their significance until he recognized the handwriting and saw they were all written by the same person.

"Holy shit," Topher said. "These are all *mine*.... You've *saved* every letter I ever wrote to you...."

"I promise it's not as creepy as it seems," Cash said. "Nine years ago when the show started, you were the first person that sent me a letter addressed to my name and not Dr. Bumfuzzle. You didn't act like the show was real, you didn't pretend I was anything but an actor doing a job, and you never asked me for any favors. You just thanked me for the work I did and treated me like a person—and I didn't get that very often. You were only eight when you wrote that first letter and I was only twelve when I read it, but your letter meant the world to me. I had the companies running my fan mail and website keep an eye out for anything else you might send. It was nice knowing there was someone out there who knew I was just a kid and not a quantum physics expert."

"I don't know what to say," Topher said. "There are letters in here that I don't even remember writing."

"Oh gosh, I was like your therapist." Cash laughed. "You wrote to me after the very first episode of *Wiz Kids* aired and told me how amazing you thought it was. You wrote to me the day you met Joey, Sam, and Mo and said how excited you were to make such cool friends. You wrote to me when your dad took his first teaching job in another state and told me how sad it made you. You wrote to me when your brother was diagnosed with cerebral palsy and told me how much it scared you. You wrote to me on your first day of high school and said how nerve-racking it was. You wrote to me senior year about how worried you were that you wouldn't be your class valedictorian. Your letters were always so descriptive I felt like I was right there with you! They were the only thing that made me feel like I was a normal kid."

Topher turned to the last page of the binder and found the letter he had written the actor the night before their trip.

"And then I invited you to join our road trip and you actually showed up," he said.

The actor teared up and gently nodded. "I needed to say good-bye," he said. "You know, in each and every letter you thanked me and gave me the credit for *your* bravery—but I think it was really *you* who was inspiring *me* to be brave all along. In an industry that makes a hobby of ripping celebrities apart, and on a set controlled by people who didn't care for me very much, knowing I had someone like you to inspire made everything worthwhile. You've been my hero as much as I've been yours."

Cash's words made Topher look at his life in a drastically different light. Everything he had ever been through seemed to have a much deeper meaning than the mediocrity it had before. Topher couldn't believe he was standing at the deathbed of his childhood hero and being made to feel so significant. It sent a wave of emotions through him that he couldn't handle in front of the actor.

"I need to find the others," Topher said. "They were parking the car when I came in and I think they got lost. I'll be right back."

He dashed through the halls of the Sunny Skies Care Center and ran through the parking lot like a crazy man. His friends were relieved to finally see him but annoyed it had taken as long as it had.

"About time," Joey said.

"Yeah, I'm so bored I could die," Mo said.

"Did you talk to Cash?" Sam asked.

"Yeah." Topher panted. "And I know you guys don't want to see him—but you really need to come inside."

"No way!" Mo said.

"We aren't changing our minds," Joey said.

"Topher, can we just get back on the road?" Sam asked. "We've got so much ground to cover—"

"CASH IS DYING!" Topher blurted out.

All the emotion he had been suppressing rushed out of him like a waterfall. It wasn't until he said the words aloud that the reality of the situation hit him. Topher leaned against the station wagon, slid down to the ground, and sobbed. His friends got out of the car and approached him like he was a wounded animal.

"Topher, is this some kind of joke?" Sam asked.

"No," he blubbered. *"Cash has been sick this whole time and we never knew! He's been putting on a show for us since we met him! He's not a bad person—he's got brain cancer! That's why he's been behaving the way he has! He cares more about us than we could have ever imagined—and we almost drove home without stopping to see him!"*

The others had never seen Topher like this before. They knew he was serious and took the news exactly like he did. It was hard to accept but made a lot of sense the more they thought about it.

"I can't believe this," Sam said.

"We need to see him," Mo said.

"Topher, can you show us to his room?" Joey asked.

Once Topher composed himself, he led his friends into the Sunny Skies Care Center and down the hall to room 828. All it took was one look at the actor and everything Topher had just said was confirmed. Even with a heads-up of what they were walking into, the others couldn't contain their emotions as well as Topher managed to.

"You don't have to feel *that* sorry for me," Cash said. "I'm on enough morphine to stop a herd of elephants. Things could be worse."

"Why didn't you tell us you were sick?" Mo asked.

The actor laughed. "No offense," he said, "but you aren't the easiest bunch to break bad news to. By the way, I'm so sorry for spilling all your secrets like I did. Just because I'm dying doesn't give me the right to be a dick. I hope you'll forgive me."

Given the new circumstances, none of them had it in their hearts to hold anything against him. It was like a magic eraser had wiped away all their grudges and hard feelings toward the actor.

"I think I speak for everyone when I say you have our forgiveness in spades," Joey said. "It pissed us off for a while, but it only brought us closer together. So we really should be thanking you."

"It's not like anything you said was a lie," Topher said. "Unlike the things people have been saying about you. Everyone's got it all wrong—when are you going to break the news to them?"

"Not until I'm gone," Cash said with a sly smile. "Which is really a shame because I'd love nothing more than to see the looks on all those asswipes' faces when they find out they've been chastising a guy with cancer. It's going to be a crow buffet! Enjoy it for me."

"Why don't you want to see it for yourself?" Sam asked.

The actor let out a long sigh. "It would just create an even bigger frenzy than there's already been," he said. "My life has always been so *crazy*, so *loud*, and so *busy*. For once, I just want everything to be *quiet*. Besides, when the whole world is tarnishing your name, that's how you learn who your true friends are. You guys are all I need."

Mo could barely get the words past her tears. "Is there anything we can do for you?"

She had to ask it even though they all knew there was nothing anyone could do. However, Cash did have a very important request for them and he was grateful he had the opportunity to ask it.

"Yes, you can make me a promise," the actor said. "Promise me you won't waste the rest of your lives pleasing other people, because if you do, you'll wake up one day and realize you've never really lived. Trust me, you don't want to learn that lesson the way I did."

Topher, Joey, Sam, and Mo gave the actor their word and it was the greatest gift they could have given him.

"Good," Cash said with a light chuckle. "Then my mission is now complete."

The Downers Grove gang were determined to stay by Cash's side until the very end. They called home and told their families they'd be returning a few days later than expected. All they said was that they had met a new friend on the road who was sick in the hospital and they were going to stay with him until he could leave. None of them felt an ounce of guilt about the claim because, just like Cash taught them, there was a difference between telling a lie and not giving the whole truth. It was a blessing that none of their parents took issue with it, because not even a meteor impact could get them to leave the actor.

As the week went on, Cash's health rapidly declined more and more each day. By Thursday the actor had lost feeling in his legs and feet. By Friday, the numbness had spread to his arms and hands. By Saturday he stopped eating and drinking water. By Sunday the actor stopped talking and opening his eyes. Then on Monday, July 10, Cash Carter took his final breath and peacefully passed away in a very quiet room surrounded by new friends. The actor had had so little control over his life, but his death was exactly how he wanted it to be.

From that day forward, when Topher, Joey, Sam, or Mo thought about Cash, they never imagined his character from television or the sick man in the hospice bed. Instead, the group pictured the actor behind the wheel of a sleek and shiny Porsche 550 Spyder, cruising down an open highway of the afterlife, pranking, peer pressuring, and corrupting every naive angel he found along the way. That was the Cash Carter no one else got to see, and that was the Cash Carter they would miss forever.

Chapter Twenty-Three

TRUSTS

On August 10, exactly one month after Cash Carter passed away, Topher, Joey, and Mo sat in the dining room of their favorite Chinese restaurant in Downers Grove, Cok with a Wok. They were there to celebrate their final meal together before splitting up for college the following day, and impatiently waited for Sam to join them. They weren't only anxious because they were all starving, but also because today was the day Sam was going to tell his mother that he was transgender, and they wanted to know how Candy Rae Gibson had reacted.

"Here he comes!" Mo said when she saw Sam through the window. "Oh gosh, I'm so nervous to hear how it went! I practically feel like I came out as transgender, too!"

"Only you could make *this* about you." Joey laughed.

Sam entered the restaurant and had a seat at the table. His friends were jumpy with anticipation and didn't even bother saying hello—they went straight for the details.

"Well?" Topher asked.

"*Weeeeeell…,*" Sam began, and all his friends leaned closer to him. "Honestly, it wasn't as bad as I expected."

"That's terrific!" Joey said.

"Don't get me wrong, there were still a lot of tears," Sam prefaced. "But for the most part Candy Rae Gibson handled it pretty well. I didn't have to explain what transgender meant like I thought, which was nice. Apparently there was a trans character on *Grey's Anatomy* last season so my mom thinks she's an expert on the subject now. There were a lot of questions, though—did it have anything to do with her, was I trans because she failed as a mother, was there anything she could have done differently that would have changed it, *blah blah blah*—but once I assured her it had nothing to do with her she was pretty much okay with it. Actually, a little too okay with it— she made me listen to Lady Gaga's 'Born This Way' with her like six times."

"Sam, I'm so happy for you!" Mo said, and gave him a hug. "You've been dreading this day for your whole life!"

"Yeah, it feels good to be open with *everyone* now," Sam said. "I told her all about the clinic I found in Providence where I'm planning to start my first round of hormone therapy. She wanted to know if she could meet me there and maybe do a round of estrogen herself—so I had to explain that it's not like getting a mani-pedi."

Joey was over the moon for his friend, but he couldn't keep some sadness from surfacing in his eyes.

"Joey, are you okay?" Sam asked.

"Totally," he said. "I'm so happy for you, Sam. I just wish it had been a little easier for me, you know?"

"Have you *still* not spoken to your dad?" Mo asked.

"Not a word," Joey said. "I've been meeting my mom for lunch every other day, though. She's so dramatic—she's always in sunglasses and a veil so no one in the church catches her. I keep reminding her I'm gay and not a terrorist."

"I know it really sucked when your dad told you to leave, but it's been *wonderful* having you at my house," Topher said. "Joey's been a huge relief to my mom and me by helping us with Billy. He also makes the best pancakes in the world on the weekends. Yesterday my mom actually referred to him as her son and didn't even correct herself."

"I can't thank you enough for letting me stay," Joey said. "I have to admit, it's been like a vacation. I'd take Billy any day over those heathens I used to live with."

Even though they were directly in front of her, Mo tapped the side of her glass with a spoon to get her friends' attention.

"I have a little announcement, too," she declared. "Today I managed to convince my father to give me my college fund to pay for Columbia."

"That's amazing!" Sam said. "How'd you do it?"

"Compassion wasn't working so I tried a different method—*blackmail!*" Mo was proud to share. "I told him if he didn't fork it over, when he was an old man I would put him in the retirement home that had the lowest Yelp score I could find. That did the trick."

There was laughter and high fives all around.

"Way to go, Mo!" Topher said.

"God, you're terrifying when you want to be," Joey said.

Mo gave him a big devious smile but it faded away when a sad thought crossed her mind.

"You know, it's really thanks to Cash that I did it," she said. "I was thinking about him a lot today. Can you believe it's been a month since he died?"

"It still doesn't feel real to me—none of the trip does," Sam said. "He was kind of like the world's worst Mary Poppins. He just flew into our lives one day, brainwashed us into doing some terrible things, and changed our lives for the better somehow. I actually went with my mom to see this psychic she gives perms to, you know, just in case Cash's spirit had something to say."

"Did he come through?" Topher asked.

"Not at first," Sam explained. "So I asked Madame Beauffont, that's the psychic's name, to try really hard at contacting him. She got a clear message from someone and I think it was him."

All his friends were on the edge of their seats.

"And?" Joey asked. "What did it say?"

"Fuck off, I'm banging Marilyn Monroe," Sam said.

They laughed so hard they made the other people in the restaurant very uncomfortable. With one vulgar statement, the afterlife was all but confirmed for them. Only the real Cash could have made a remark like that.

"Not to be a downer, but did anyone watch the footage from Cash's funeral today?" Mo asked.

"Why did they wait a whole month to have it?" Topher asked.

"Because it was sponsored by Canon and their new camera comes out this week," Mo said. "Well, I watched it until Damien Zimmer gave the eulogy, then I had to turn it off. It was a good move, too, because apparently Kylie Trig sang 'Wind Beneath My Wings' right after he spoke."

"Sounds more like Cash's execution than his funeral," Joey said. "How does the same person who started a worldwide hunger strike when *Wiz Kids* got canceled get invited to sing at the lead actor's memorial? And she can't even sing!"

"I didn't see any video but I did see the pictures," Sam said. "And I'm sorry, but it's just *tacky* having a red carpet at a funeral. Did Amy Evans *really* need to wear that Pharrell hat to his service? So disrespectful."

The whole table nodded at the notion.

"Wednesday nights aren't going to be the same," Topher said. "Maybe we should still video message one night a week and start a new show, like *Doctor Who* or *Supernatural*. We can even rope Huda and Davi into it!"

"That's a great idea," Mo said. "And don't forget, we're all meeting Sam in Rhode Island on the weekend of Thanksgiving, then we'll be coming back here to see you guys for Christmas, and spring break you'll be visiting me in New York."

"I'm so glad you decided to stay in Downers Grove for school, Joey," Sam said. "Oklahoma wouldn't have been a very fun place to meet up for a holiday."

"Yeah, I'm glad I'm staying here, too," Joey said. "Topher and I are both going to get our GEs and then transfer somewhere fancier in the future. Hopefully someplace on the East Coast close to you guys so vacations will be easier."

Topher looked around the table and smiled at his friends. They'd stuck to the promise they made Cash and had come a long way in just a month's time. He hoped wherever the actor was, he was watching them with a lot of pride. He didn't reminisce for very long, though, because the moment was interrupted when his phone began buzzing in his pocket.

"Someone's calling me with a 323 number," Topher said. "Anyone know where that's from?"

"I think that's Los Angeles," Mo said.

"Hello?"

"Hi, am I speaking with a Christopher Collins?" asked a man on the phone.

"Yes, who is this?" Topher asked.

"I'm so relieved to finally touch base with you, Mr. Collins. I've been trying to track you down for a couple weeks. My name is Carl Weinstock, I was Cash Carter's lawyer before he passed away."

"Hi, Mr. Weinstock," Topher said, and then covered the phone to address the curious looks on his friends' faces. *"It's Cash's lawyer."*

"What does he want?" Joey whispered.

Topher shrugged. "What can I do for you?"

"I hope I'm not interrupting anything," Mr. Weinstock said. "I'm the executor of Mr. Carter's will and need to finish distributing his assets by the end of the week. He left a trust behind in your name—if I flew into the Chicago area tomorrow, would you be free to meet?"

292 ★ CHRIS COLFER

"Oh, sure," Topher said, then glanced at his friends. *"Cash left me something in his will."*

"Fancy!" Sam said.

"You wouldn't happen to be in contact with a Mr. Joseph Davis, a Ms. Samantha Gibson, or a Ms. Moriko Ishikawa, would you?" Mr. Weinstock asked.

"As a matter of fact, all three of them are sitting in front of me," Topher said.

"What does he want with us?" Mo asked.

"That's terrific!" Mr. Weinstock said. "Mr. Carter left trusts behind in their names as well. Could they accompany you if we found a time tomorrow that worked for everyone's schedule?"

"Let me ask," Topher said. *"Sam, what time am I taking you to the airport tomorrow?"*

"Not until four," he replied.

Topher gave him a thumbs-up. "We're free until around three o'clock," he said into the phone.

"Super," Mr. Weinstock said. "I'll go ahead and book my flight this evening. I have an associate in Chicago who will let us use their meeting space. I'll reach out tomorrow with a time and an address once I confirm it."

"Sounds good," he said. "We'll see you then."

Topher hung up the phone. His friends were staring at him like they had just watched a Hitchcock movie with the sound turned off.

"What was that all about?" Mo asked.

"Apparently Cash left something behind for *all* of us in his will," he said. "His lawyer needs to meet with us tomorrow in Chicago so he can distribute the trusts he put aside."

"Wow," Sam said. "I wonder what he left us."

"I hope it isn't more of that weed he made us smoke," Mo said.

———

At ten o'clock the following morning, Topher received a text message from Carl Weinstock with a time and address to meet him at. Topher passed the message along to his friends and at two o'clock they met him on the twenty-third floor of a towering office building in downtown Chicago. The floor belonged to a swanky firm called Meredith Brown and Associates and a receptionist at the front desk escorted them into a long and intimidating boardroom. Carl Weinstock was waiting for them inside with an open briefcase. He was a short and chubby man with a thick mustache.

"Thank you all so much for meeting me on such short notice," he said, and shook their hands. "Why don't you have a seat and I'll get through this as quickly as I can."

Topher, Joey, Sam, and Mo sat across from the lawyer and he passed them each a manila folder with their name on it.

"First off, let me tell you how sorry I am for your loss," Carl said. "I've been working with Cash since he was just twelve years old, so this has been a difficult time for myself and others at my firm. Shortly before he died, Cash set aside some funds for each of you to help pay for your education. Go ahead and take a look."

They each opened the folder in front of them and stared down in shock at the absurd amount of money the actor had left them.

"Holy fuckballs," Joey said.

"This . . . this . . . is for us?" Sam asked.

"Yes," Carl said. "Mr. Carter wasn't sure how much your specific tuitions would cost, as you all had plans to attend different schools, but he wanted to leave enough so you didn't have to worry."

"Where did he think we're going to school?" Mo asked. *"Buckingham Palace?"*

"This is about three more zeros than I would ever need," Topher said.

"There's a *second* page," Carl said.

The teenagers turned their pages and discovered another generous inheritance from the actor.

"As you can see, the second page is more individualized to your specific needs," Carl said. "Mr. Davis, Cash has left you his apartment on the Upper East Side of Manhattan, should you pursue performing arts in New York City. Ms. Ishikawa, Cash has left you the official rights to his life story, should you choose to write a biography of the actor someday. And as for Mr. Collins and Ms. Gibson, Cash has left you both an additional trust. The second trust for you, Mr. Collins, is titled the Billy Trust, which is enough to hire a full-time caregiver for your brother so you can focus on your education. Ms. Gibson, Cash left no instructions on how he wishes you to use the second trust under your name, but he's titled it the Transitioning Trust."

After all the bombshells the teenagers from Downers Grove had endured over the summer, they didn't think anything could ever shock them again. However, all four of them stared down at the legal documents with wide eyes and open mouths—they weren't used to *happy surprises*.

"I can see you're all rather stunned," Carl said. "I'll leave you alone for a moment while you *absorb* this information. If you have any questions, I'll be right outside the door."

The lawyer left the boardroom to give them a few minutes of privacy. It took a while before Topher, Joey, Sam, and Mo realized they weren't dreaming and even longer for them to form words to speak to each other.

"Holy fuckballs," Joey said again—as if all other words in the English language had escaped him.

"Can we even accept this?" Sam asked.

"Of course we can," Joey said. "It'll probably all go to taxes and stuff if we don't, right, Topher? *Topher?*"

"Sorry, I'm really overwhelmed," he said. "I never expected Cash would do this for us. How about you, Mo? You're the creative one in the group. Did you ever imagine something like this could happen?"

Despite her overactive imagination, Mo was just as shocked as everyone else. The aspiring writer felt like she and her friends were living a ridiculous happy ending straight from the final page of one of her outlandish stories.

"Definitely not," Mo said. "I don't care what Cash said on the first day in the car—everything that's happened to us this summer, well...it's all been *stranger than fanfiction*."

AUTHOR'S NOTE

Stranger Than Fanfiction is the story of five young adults who face unique social challenges. Several sensitive topics are discussed in hopes of providing comfort and inspiration to readers who have experienced similar issues, as well as awareness and understanding to readers who haven't.

However, for the purpose of good storytelling, the characters' opinions and choices are sometimes flawed. Please do not view their actions as generalizations or examples to follow, but as the mistakes and triumphs of individuals.

And if you're a parent, I promise your child already knew all the bad words in this book....

ACKNOWLEDGMENTS

I'd like to thank Rob Weisbach, Alvina Ling, Alla Plotkin, Melanie Chang, Megan Tingley, Derek Kroeger, Will Sherrod, Heather Manzutto, Rachel Karten, Nikki Garcia, Jerry Maybrook, Joey Garcia, Kheryn Callender, Collyn Dungey, Fox Benwell, Jen Graham, Karina Granda, Ruiko Tokunaga, and all my friends and family.

And, of course, to all the writers of fanfiction my likeness and I have had the privilege of being included in. Thank you for the inspiration...and for describing me with abs.